"What are . . . Lauren?"

"Nothing. Please, just go."

She was protecting something inside that bedroom. Or someone. He was certain of it. She was no longer living here alone. Another man? He was gripped by a sudden spasm of jealousy.

When he strode purposefully towards the bedroom door, Lauren tried to cut him off. "You have no right!" she cried in panic.

He opened the door, walked into the room. There was no other man. Nothing out of the ordinary. Except for a crib located near the window.

Ethan was only dimly aware of Lauren behind him, plucking at his sleeve in a futile effort to stop him. He reached the crib, the breath sticking in his throat as he looked down into its shallow depth.

A pair of blue-green eyes—*his* eyes— gazed back at him innocently.

Available in November 2005
from Silhouette Intrigue

Full Exposure
by Debra Webb
(Colby Agency: Internal Affairs)

Paternity Unknown
by Jean Barrett
(Top-Secret Babies)

Bridal Reconnaissance
by Lisa Childs
(Dead Bolt)

Spellbound
by Rebecca York
(Eclipse)

Paternity Unknown
JEAN BARRETT

SILHOUETTE®
INTRIGUE™

To my readers
I never forget that you make it all possible

*First published in Great Britain 2005
Silhouette Books, Eton House, 18-24 Paradise Road,
Richmond, Surrey TW9 1SR*

© Jean Barrett 2005

ISBN 0 373 22842 2

46-1105

*Printed and bound in Spain
by Litografia Rosés S.A., Barcelona*

JEAN BARRETT

If setting has anything to do with it, Jean Barrett claims she has no reason not to be inspired. She and her husband live on Wisconsin's scenic Door Peninsula in an antique-filled country cottage overlooking Lake Michigan. A teacher for many years, she left the classroom to write full-time. She is the author of a number of romance novels.

Write to Jean at PO Box 623, Sister Bay, WI 54234, USA. SAE with return postage appreciated.

CAST OF CHARACTERS

Lauren McCrea—The frantic mother has no choice but to join forces with the one man she is unable to trust.

Ethan Brand—He has sworn to find his little Sara...and prove his innocence to the woman he never forgot.

Sara—The innocent baby is a pawn in a desperate game.

Hilary Johnson—What terrible secret is the housekeeper concealing?

Sheriff Howell—He resents any interference in his cases.

Marjorie Landry—The FBI agent ends up being a disappointment.

Anthony Johnson—He is the key to everything.

Buddy Foley—The Seattle cop is a friend from the past.

Charlie Heath—The pompous lawyer isn't all that he seems.

Prologue

He was in the wilderness, he was lost, and it was snowing.

Okay, so there was still some question about the first two, but there was no mistaking the snow. The skies had been a clear, brittle blue when he'd left the airport near Kalispell. Somewhere along his route, though, a cloud cover had sneaked in over the mountains, obscuring the sun.

He hadn't been worried when the first white flakes swirled through the air. Hell, it was November, and this was Montana. It was supposed to snow, wasn't it? The car rental agency hadn't mentioned anything about the possibility of a storm on the way.

But the snow had thickened and for the better part of an hour now, the stuff had been falling at a serious rate. No weather report on the radio. All he could seem to find was music.

The wilderness part was a matter of definition. He knew there were rugged mountains out there—the Flathead Range, according to the map he'd found in the glove compartment. He just couldn't see them through this curtain of white.

For that matter, he could barely make out the ranks of evergreens pressing in on him. They crowded both sides of the winding road, a forest unbroken by any clearing or a sign of a building. For a man who had spent most of his life in a large city, that translated into his version of a wilderness.

As for being lost…yeah, it felt like it.

He couldn't remember when he had last met another vehicle. There was just him and this narrow ribbon climbing through the hills. It seemed more like a back road than a highway. Had he missed a sign, taken a wrong turn? The map was of no use; it wasn't specific enough.

Nor could his cell phone help him. He'd tried to raise the state highway department to learn about the weather conditions and to ask directions, only he was unable to get a signal. The weather was probably to blame—maybe a tower was down.

As if all that weren't bad enough, the light was rapidly fading. No surprise at this time of the year when the days were so short, but it made his situation all the more treacherous.

Any fool would have turned back long ago, but he didn't consider it. He *couldn't*. Whatever the risk, the urgency of his mission forced him to go on. He had to reach the woman whose knowledge meant his survival.

No time to lose, either. They must be searching for you by now, and if you don't get to her before they find you...

Forget about that. Take it one step at a time.

At this moment, that meant concentrating on the road. It wasn't good. The snow was piling up. How much longer would the route remain passable?

Whether it was the instinct that had served him so well in the past or merely blind luck that enabled him to glimpse the sign at the side of the road a moment later, he couldn't say. The point was, he saw it, and he could have easily missed it in the driving snow.

Easing the car to a halt, he peered through the windshield where the wipers swished across the glass. The beams of his headlights penetrated the snow and gathering darkness just enough for him to make out the old, faded sign.

It wasn't a directional sign. It was a small billboard. Straining, he could see that it advertised vacation cabins for rent. The cabins were of no interest to him. Their location was. Elkton, Five Miles Ahead, the sign read. His destination. He was on the right road.

Relieved, he moved on. The conditions worsened with each bend in the road as the snowfall accelerated to a furious blizzard. It was full night now. He could barely see the route. Feeling his way, he crested a rise and almost missed a sharp curve. He swung the wheel in time and rounded the turn.

Though alert for trouble, he wasn't prepared for the cow that loomed directly in front of him. Or maybe it was a moose. It didn't matter. Whatever the animal was, it was a large threat frozen in the glare of his headlights that sliced through the screen of snow.

He cursed as he hit the brake to avoid a collision. Mistake. There was ice under the snow. The vehicle went into a skid, its nose spinning to the right. Before he could correct it, the car leaped the shoulder and plunged down a long, steep embankment.

Pine boughs slashed the sides of the rental sedan, failing to slow its descent. In the end, the car slammed against the trunk of a tree. Bouncing off, it lurched over onto its side.

He felt a sharp jolt as his head struck the doorframe. A second later, his pain was obliterated by the blackness that swallowed him.

Chapter One

Somebody had gone and changed the rules, Lauren thought. Either the power could be out or the phone could be out, but never both at the same time. That the two of them were just that on this occasion was an indication of how major the storm was.

Has to be the ice, she decided, replacing the receiver in its cradle after testing her phone and finding it dead. There had been a lot of it in the area in the form of frozen rain before it turned to snow. It must have brought down lines everywhere, which meant it was anyone's guess when her services would be restored.

Lauren wasn't worried. This wouldn't be the first time she had been without either a phone or electricity. Hey, you had to expect such inconveniences when you lived in a place this remote.

Anyway, she knew the drill and had already fired up the gas-powered generator out back. Although it was small, it would keep the water pump and the refrigerator going. Nothing else that depended on electricity was essential.

She had also lit the oil lamps and placed them in strategic positions around the combination living room–kitchen that overlooked the frozen lake. The doors to the two bedrooms were closed to conserve heat. Without the electric furnace, she would have to rely on the fireplace at this end of the living room and the old cookstove on the kitchen side. Both were cheerfully blazing.

Needing to make sure there was plenty of firewood inside, Lauren eyed the split logs heaped beside the hearth. They seemed to be a generous supply. They weren't. She knew how fast the pile could sink when you had to feed both the fireplace and the stove.

Snagging her coat from a peg beside the door, she bundled into it, seized the log carrier, and left the cabin.

The wind was howling off the lake, the snow was flying and it was brutally cold. Definitely a night to stay indoors. But since the covered porch that stretched across the front of the cabin was as far as she had to go, she didn't complain. Firewood was stacked along its entire length against the log wall.

Lauren was filling the carrier when she noticed it. A strange glow off the far end of the porch.

What in the world—

Leaving the carrier, she moved toward the light. When she reached the corner of the building, she leaned out over the rail for a better look. Whatever its source, the glow was some distance off. It came from the direction of the road up along the ridge above her cabin.

Puzzled, Lauren went on gazing into the night, trying to figure it out. The obstruction of the trees and the falling snow made it impossible to identify. It wasn't until there was a brief lull in the snowfall that she realized what she was seeing.

Not one light. *Two* lights. She was seeing the twin beams of a car's headlights. Only there was something wrong with them. They weren't horizontal. They were turned upward, like a pair of fixed lamps searching the night sky through the tall spires of the trees.

And that's when Lauren realized what must have happened. A car had run off the road and landed at such an angle that—

Dear God, an accident! Maybe a serious one, with people

injured. There would be no help from a passing vehicle, either. With the new highway to Elkton, this was no longer the
main route. The road up there was rarely traveled now, and
in weather like this it could be forever before someone came
along. Probably not until after the plow came through, and
who knew when that would be.

That leaves you as the only available help.

As much as she disliked the thought of going out into the
storm, Lauren didn't hesitate. She was already forming her
plan as she left the railing and sped back into the cabin.

Blankets. She would need blankets. She pulled three of
them off the shelf of the closet next to the bathroom. Throwing them down on the floor beside the front door, she traded
her coat for her snowmobile suit, boots and helmet.

She would have to take the snowmobile. Her car would be
useless in this stuff, her driveway already blocked. And she
would need the toboggan. She used it when the snow was
deep to haul supplies from her car to the cabin or to replen-
ish the wood on the porch from the shed out back.

The toboggan was leaning against the porch. When she
came away from the cabin, she lowered it and piled the blankets on it. Then she drew the load around the corner of the
building to where her snowmobile was parked. Removing the
protective cover from the machine, she roped the toboggan
to its rear bumper.

The engine kicked in with a roar on her first try with the
pull start. Straddling the saddle, she wove a trail up through
the snow-laden firs and pines. The headlights of the helpless
car guided her like a beacon.

Their glow seemed to grow weaker the closer she got, which
had to mean the car's engine wasn't running and that the headlights were operating on a battery whose power was dwindling.

Topping the last rise, she arrived at the scene of the accident. A silver sedan lay half on its side, with its back end buried down in a drift and its hood pointed upward.

Braking her snowmobile and leaving the engine idling, Lauren trudged through the snow, fearing what she would find as she approached the vehicle.

She had a flashlight with her, and when she reached the car, she directed its beam through one of the windows. The driver was still inside, sprawled behind the wheel. He was either unconscious or—

But Lauren refused to consider the worst.

She played the flashlight around the interior. No other occupants. That meant she had only the one victim to rescue. And, providing it wasn't already too late, she could lose him if she didn't hurry.

With the car's motor stalled, he couldn't have had the heater to keep him warm. There was no telling how long he had been out here in the cold. Certainly he would never have survived the night if, by pure chance, she hadn't spotted his headlights.

Lauren didn't stop to question the risk. Stranger or not, she had to transport him to the warmth of her cabin. There was no other option.

It was a decision easier made than executed. Just getting at him was a challenge in itself. The driver's side was jammed down into the snow, which left that door inaccessible. The passenger door was her only entry, and a difficult one when it was at an angle and several feet off the ground. Lauren somehow fought it open and lifted herself inside, noticing the air bag hadn't deployed. Well, technology wasn't infallible.

The driver never stirred. Removing her glove, she groped inside the collar of his expensive-looking leather coat. Her fingers pressed against his strongly corded throat, feeling for a pulse. She got one, slow though it was. He was still alive.

But her relief was dampened when she encountered a trickle of blood. The flashlight revealed its source as a wound on the side of his head. Just how serious it was she would need to try to determine when she moved him into the cabin.

The easy part was clambering out of the car, releasing the toboggan from the snowmobile, and positioning it below the open door.

The tough part was placing him on the toboggan. From what she could judge, he had to be all of a solid six feet in length. And a deadweight. But with a combination of tugging, dragging and sheer stubbornness, Lauren managed to wrestle him out of the car and lower him onto the toboggan. What damage she might be inflicting on him in the process she didn't dare to think about. It couldn't be helped.

After trussing him up in the blankets and hitching the toboggan to the bumper of the snowmobile again, she went back to the car to switch off its headlights and remove the keys from the ignition.

Pocketing them, she had a last look around the interior. Her flashlight disclosed a small travel bag on the backseat. She took it and placed it on the toboggan with her unconscious passenger.

It was time for her sled to go into action again.

ONCE SHE'D RECOVERED enough wind to do more than wheeze, Lauren addressed her patient.

"A few words of congratulation would be nice."

He didn't answer her plea. He remained inert.

"Please."

No response. Not so much as a flutter of his eyelids.

It really wasn't his approval she needed, only some form of reassurance from him that he wasn't going to expire on her. Though, considering what she had undergone to get him here, she was entitled to that congratulation.

The trip itself back to the cabin hadn't been eventful. It was what Lauren had achieved after the snowmobile delivered them to the cabin that deserved recognition. Since she'd had to get him inside, and since he was far too heavy for her to carry, she'd used the only means she could think of.

Filling the steps and the floor of the porch with snow, huffing and straining, she had hauled the toboggan and its load up onto the porch. Dragged it across the porch, over the threshold of the front door, and somehow arrived with her burden in front of the hearth.

Only then had Lauren permitted herself to collapse on the floor of the living room. It was where she huddled now beside the toboggan. And where, exhausted, she longed to go on huddling. But, whoever he was, the man she had rescued demanded immediate attention.

The fire first. It had shrunk to embers in her absence. Heaving herself to her feet, she placed fresh logs on the grate, made sure they caught and then went off to the bathroom.

When she returned, first aid kit in hand, the fire was blazing again, radiating a welcome warmth. She started to crouch down beside the toboggan and then stopped.

This is no good. You can't just let him go on lying there on that hard thing.

Yes, but there was no way she could manage to get him up onto one of the beds. Besides, the bedrooms had to be like freezers now.

All right, if she couldn't take him to a bed, then she'd bring the bed to him. Or the part that mattered, anyway.

Lauren felt like a player in a comic performance as she tussled a mattress off one of the twin beds in the spare bedroom, squeezed it through the doorway, and stumbled over it twice before she was able to deposit it on the floor between the sofa and the toboggan.

Stripping off her boots and snowmobile suit, she knelt beside the sled and unwrapped the blankets from the figure stretched on it. Then, sliding her hands under his back, she heaved him up and over onto the mattress. It took another effort before she was able to roll him over onto his back again.

There. Much better.

Or maybe not. There was still the matter of his head

wound. And who knew what other internal injuries he might have sustained. If he had, there was nothing she could do about them.

Leaning over him, she turned his head toward the light of the oil lamp on the table above her. The wound on his temple had stopped bleeding, but it was a nasty-looking gash. She cleaned it with antiseptic from the first aid kit, applied an antibiotic ointment for good measure and decided not to try to dress it with a bandage.

Lauren was no nurse, but his color looked all right, and when she checked his pulse again, it seemed steady enough.

But he never stirred, and that continued to worry her.

His coat. He'd probably be more comfortable if she could get him out of that coat. Lifting his head and shoulders, she set to work peeling away the leather coat. It was another struggle, but she succeeded in removing the garment.

Two items stuck in one of the coat's pockets landed on the floor. A map and a newspaper clipping. She set them aside with the jacket.

Sinking back on her heels, Lauren considered her patient. She knew he ought to have a doctor, maybe be admitted to a hospital. But there was nothing she could do about that. If he didn't come around by morning, she would have to think about going to Elkton for help. Providing, that is, she could get that far, even on the snowmobile. With the weather worsening, it was doubtful.

For the moment, though, she had done all she could.

You don't think you're finished here, do you? There's the little matter of his wallet.

Lauren had noticed the bulge in his back pants pocket when she had turned him over on the mattress. A wallet would provide her with identification, and she was entitled to know who he was.

Right.

But she hesitated. Her contact with him until now had

been necessary and strictly impersonal. However, groping around that particular area of his body seemed…well, somehow too familiar.

Just get on with it.

She did, squeezing her hand under his backside and working the wallet out of his pocket. There was fabric between her fingers and his firm flesh, but it didn't matter. The sensation of heat and intimacy had her gulping like a teenager.

The wallet in her hand, she scooted away from him.

Idiot.

Drawing a safe breath, she opened the wallet. She found a driver's license inside with a Seattle, Washington, address. It was issued in the name of Ethan Brand. She looked down at him.

Well, you have an identity now, Ethan Brand. I know who you are, but I don't know what *you are.*

For one thing, he was twenty-seven, according to the birth date on his license. He also didn't have to worry about his looks, Lauren decided.

Until this moment, she had been far too busy saving him to acquire more than a brief impression of his face and form. But now she had the opportunity to gaze at him in earnest. She liked what she saw.

Long-limbed and lean, he had a body that she supposed could be defined as athletic. It was his face, though, that she found interesting. And definitely appealing with its square jaw, cleft chin and thatch of dark brown hair.

That strong face also had a wide mouth with a boldly sensual quality. It would probably be wise, though, not to dwell on that.

And, anyway, it didn't seem fair for her to go on gaping at him when he was lying there unconscious and vulnerable.

Getting to her feet, Lauren placed his wallet and jacket, together with the map and clipping, on a chair. Then, covering him again with a blanket, she put on her coat, returned the toboggan to its spot below the porch, made sure her snowmobile was secure and resumed her interrupted job of bringing in a fresh supply of wood.

It was afterward, seated at the table eating the soup and sandwich she'd fixed for her supper, that she thought again about her silent visitor.

Ethan Brand. She knew his name and looks now. What she didn't know was his character. And to be honest about it, that concerned her. In his present condition, he certainly posed no threat. Nor had she a reason to think he was anything other than the harmless victim of an accident. Still…

Her gaze strayed in the direction of his travel bag she had dumped on the floor below the sofa. Should she? No, unlike her essential investigation of his wallet, digging through the contents of that bag struck her as a blatant invasion of his privacy.

Then she remembered the clipping and the map. They were there on the chair, out in the open, with no guilt involved and enticing her with the offer of possible clues.

Unable to resist the temptation, Lauren left the table and went to look at them. The clipping was no more than a ragged scrap hastily torn from a newspaper whose identity was missing. Most of the story wasn't there, either.

There was only one intact, small paragraph. It named a witness who had returned from Seattle to her home in Montana. Hilary Johnson. Lauren didn't recognize the name. Nor did this portion of the story include just what Hilary Johnson might have witnessed.

Lauren turned to the map. It was a road map of Montana, folded so that only one area was visible. *This* area. The town of Elkton was circled. *Heavily* circled, as if there had been a fierce determination in the action.

The clipping and the map smacked of —

Well, Lauren didn't know what they suggested. Something desperate? A mystery certainly.

And, when you get right down to it, none of your business.

She put the clipping and the map back on the chair. Wishing she hadn't looked at them, she tried not to let them make her uneasy. In all likelihood, there was an innocent explanation.

She returned to the table and her supper. Afterward, while cleaning up, she turned on the portable radio. Wanting to conserve its batteries, she listened only to the weather report.

It wasn't encouraging. The storm was expected to last through tomorrow and perhaps on into the next day. But then, she didn't need the radio to tell her just how bad the conditions were. She could hear the snow hissing at the windows, the wind snarling around the corners of the cabin.

Fortunately, the thick logs of its walls made the cabin snug and warm. As long as she kept the fires going, that is. She added fuel to both of them before deciding to call it an early night. She had earned a long rest after this evening's ordeal.

Long maybe, but not without interruptions, Lauren reminded herself. She would have to get up periodically to tend to the fires. Otherwise, in these temperatures the water lines would freeze.

Also, she needed to check regularly through the night on her patient. She went now to look at him. There was no change. He continued to lie there without any sign that he was either worse or better. As she crouched beside the mattress looking down at that still face, she was troubled by something that hadn't occurred to her before.

There are probably people somewhere worried about you, Ethan Brand. Maybe a family waiting for you, wondering where you are and why they haven't heard from you. If so, they must be frantic.

As disturbing as that possibility was, there was nothing Lauren could do about it. Not until the roads were cleared and she had a working telephone again.

Accepting the inevitability of their plight, Lauren rose to her feet. She fetched a pair of blankets and a pillow for herself, set the alarm clock to wake her in an hour, lowered the wicks on the lamps and stretched out on the sofa where she intended to spend the night.

Her last act before she drifted off was to lean over and murmur in the direction of the mattress, "Lauren McCrea wishes you a good night, Ethan Brand."

It would have been nice to hear a response, but of course there was none.

THE COLD, GRAY LIGHT of early morning was stealing through the windows of the cabin when Lauren was roused again by the buzz of the alarm clock. Stretching out a hand, she silenced the blasted thing.

She lay there for a moment, reluctant to stir. Then, remembering her patient, she lifted her head from the pillow to look down over the side of the sofa. And was startled out of her lingering drowsiness by a pair of riveting, blue-green eyes gazing back at her from the mattress.

Chapter Two

The only sound in the taut silence was the rustle of the embers in the fireplace as they sifted through the bars of the grate.

Swallowing nervously, she finally managed to find her voice. "You're awake."

It was hardly a necessary observation since he continued to regard her with those mesmerizing, blue-green eyes. Whether he was *lucidly* awake was another matter.

Concerned about that, she watched him lift his head from the mattress. The remarkable eyes narrowed in puzzlement as he cast his gaze around the room.

Then, looking at her again, his voice deep and raspy, he responded with a slow, "You mind telling me something?"

"What?"

"Just who the hell are you, and how did I get here? Wherever *here* is."

It wasn't a very friendly beginning—pretty brusque, in fact. But, considering how confused he must be, she was prepared to understand.

"The name is Lauren McCrea. The cabin is my home. And you don't need to tell me who you are. I checked on your identity in your wallet."

He considered her confession, maybe was briefly troubled by it—she couldn't tell—and then nodded his acceptance. "Fair enough."

"You had an accident. Do you remember it?"

"Oh, yeah. Skidded off the road while avoiding a collision with a—I don't know, either a cow or a moose. Something like that."

"It wouldn't have been a cow. There are no farms around here. Might have been a moose, but more likely an elk." The injury to his head hadn't left him disoriented, anyway. That much was a relief. But she was still concerned about other possible injuries. "How are you feeling?"

"Like that elk went and walked all over me after I smacked into the tree."

Lauren was alarmed when he shoved himself into a sitting position on the mattress. Throwing back the blanket that covered her, she swung her legs to the floor and sat up on the sofa.

"You shouldn't be moving! Not with that cut on the side of your head!"

"A cut, huh?" Only then did he seem to be aware of his wound. He fingered it carefully. "Yeah, it's kind of tender."

"Maybe more than just that. You've been unconscious since the accident."

He frowned, and as he glanced in the direction of a window, she could see him realize something else. That it was daylight.

"You telling me I slept around the clock?" He looked worried by that.

"You must have needed it."

"It was probably a result of exhaustion as much as the accident. It all caught up with me."

She waited for him to tell her what had caught up with him. But instead of explaining, his frown deepened, as though he regretted a careless admission.

"Whatever it was," he continued, trying to sort it out, "I'm missing something. I still don't know just how I ended up here and who I have to thank for—"

He broke off, looking around again, as if searching for his rescuer.

"No, there is no one else," she said.

He swung his attention back to her. "Are you telling me—"

"That it was me who brought you here, yes." She went on to inform him how she had spotted his headlights, traveled to the scene on her snowmobile and transported him back to the cabin.

"I'll be damned." He stared at her in wonder. "Nothing ordinary about you, is there, Lauren McCrea?"

She could see admiration in his gaze. It was silly of her to experience a sudden rush of warm pleasure. She tried to deny it with a shrug. "There's nothing extraordinary about doing what you have to do."

"Yeah," he said soberly. He stroked the stubble on his jaw and looked thoughtful. "You report the accident?"

Lauren shook her head, not liking to admit it but knowing he had to be told. "The telephone is out. The power, too."

"And the roads?"

"There's no way to get through, and no knowing when everything will get back to normal."

"You telling me we're stuck here?"

"Until the plows are able to open the roads, and as bad as this storm is… Look, I'm sorry. You must be anxious to let family or friends know what happened and where you are, but I'm afraid that isn't—"

"Don't worry about it. It doesn't matter."

Odd. She would have thought it mattered a great deal. Before she could pursue his lack of concern in that direction, he pushed aside the blankets and got to his feet.

"What are you doing? You should be resting."

"Right now, I need something…uh, more."

"Oh," she said, understanding.

"Uh-huh, a bathroom."

"Through there." She pointed in the direction of the hall that connected with the bedrooms and the bath. "But I don't know how smart this is."

He looked down at her from his six-foot height, a grin on his wide mouth. "You offering to go along and help, Lauren?"

The grin was slow, unexpected and decidedly sexy. It also left her flustered. He took pity on her.

"Relax. This body of mine may be suffering a few aches, but not enough to keep it down." He eyed his travel bag where she had left it on the floor. "It could do with a cleanup, though. But I don't suppose without power…"

"There's running water," she assured him. "I have a generator for the pump, but it's too small to operate the water heater."

"I've had cold showers before."

There was no note of humor in his tone, as if the subject of cold showers raised some grim memory. Scooping up his travel bag, he headed for the bathroom, leaving her mystified.

But not for long. The temperature in the room had dropped, reminding her that the fires needed her attention. She could hear the shower going in the bathroom as she busied herself fueling the stove and the fireplace. She thought about him, hoping he was all right in there.

There was something else she thought about, as well. Ethan Brand seemed to be a man with secrets. He had been vague about several things, reluctant to—what? Trust her?

And had she imagined it, or had he been relieved to learn she'd been unable to report his accident? If that were true, it didn't make sense. Unless—

Will you just listen to yourself?

She was getting all worked up without cause. All right, so she was trapped here with a stranger. But that didn't mean he was in any way dangerous just because he chose to keep his affairs private.

Except there was one little thing that genuinely bothered her. Ethan Brand was far too potent for comfort with those breath-robbing eyes and that provocative grin. And with this intimacy that had been forced on them.…

SHE HAD COFFEE finished on the stove and eggs ready to go into the frying pan when he emerged from the bathroom. The stubble was gone from his jaw, which meant he had managed to shave. He had also changed into a fresh shirt, its cuffs rolled back on his forearms.

"What's the weather doing?" he asked, placing his travel bag on the floor again. "The bathroom window was too frosted for me to tell."

"Still coming down hard, I'm afraid. How do you like your eggs?"

He didn't answer her. In the act of reaching for his wallet on the table, he had discovered the clipping and the map where she had left them next to the lamp. He picked them up and gazed at her questioningly.

"They fell out of your coat pocket," she said, explaining why they were there.

Except for the snapping of a log in the fireplace, there was a long silence in the room. He moved toward her where she stood by the stove, the map and the clipping still in his hand.

"Did you read it?" he asked, referring to the clipping.

There was no accusation in his tone, nothing menacing in his eyes. No reason for her to feel uneasy, but she did, as if he had caught her prying.

"I glanced at it," she admitted.

"And?"

"Nothing. It's none of my business." He was so close now that she could detect the clean scent of him after his shower. It was unsettling.

"But it must have left you wondering just who you've taken into your home. Whether you could be at risk having me here."

"Am I?"

She thought he might explain then about Hilary Johnson, about what exactly the woman had witnessed and why he needed to reach Elkton. Maybe even tell her he was a kind of investigator on a sensitive mission. Something like that. But he had no explanation for her.

"No, you're not," he said. "But if you want to throw me out in the snow, I'll understand. *Would* you like me to leave?"

"Don't be ridiculous. Where do you think you could possibly go in this storm?"

"All right, but I don't want you to be afraid of me. I promise you, Lauren, that I'm not dangerous."

She looked into those pure, blue-green eyes, and she believed him. Maybe she was a fool, but whatever trouble shadowed him, she sensed an innate decency in this man. He wouldn't hurt her.

"So, how *do* you like your eggs?"

"Surprise me. I'm not fussy. What can I do to help?"

"You can sit down at the table. If you won't stay in bed, then at least get off your feet."

Her concern apparently amused him. He wore that treacherous grin again. But he obeyed her, swinging around one of the captain's chairs and placing himself on it.

"How is the head wound doing?" she wanted to know as she went to work scrambling eggs.

"A little sore, that's all."

She poured coffee into a mug and brought it to him. "I'm not sure I shouldn't have covered it with a bandage. For all I know, it ought to have had stitches. Do you have a headache? Any dizziness?"

"Lauren?"

"What? Do you need milk? Sugar?"

"No, I need you to stop worrying about me. And you don't have to wait on me. I can help myself."

Cradling the coffee mug in his big hands, with long jeans-clad legs stretched out in front of him and crossed at the ankle, he gazed down the length of the room, as if noticing it for the first time.

"Nice place," he said. "But, uh…"

"What?" she asked, taking several slices of bread from the loaf to toast on the rack inside the cookstove's oven.

"I guess I'm just wondering what a woman is doing here all on her own in the middle of nowhere."

"Oh. Well, my grandfather left the cabin to me. When I was growing up, I would spend my summer vacations here with him."

He raised the mug to his mouth, sipped from it. "And the rest of the year?"

"My father's company moved us all over the map. He and my mother loved it. He's retired now, a condo in Florida, but the two of them still prefer traveling around the globe."

"And you didn't love it," Ethan guessed.

She glanced at him. He was perceptive. Maybe he *was* an investigator.

"I hated it," she admitted. "It was so impermanent, I never had time to put down any roots. I suppose that makes me disgustingly traditional, no taste for adventure."

"So that's what the cabin means for you? Roots?"

"It's home now. The only real home I felt I ever knew."

She had come home to Montana, yes, but that wasn't the whole story. Lauren knew she didn't have to tell him the rest. There was no reason for him to hear it. No sense in sharing something private and painful with a man she had known less than a day.

On the other hand, she thought, dishing up the eggs, removing the toast from the oven and joining him at the table with their plates, telling him might encourage him to be open with her. Face it, she was still curious to know what he was withholding from her. She decided to risk it.

"Being here, though, is a little more complicated than that," she confessed. "Before the cabin, I was working in Helena. Not a very satisfying job, but there was this guy…well, let's just say I thought it was the real thing. He didn't. The real thing for him turned out to be his ex-wife he ended up going back to."

"Are we talking about a broken heart?"

Lauren laughed. It wasn't funny, but she was long past the stage of tears and laughter did seem like a better remedy. "Absolutely. One that required mending. That being the case…"

"You came home to heal. Has it worked?"

"Can't even remember his name."

Not quite true, but she was no longer hurting. Which just went to prove that Kenneth had never been right for her in the first place.

There was a long moment of silence while they concentrated on their eggs and toast. Lauren was conscious of how he kept eyeing her over his coffee mug. His bold curiosity made her squirm. But she had no right to complain. Not when she kept sneaking her own looks at him in return.

Her interest wasn't very smart when the man was just passing through her life. Once the storm was over and the road cleared, he would be out of here and they would forget all about each other.

But until then, the two of them were caught here. Snowbound and aware of each other. Well, she was intensely aware of him, anyway. Little things, like the way his Adam's apple bobbed when he swallowed, how his wide shoulders hunched forward, and a look in his eyes that was…what? Haunted somehow?

"So, tell me," he said, breaking the silence, "what do you do with yourself all alone here in the wilderness? When you're not rescuing accident victims, that is."

She looked at him in surprise. "Why, I work, of course."

"You mean you commute to a job?"

"I don't have to. My work is right here."

He twisted around when she nodded in the direction of the book-lined alcove at the far end of the living room. Her computer sat there on a table beneath a window that overlooked the lake.

"See the row of books on the middle shelf over to the left? Those are mine."

"Are you telling me you're an author?"

"In a manner of speaking."

"I'll be damned."

She laughed. "Don't be impressed. My name doesn't appear on the spines. I'm a ghostwriter. Autobiographies mostly, and sometimes how-to books, all for professionals who haven't the time or the skill to write their own. They communicate by e-mail, and I put it together for them."

"And they get all the credit on the title pages? That doesn't seem fair."

"I'm not complaining. It pays the bills until someday when I hope to have my own name on the covers. How about you?"

"Nothing so interesting."

He helped himself to more coffee. She waited for him to tell her about his work. To tell her anything at all about himself, but he changed the subject.

"Still blowing out there," he said, glancing toward the window.

Talking about herself hadn't worked. He wasn't going to share his own secrets. She had to accept that.

"And drifting badly on the roads, I'm afraid." She checked her watch. "It should be time for a local weather forecast. Let's see."

Did she imagine it, or did Ethan suddenly stiffen when she rose from the table and moved toward the counter where her portable radio was tucked between the toaster and the microwave?

They listened to the weather portion of the broadcast that reported downed lines, closed roads and the likelihood that the storm would not end before tomorrow. Mindful of the batteries, Lauren switched off the radio without waiting for the news.

Her imagination again, or did he look relieved this time? *Should* she be worried that he was hiding something from her?

ETHAN WAS FRANTIC as the day wore on, the snow outside building to a depth that made him wonder just when he would be able to leave. When he could do what he had come here to do before it was too late for him.

Lauren heated water for herself on the wood-fueled cookstove and carried it into the bathroom to bathe and change. Afterwards, installed on the sofa with pad and pencil, she worked on notes for her latest project.

Ethan kept the fires going for them and paced. Though she didn't complain, he was probably driving her wild with the tension that kept him moving restlessly from one end of the long room to the other like a caged animal.

He couldn't help it. Everything counted on his reaching Hilary Johnson, getting her to commit to the truth.

That was part of his need to get out of here, a *big* part, but there was something else. There was Lauren McCrea. In just the few hours he'd known her, she had brought him dangerously close to losing his head.

He wondered even now, gazing at her curled up in a corner of the sofa with her feet tucked under her, if she had any idea how alluring she was with her long, auburn hair, that slim, woman's body with its surprising strength, and those warm brown eyes. He doubted it. She struck him as much too modest to realize her worth.

There was her smile, too. The kind of smile that made a man feel good about himself.

What a fool that guy in Helena had been to let her get away. Even if he hadn't appreciated her looks, he should have cherished all her other qualities. Things like the courage that had sent her out into a howling blizzard to rescue a stranger, and then to care for him with a generosity that no man should have failed to value.

What are you doing?

This was crazy. He couldn't have chosen a worse time to be so strongly attracted like this to a woman, particularly someone as special as Lauren. She deserved the interest of a man who could be open and honest with her.

And Ethan had been neither. Because if he had told her the truth, he would have risked involving her in his mess. He didn't want that. Didn't want her to learn she had a fugitive on her hands. She was already vulnerable enough just having him here.

But Lauren must have already realized that. She couldn't have missed his concern about the radio, and must have wondered about it, even if there had been no way for her to guess he feared a newscast naming him as a wanted man. Probably not much chance of such a report, though, when Seattle and what had happened there were a long way off. Still, there was always the possibility.

No, he didn't want to hurt her. So he had withheld an explanation, even though she was entitled to one. But she hadn't demanded answers from him. She had accepted his evasive silence, even respected it. Amazing woman.

She's not for you, Brand. Just stop looking at her, will you?

Fine. He'd look elsewhere. Admire instead the cabin her grandfather had left her. They must have been very close, Lauren and her grandfather. Shared a lot of good times together that left her with sweet memories. Thinking of his own grandfather, and how vastly different their relationship had been and how it had ended, Ethan envied her that.

Yeah, he liked the cabin with its stone fireplace and rough log walls. It was solid and honest. But not austere. Probably because Lauren had added her own personal touches, such as the colorful rugs on the polished plank floor, the cheerful curtains at the windows, the watercolors on the walls, the wealth of books on the shelves. Things that made the place safe and inviting. Like its owner.

Here he was back to thinking about her again. This was no good. No good at all.

Damn it, why couldn't it stop snowing? He needed it to stop snowing. He needed to get away before it was too late, before he wound up losing his sanity along with his self-control. He needed to leave her while she was still untouched by the trouble he had brought with him to this place.

"THE LAMPS ARE getting low on oil," Lauren said.

They had been burning the lamps all day against the gloom of the storm. It was late afternoon now, and the light outside was beginning to fail.

"There's kerosene in the shed. I'd better bring in a fresh supply."

"I'll go," Ethan volunteered. "It's about time I started to earn my keep."

She looked down pointedly at his shoes. "In those? I don't think so."

Yeah, he thought, following her gaze, he'd been in too much of a hurry to leave Seattle to think of taking a pair of boots with him. "So I'll get wet feet."

"Just when I've got you on the road to recovery, you want to go and risk a relapse."

"What? You think you'll have to nurse me through something like pneumonia just because I get wet feet?"

"We're not going to argue about it." She headed for her coat and boots located beside the front door. "Besides, I know how to deal with that shed door and just where to lay my hands on the kerosene when I get inside."

She was a stubborn woman. And, in her determination, also a damn appealing one. He was reluctant to let her go.

"You be careful out there," he cautioned her.

"You forget," she said, tugging on her boots, bundling into her coat, "I'm used to wading through drifts. Be back before you can miss me."

She was gone then, out the door and clomping across the porch. And he already missed her.

Ethan was starting for the fireplace to lay another log on the blaze when he heard it. A slow rumble overhead that escalated to a rapid roar.

What in the name of—

His gut tightened on him as, beginning to understand what had just happened, he raced to a window that overlooked the side of the cabin. It was true! The snow that had been accumulating on the roof all day had surrendered under its own weight, sliding from the steep slope like an avalanche off the side of a mountain.

Worse than that, Lauren had been passing under it when it collapsed. He could see one of her arms sticking out of the mound. Nothing else. The rest of her had been buried.

He didn't stop to snatch up his coat. Didn't care how exposed he was to the unforgiving cold. All that mattered was digging Lauren out of that pile before she suffocated.

He never felt the wind that blasted at him as he tore out of the cabin and around the corner. Never felt anything but an urgency to reach her. Dropping to his knees when he got to the mound, he clawed at the snow, pulling it away in great handfuls.

The top of her head appeared. Then her face. And finally her shoulders. When he could get his hands under both of her arms, he heaved, dragging her up out of the mass that had imprisoned her.

Ethan staggered to his feet with his precious load, fought his way back to the front of the cabin, up the steps, across the porch and inside. Kicking the door shut behind him, he strode across the room and placed her on the floor close to the hearth.

And all the while, as he hunkered down in front of her, lifted her up and struggled to free her of her coat and boots, he was sick with fear.

God, she looked so white and frail, felt so cold and wet!

He stripped off her mittens, seized both her hands and began rubbing her limp fingers. Her eyes were closed. Was she unconscious?

"Lauren, can you hear me?"

"Okay," she muttered, her eyes drifting open. "I'm okay."

His relief was immense.

He didn't know when it happened. When his hands were no longer holding hers. When, instead, they were on either side of her head, his fingers in her silky hair. The two of them were face-to-face now, mere inches apart.

There was a long silence, her eyes searching his, questioning. It wasn't a total silence. He was dimly aware of the crackling blaze in the fireplace behind her, the muffled hum of the generator somewhere out back.

"Ethan?" she whispered.

It wasn't a question as much as it was a plea. That's how he chose to read it anyway. And he answered it, surrendered to the thing that had been thrumming between them all day.

Head angled, he brought his mouth down to hers. Kissed her, at first gently and then with abandon. Tasted her sweetness, savored her flavor with his tongue.

He was aware of her scent, something as subtle as wildflowers. Aware, too, as he deepened their kiss, that her lush body pressed to his was no longer cold. It radiated a heat that ignited his senses.

Was Lauren the first to recover her sanity? Him? Or both of them at the same time? It didn't matter. Either way, he felt the loss when they drew apart.

She stared at him, clearly shaken.

"It's what happened," she said, eager to explain the madness that had seized them. "Not just now with your digging me out of the snow and carrying me back inside. It's the whole thing. Our being caught here like this together in the storm. It isn't reality, so it's done things to our emotions, made them reckless. You see?"

Ethan nodded. Agreed that their kiss had been the result of an irrational, temporary behavior, because that's what she seemed to need. But he didn't believe it. For him, it had been very real. In just a few hours, Lauren McCrea had become vital to him. And, with time running out on him, he could do nothing about it.

Chapter Three

"Why don't you confess, Ethan? Think of how much better you'll feel after you tell me all about it."

The voice that taunted him was as soft as silk. And as deadly as a cobra. It was also familiar. He knew that voice, didn't he? But how could he match it to a face he couldn't see? A face that was hidden in the blackness behind the glaring, white-hot lights that blinded him.

If only he could sleep. But they wouldn't let him sleep. Whenever he closed his eyes, they would rouse him. Sometimes by slapping or kicking him awake. At other times by subjecting him to those frigid showers.

The interrogation was endless. But he hadn't broken. He had been trained not to tell them what they wanted to know.

"We already know the truth anyway, Ethan. Your hands told us the truth. Look at your hands."

He looked down at his hands. Horrified, he saw that they were covered with blood.

"His blood, Ethan. You have his blood on your hands."

This time, his tormentor thrust his face down into the light. Ethan recoiled from the sight of it. Koh!

So he had been right about the voice. But what was that monster doing here in Seattle? He had left Koh back in the bleak, North Korean cell where they had held him all those weeks of pure hell.

"Tell me you did it, Ethan. Tell me you killed him, and then you can sleep."

Lack of sleep. It had him confused. Koh couldn't be here. Not in Seattle. Whatever the explanation, he held on to his determination. He refused to talk.

His interrogator sighed with a regret that belied his brutality. "You leave us no choice, Ethan."

He heard the sound of a door opening in the blackness. Then someone stumbling as he was pushed forward into the light. Ethan recognized the figure and was shocked. Hands bound behind him, the man's face was a mess of bruises and raw cuts. They had beaten him.

It was Zach, of course, who had been on the reconnaissance mission with him. Who had been captured along with Ethan by the North Koreans. Why had they brought Zach to Seattle?

"Don't tell them, Ethan," Zach pleaded with him. "Whatever they do to you, don't tell them anything."

"Oh, but he will," Koh insisted. "When he watches what we are going to do to you, he will talk. Won't you, Ethan?"

Ethan had withstood it all, every punishment they'd inflicted. Was prepared to go on resisting them whatever they made him suffer. But to torture Zach while they forced him to watch—

"Bastards!"

Surging up from the hard stool, he struck out at them, fists swinging in an explosive rage…

"IT'S ALL RIGHT. Ethan, it's all right."

A pair of hands. He felt a pair of hands on his tight fists, striving to restrain him. They weren't cruel hands. They were gentle.

"You were having a nightmare."

The voice was gentle, too. And deeply concerned. He went still, his fists uncurling as a blessed reality replaced the nightmare. The darkness of another night had wrapped itself around the cabin where he was sitting up on the mattress. Lauren had slipped off the sofa and was kneeling in front of him.

They had left one of the lamps burning on the table above them, its wick turned low. In the feeble glow, he could see her troubled face.

"It's okay," she assured him, "you don't have to tell me about it, but it must have been some awful nightmare. You were shouting in your sleep."

Awful? Yeah, just about as bad as it could get. His imprisonment in North Korea over a year ago had somehow gotten mixed up in his dream with what happened just days ago in Seattle. Only he was no longer in the service. There would be no one this time to negotiate his release.

Another cell. He couldn't be locked away in another cell. After what he had endured in North Korea, it would destroy him. But it could happen. It *would* happen if—

"Your hands are shaking," she said.

She must have sensed how desperately he needed her comfort in that moment. That's why she did a wonderful, impulsive thing. Still clinging to his hands, head bent over them, she covered their backs with slow, soothing kisses.

He shuddered over the heat of her mouth on his flesh. She felt so good, so right. A lifeline of sanity in a world that had become demented for him. He didn't know how he was going to bear leaving her when the time came for him to go.

"Lauren," he said, his voice gruff with emotion.

She lifted her head and met his gaze. He looked into her eyes and read understanding there. She knew what he wanted, what was tearing him up inside: her. He needed her as he had never needed any other woman.

It was wrong of him to take advantage of her just because she was receptive to that need. He realized that. But, in her generosity to offer him what would bring him relief from his anguish, however temporary, he was unable to resist her.

With a groan of submission, snatching his hands away

from hers in order to gather her into his arms, he reached for her. Hauled her softness tightly against his hardness, crushed his mouth over hers.

Alternately fierce and tender. That's how Ethan kissed her, and how she responded with her own kisses.

They must have shed their clothes between those fevered kisses. He didn't remember. He only knew that at some point they were both naked, that he was swollen with desire, his senses inflamed by the taste and feel of her.

He should have been beyond all hesitation by then, but some shred of conscience did make him pause. "It's not too late," he rasped. "We don't have to—"

"Yes," she whispered. "Yes, we do."

Her own urgency robbed him of all reason then, leaving him with only one scrap of responsibility. At least he had that much, he thought, his hand groping for his wallet on the table beside them.

Fumbling for the condom inside, slitting it open and removing it, he sheathed himself. There was no self-control after that. All the rest was a mindless, rapturous joining. Their two bodies consuming each other, straining for release and finding it in a roaring fulfillment.

Afterwards, holding her securely against his side as she slept, Ethan knew he should regret what had just happened. But he didn't. He couldn't.

COLD WATER pelted his body, reviving him. He was able to think clearly as he soaped himself and turned under the shower spray.

The first light of morning had revealed that the storm had ended. That meant the plows would soon be out clearing the roads, maybe already were.

Ethan didn't think there was much chance of one of them spotting his rental car down among the trees. It must be snow-covered by now. But there was always that risk.

And if it were sighted and its presence reported, it would

be investigated and identified as a rental car. Its license would be easily traced to the agency in Kalispell. The police would be told who had rented the vehicle. They would run a check on him, learn he was wanted in Seattle. And since the sedan had been abandoned, and the cabin the only nearby shelter in the storm, it was only logical…

It can't happen that fast. You still have time.

Okay, that was probably true, but he couldn't waste that time. He was defenseless here. He had to get away just as quickly as possible. How? The rental was useless.

Lauren's car, he thought. She had told him over dinner last night that she'd left it parked up at the mouth of her driveway where it joined the road, just as she always did whenever there was the threat of a heavy snow that made her lane impassable. He didn't want to involve Lauren, but there was no other way. He'd have to ask to borrow her car, dig it out of the snow, and drive into Elkton.

Things would be all right if he could just reach Hilary Johnson. He would *make* them all right.

And then what? What was he going to do about Lauren? Running out on her after last night was unthinkable. But with what he was facing, how could he do otherwise? Anything else would be unfair to both of them.

And just how fair is it to go without a word of explanation, to leave her hurt and wondering? You can't do that. She deserves to know.

Ethan made up his mind. He would tell her everything over breakfast. She might react very badly to the truth, order him out of the cabin and her life. He wouldn't blame her if she did, even though it would kill him if she turned away from him now. No other choice, though. He would have to take his chances with her.

It was when he turned off the shower that he was able to hear a kind of reverberating noise somewhere outside the cabin. Sounded like machinery.

A snowmobile? he wondered. Had Lauren fired up her snowmobile?

Puzzled, he flung back the shower door and grabbed a towel. It wasn't until he emerged from the stall and was swiftly drying himself that he realized what he was hearing was a heavy-duty vehicle of some sort.

The thing suddenly went silent, as if it had arrived at its destination. Seized by a grim understanding, his stomach lurched.

Ethan dragged on a pair of jeans. He didn't bother with any other clothes. He could hear voices out in the living room. He knew there was no point in trying to make a break for it. He wouldn't get ten yards.

His chest and feet bare, he left the bathroom, walked into the living room. He had been wrong in his judgment. Time had already run out on him.

There were two of them, both of them with faces like stone. Maybe they were state troopers, or maybe they were from the local sheriff's department. He didn't know, didn't care. All that mattered was Lauren. She stood there staring at him with an expression on her face that chewed him up inside.

One of the uniforms held a gun on him while his younger partner approached him and began to cautiously check his jeans for any weapon he might be carrying.

The officer with the gun addressed him, solemnly intoning, "Ethan Brand, you're under arrest as a suspect in the murder of Jonathan Mortimer Brand. You have the right to…"

Ethan didn't listen to the rest, didn't even look at their faces as he stood there without moving. The only face that mattered was Lauren's. She still wore that stricken expression.

He tried to meet her gaze, tried to send her a silent message of appeal, imploring her forgiveness. But she turned away from him. He had never felt such a miserable sense of abandonment.

Eleven months later

IT WAS ANOTHER Montana. The mountains and the forests were still there, just as he remembered them. But they weren't wrapped in deep snow. The gaudy colors of early October tinted them now, the hardwoods ablaze with crimson and gold against the drab green of the pines. The air was kinder, too, almost balmy and wearing a faint autumn haze.

Yeah, it was different, although Ethan was able to recognize the road he traveled, this time in a rental sedan that almost matched the clear blue of the sky. There were familiar landmarks, like the sign that advertised vacation cottages for rent in Elkton.

Elkton. That was why he'd come back to this place. He had unfinished business with Hilary Johnson, who now lived permanently in her hometown.

His grandfather's former housekeeper had lied on the stand when they'd brought her back to Seattle as the chief witness in Ethan's trials. Both juries had believed her, but her testimony hadn't been enough to convict him. Insufficient evidence. He'd been acquitted in the end.

Ethan should have let it go at that, gotten on with his life. He couldn't. Whatever the final verdict, he knew that the police and the public continued to doubt his innocence. He had to know why Hilary Johnson had lied. Had to do whatever he could to clear himself, or this cloud of guilt would shadow him for the rest of his days.

Hell, why was he playing games with himself? He had realized the moment he'd boarded the plane, even before then, that it was not just Hilary Johnson who was bringing him back to Montana. Lauren. He had to try to make it right with Lauren.

The road climbed the ridge and swept around a bend. Ethan slowed the car. Another landmark. This was the spot where he had skidded and gone over the embankment.

Recollections. And the worst of them was the gut-wrenching memory of Lauren's face when those two cops had hauled him away from her cabin in cuffs. The look of betrayal on her face had haunted him all those long months they had kept him in jail.

He had to try to make it right with her. If she would let him.

He was seething with that hope when he reached the turn into her driveway and descended the long, winding lane. Maybe she wouldn't be here. He hadn't considered that.

Swooping around a curve, he emerged from the trees. Another vehicle, a green compact, was parked at the edge of the clearing. He figured it had to be hers. He pulled in behind it and climbed from the rental.

The ground here had been white when he'd last seen it, the lake frozen. Now the clearing was a golden brown with drifting leaves and the open waters of the lake a deep blue. No wind, either. The morning was tranquil.

Ethan was aware of the stillness as he crossed the clearing to the cabin, mounted the steps of the porch and arrived at the front door. The door was slightly ajar. When he rapped on it, it spread inward.

"Lauren," he called softly. "You here?"

No answer. The open door was an invitation. He probably had no right to look at it that way, but he did.

Ethan walked into the living room and was immediately assaulted by memories. Some of them were raw and painful. Most of them were good memories. He tried to hang on to those, just as he had clung to them all those months in jail.

The cabin was silent. There was no sign of Lauren. But sacks of groceries stood on the bar that divided the kitchen from the living room, as if she had recently arrived home from the store and hadn't had time to unpack them.

A movement through one of the windows at the side of the cabin captured his attention. Ethan went to the glass and looked out. Lauren was there in the yard putting seed in a bird feeder. The sight of her slim figure had emotions welling up inside him. They threatened to spill over when she left the feeder and trotted back around the corner of the cabin.

She hadn't heard his car, didn't know he was here. He turned away from the window, waiting for her. When she came through the door and discovered his presence, she stopped, a look of naked shock on her face.

Swiftly recovering herself, she challenged him with a sharp, "How did you get in?"

It was not the greeting Ethan wanted to hear, even if he did deserve it. "The door was ajar. I didn't think you'd mind."

She set the container of sunflower seeds on a small table just inside the door and then moved away toward the far end of the living room, as if she didn't trust him to be anywhere near her.

"How long have you been here?" she demanded.

"I just got—" He broke off. He could see she was trembling. She was afraid. Afraid of him. Stung by her fear, he tried to reassure her, saying solemnly, "I told you once, Lauren, that I wouldn't hurt you. I meant it. I mean it now."

"You turn up like this out of nowhere just to tell me that?"

She was right. He should have phoned her first, asked if he could see her. Why hadn't he? Maybe because he'd feared she would hang up on him.

She raked her fingers through her auburn hair. That's when he noticed she had cut it and that this shorter length suited her. Her action was evidence that she was still apprehensive. He tried again to ease her.

"I wouldn't hurt anyone, Lauren, and I didn't. What I was accused of when they arrested me last year… well, I stood trial for that and was—"

"I know. It was all over the news."

Yeah, given his grandfather's wealth and prominence, he supposed the whole thing was sensational enough to have been covered even here in Montana

"Then you know I'm no longer a wanted man."

"What I don't know is what you're doing here."

This was all going badly. They were stiff and awkward with each other, not what he'd planned. "We're unfinished business, Lauren. Whatever happened, I cared about us. I still care."

"You had a strange way of showing that. Eleven months of silence."

She was angry now. Unable to forgive him. He couldn't blame her. No, he hadn't tried to call her or write her. How could he, with a prison sentence looming over him every day of those eleven months?

Almost a year. A whole year locked away in a Seattle jail. Held without bail because not only was the charge murder, he'd been a suspect who had fled the state of Washington with the intention of badgering a witness. Hilary Johnson, who, after her deposition, had come home to Montana until her testimony was needed.

She *had* testified, but only after lengthy delays that had preceded the first trial, which had ended in a hung jury. Then more delays followed until the second trial, when the jury this time had brought in a reluctant verdict of innocence. The prosecution had failed to prove Ethan's guilt beyond any reasonable doubt.

And throughout those eleven months, he had made no effort to contact Lauren. He'd been convinced it wouldn't be fair to her, that with the threat of prison he'd only be hurting her more than he already had. She hadn't needed him messing up her life again.

This was what Ethan had thought, and he realized now how wrong he had been.

"You're right," he said. "I owe you an explanation."

"I don't want to hear it. I don't need it. I just want you to go."

Hoping an appeal would work, Ethan started toward her.

She backed away from him. That's when he realized she was more than just hurt or scared. She was worried about something. Her gaze nervously, briefly slewed in the direction of the door to the master bedroom. Ethan could see that door now. It was closed.

"What is it, Lauren? What are you hiding?"

"Nothing. Please, just go."

She was protecting something inside that bedroom. Or someone. He was certain of it. She was no longer living here alone.

Who? Another man? Was the guy from Helena back in her life?

He was gripped by a sudden spasm of jealousy. Stupid. He wasn't entitled to such an emotion. Lauren was a young, vibrant woman. Why shouldn't she have someone in her life?

But as unreasonable as he knew his jealousy to be, it persisted, resulting in an equally irrational action.

When he changed direction and strode purposefully toward the bedroom door, Lauren tried to cut him off. He was too quick for her, arriving at the door before she could prevent his intention.

"You have no right!" she cried in a panic.

No, he didn't. No right at all to confront some concealed lover like an outraged husband. He could end up making a thorough fool of himself. Probably would. He didn't care. He opened the door, walked into the room.

There was no other man. Nothing out of the ordinary. Except for a crib located near the window.

Ethan was only dimly aware of Lauren behind him, plucking at the sleeve of his sweater in a futile effort to stop him. Shrugging her off, he moved numbly across the room.

He reached the crib, the breath sticking in his throat as he looked down into its shallow depth. A pair of blue-green eyes, *his eyes*, gazed back at him innocently.

Chapter Four

Lauren drew back when he swung around to confront her. It wasn't the hard look on his face that made her shrink from him, although that was intimidating enough in itself. It was the way he stood there with feet braced slightly apart, lean body rigid, hands rolled into fists down at his sides.

Like a man ready for battle.

She had watched him assume this tough attitude once before. It had happened eleven months ago on that awful morning when he had emerged from the bathroom to find the two state troopers waiting for him. Brief though it had been, Lauren had never forgotten it. It was as daunting now as it had been then.

"The baby," he said, his voice like gravel. "It's mine, isn't it?"

It would be useless to deny it. Even at two months old, Sara not only had Ethan's eyes but his face, as well, including the hint of a cleft in her chin.

"Yes," she admitted reluctantly.

She could see memory surfacing behind his frown. "But we used protection."

"And sometimes protection fails."

"My kid," he muttered, struggling to accept it.

As though needing further verification, he turned back to the crib, leaning down for a closer look. No longer fearful of him, aware only of a maternal need to protect her child, Lauren flew to the crib. She hovered there, prepared to defend Sara against any threat.

She needn't have been worried. Her daughter certainly wasn't. Her wide, blue-green eyes gazed up at the face of the man above her with trust and interest, her tiny fists waving in contentment.

And Sara's father?

Lauren turned her head to glance at him. Ethan's face had softened, the expression on it tugging at her in spite of her resistance.

"The blanket is pink," he said. "Does that mean—"

"Yes, a girl. Her name is Sara."

The precious moment they shared didn't last. Ethan straightened, his bold mouth hardening again as he faced her.

"And just when were you planning to tell me I had a daughter?"

The thing that had terrified Lauren all these months was no longer just a possibility. It had arrived in the shape of a formidable Ethan Brand. She knew she had to meet his inevitable demands with courage and determination, but she couldn't seem to find her tongue. Her silence condemned her.

"You weren't going to tell me, were you? You were going to go on preserving this little secret."

He would never understand the torment that had prefaced her ultimate decision. Wouldn't think, as major as all this was to him, that she deserved his sympathy. She didn't try.

"Damn it, Lauren, you should have contacted me when you realized you were pregnant. I had a right to know about Sara."

Here it was, the angry accusation she had prayed she would never have to hear and deal with. "Yes, you did," she agreed, "but —"

"But *what?*"

Lauren drew a slow breath to steady herself. When she

spoke again, she tried to choose her words with care. But there was no way to ease their inherent cruelty.

"I felt I had to keep Sara's paternity a secret from everyone. Even from the man who fathered her."

"Is this supposed to make sense?"

"Think about it, Ethan," she said, pleading for his understanding. "You'd been arrested for murder. The opinion of every news report I heard was that you would be convicted, sentenced to years in prison."

She had been unable to avoid wounding him. She could see it in his eyes.

"Yeah, I get it," he said. "The guy you'd made the mistake of going to bed with had been branded a killer, and no way did you want to be associated with that."

"For Sara's sake!" she cried. "Don't you see how that knowledge would have hurt her growing up in a conservative place like this? I wasn't going to do that to her."

"The daughter of a man who'd murdered his own grandfather, huh? Not a very nice reputation. Okay, I can buy that. Public opinion can be pretty nasty. But what about you, Lauren? What was *your* opinion while I sat there in jail?"

She was silent again. Helplessly silent.

His mouth twisted in a bitter smile. "So you condemned me, too."

"No, I—I didn't know what to think. When all was said and done, you were a stranger. I knew next to nothing about you, and I couldn't take the chance of—"

"Believing I might be innocent. All for the sake of Sara, wasn't that it? Well, I wasn't convicted and I *am* innocent. And if there are any lingering doubts about that, and I guess there are, I'm going to see to it that you, along with the good people of both Elkton and Seattle, are relieved of them. With or without the help of Hilary Johnson. And when I'm done clearing myself…"

There was a decisive look now on his face that scared her.

She didn't want to hear what he intended, but he went on to tell her in words that were as sharp as razors.

"Whether you like it or not, Lauren, I'm going to play a role in my daughter's life. Make no mistake about that."

Trembling, she refused to listen to another word. "Get out," she commanded him angrily. "Just go."

"I'm leaving, but I'll be back. You can count on it."

And with that forceful promise cutting into her heart, he turned and strode out of the bedroom, out of the cabin. From a side window, she watched him climb into a blue sedan and drive away. He was gone, but he was not out of their lives.

What was she going to do about him? What *could* she do?

Sara was beginning to whimper. She wanted to be fed.

It was while Lauren was fixing her daughter's bottle that she made a decision. She needed professional advice.

WITH OR WITHOUT the help of Hilary Johnson.

Ethan's rash pledge to Lauren mocked him as he headed back to his motel two discouraging hours later. At this moment, after trying to track down the elusive ex-housekeeper without result, he was beginning to think he *would* have to clear himself without her.

He had started with her address in Elkton, an old frame house in need of paint. Like its neighbors who shared the quiet residential street, the place was shaded by maples in the full blaze of autumn.

Hilary wasn't at home. Ethan had parked himself on the front porch, hoping she would turn up. The old man next door, curious about his presence, had stopped raking the leaves in his yard and come over to speak to him. He'd been reluctant at first to answer questions, but Ethan had finally convinced him that it was important.

"She keeps to herself," the old man had told him, tugging at the brim of a baseball cap that was splitting at the seams.

"Just like her parents, who left her the property. Used to be a sister, but I think she died, too."

"Any idea where I could locate her?"

"Could be she's at one of those temp jobs. You know, filling in for secretaries and the like at offices around town. I know she does that sometimes."

Ethan wasn't surprised by this information. He knew that Hilary had on occasion helped his grandfather in this capacity when her duties as a housekeeper had permitted it.

"Which offices would those be?"

The old man had offered him several suggestions. Ethan had waited for another fifteen minutes on the porch, but when Hilary failed to return, he went off to try those offices.

It was while driving from insurance agents to real estate operations, none of which had employed her today, that Ethan realized he knew next to nothing about Hilary Johnson. Although she had served as his grandfather's live-in housekeeper for over two years, she remained essentially a mystery to him.

The questions that had troubled him even before his arrest continued to haunt him. Why had Hilary risked perjury charges by lying in her deposition and on the stand at both of his trials? He could see no possible motive. Nor could she, herself, have brutally struck down his grandfather like that. Whatever his age, Jonathan Brand had been a large, strong man and his housekeeper delicate almost to the point of being frail. Also, she hadn't benefited in any way from his death.

Just the same, Ethan couldn't shake his conviction that she was in some way the key to everything. Providing he could find her. And providing she would even agree to talk to him. He could be in trouble with the law again if she complained about him. It was a possibility he was prepared to risk.

But right now, he needed a shower and then something to eat. He had missed breakfast, and it was long past noon. Once revived, he would go back to hunting for his objective.

His motel was off the far end of Elkton's main street, but getting there was proving to be a slow crawl. The business district was heavy with traffic, both sides of the street crowded with shoppers.

Must be the weather that brought them all out, Ethan decided as he halted at a traffic light. The afternoon was as warm as summer.

If the circumstances had been otherwise, he might have been tempted to join all those people strolling along the sidewalks. Elkton was an attractive place.

Situated between majestic mountain ranges, the town had once been a thriving lumber center. But now, as one of the gateways to Waterton-Glacier International Peace Park, it was more tourist-oriented. The stores that in the frontier days had contained saloons, boarding houses and pool halls behind their brick fronts had been turned into gift shops and ice-cream parlors. Elkton was currently as respectable and picturesque as one of the postcards sold in those shops. Yeah, he could see why Lauren had come back here to live.

Lauren. The sudden image he conjured of her brought both pleasure and pain. Not that he needed her image to be reminded of her. She had been in his thoughts all day.

He had to face it. She was as much responsible for his low mood as Hilary Johnson. More so. He was suffering miserable guilt because of her, unable to get that scene in the cabin bedroom out of his head.

What were you thinking to turn on her like that?

But that was the trouble. He *hadn't* been thinking, only feeling. And his emotions had resulted in a harsh anger that must have hurt her. He was sorry about that, just as he regretted not having been there for her during the months she was carrying his child. Independent though she was, it couldn't have been easy for her dealing with that all on her own.

The light changed. Ethan drove on to the end of the street, turned a corner and arrived at his motel in the middle of the block. It was a long, two-storied affair, with each of its rooms opening directly onto outdoor galleries.

At this hour, there were no other cars in the parking area that adjoined the street. He was able to park the rental sedan in front of his ground floor room.

His travel bag was waiting for him just inside the door, where he had hastily dumped it when he'd checked into the motel before starting his search for Hilary. Instead of grabbing it and heading into the bathroom for that shower, he stood there in the quiet dimness of the room.

He couldn't stop thinking about Lauren. Wondering if there was any chance of mending this thing between them.

A baby ought to bring two people together, not divide them.

Poor Sara. It wasn't her fault she was the subject of a strong conflict between her parents. But, damn it, was he so wrong in wanting to be a part of his daughter's life? The daughter whose existence still had him in a state of disbelief.

Ethan didn't think he was wrong, that he was entitled to share Sara. But as ferociously protective of her daughter as she was, Lauren wasn't going to give him an easy time over that issue.

Later. You can worry about it later.

He decided that at this moment he needed an action more diverting than a shower to get his mind off a problem that seemed to have no solution. It wouldn't hurt to check in with his office back in Seattle, learn how the current operation was going in his absence. That would claim his attention.

Ethan was reaching for his cell phone when there was a pounding on his door. It had the sound of a pair of fists driven by a furious urgency.

What in God's name—

His long legs carried him swiftly to the door. Pulling it back, he found himself confronted by a wild-eyed Lauren.

"Where is she?" she demanded, her voice shrill with something close to hysteria. "What have you done with her?"

Before he could open his mouth to ask her what she was talking about, she had thrust her way past him into the room. By the time he turned away from the door, she was searching the place, her frantic gaze raking every corner.

"Lauren, what are you looking for?"

He didn't know why he wasted time in asking her when his initial bewilderment had already given way to a deep sense of uneasiness about *exactly* what she was looking for.

"She isn't here!" She whipped around to face him, her eyes registering her incredulity.

"Are you telling me—"

"Sara! Sara is missing!"

Ethan's uneasiness was replaced by an understanding that had his insides knotting with a sour alarm. "What do you mean she's missing? How can she be missing?"

Lauren didn't answer him. She started for the door, but he blocked her path.

"Get out of my way! I've got to find her!"

"Lauren, calm down and tell me what happened."

"I told you! She's gone!"

"How? From where?"

"Her car seat! She was there in the back when the bicycle went down and I rushed out to help, and then when I came back, she wasn't there! And if you don't have her—"

Her voice cracked on a note of desperation, threatening to slide into uncontrollable sobs. Ethan could see she was in no state to make sense. Sorting it out would have to wait. There was something more immediate that needed attention.

"Hang on," he said grimly.

He went to the phone on the stand beside the bed, lifted the receiver and punched in the number for the front desk. When the attendant on duty answered, he asked her to send for the police, stressing it was an urgent matter.

Lauren was still standing in the middle of the room when he hung up, fists pressed tightly to her mouth in an attitude of bleak despair. The sight of her like this tightened the knot in his stomach.

"Sit down," he commanded her.

She shook her head. He went to her, placed his hand on the small of her back and guided her over to the bed.

"Sit down before you fall down."

She didn't resist him this time. She sank on the edge of the bed, hands in her lap. Ethan hunkered down on the floor in front of her, taking her limp hands in his. They were cold with shock.

"The police are on their way. Now tell me exactly what happened."

"I can't. I should be out—"

"We have to wait for the police, Lauren. There's nothing we can do until they get here. Now tell me."

Maybe telling him would ease her shock, prepare her for the detailed account the cops would want when they arrived.

She hesitated, then made the effort to give him what he asked for. "I came into town to keep an appointment with a lawyer. His office is just across the street. I was turning into the parking lot when this bicycle…well, it just seemed to shoot in front of me out of nowhere."

"You hit it?"

"No, I slammed on the brakes in time. But the rider lost her balance and went down. The first thing I did was check on Sara behind me. She was all right, still asleep in her car seat."

"Then what?"

"I got out to see to the woman. She was on the ground. I asked her if she needed medical aid, but she kept insisting she wasn't hurt, just needed a minute to collect herself. She wouldn't let me call anyone. I helped her to her feet, and we looked at the bicycle. She said it was fine. She got on it and pedaled off."

"And when you got back to the car?" Not that he needed to

ask. Hadn't he already heard the worst before he called
the desk?

"Sara had disappeared! Vanished!"

Her voice rose again as she relived the horror that must
have gripped her. Ethan squeezed her hands.

"Easy," he said.

She shook her head in disbelief. "I don't see how it could
have happened. Not without my knowing, not when I couldn't
have had my back to the car for more than a few minutes. But
she was gone, lifted right out of her harness."

"Did you see anyone else in the area? Anyone at all?"

"No, there was no one by then but me. I started to run toward the corner, thinking I might catch up with whoever had
taken her. And that's when I saw—"

She broke off. There were tears now on her cheeks.

"What?" Ethan insisted, already guessing what she'd seen
but needing to hear it. "What did you see?"

"Your car across the street in front of the motel. I recognized your car."

He knew the rest now, didn't he? How she'd raced across
the street, banged on his door, accused him of—

Feeling a sudden anger surging through him, Ethan tried
to steady himself. Tried to remember that, in her panic,
Lauren had been beyond logic. Even so, how could she
have considered him capable of abducting his own daughter like that?

"This appointment with the lawyer," he said quietly. "It
couldn't have been about me, could it?"

Looking up into her face, he could see by the sudden,
wary expression in her moist, golden brown eyes that it was.
Only then did she seem to realize he was holding her hands.
She drew them quickly away from his grasp.

"The things you said back at the cabin...you scared me
with them. I had to learn just what rights you had about Sara,
whether you could—"

"You thought I might try to take her away from you? That I'd actually do something like that?"

"I was worried. I didn't know whether, with all your money, you could end up winning custody of—"

"Lauren, I'm not rich. Nothing like it."

What was he doing? This wasn't the time to argue about something like that. Not when she was suffering from the loss of her daughter, and he was as sick about that as she was. Not when all that mattered was concentrating their energies on recovering Sara.

Any explanation about the inheritance he had renounced wouldn't have been possible anyway. There was someone knocking on the door.

Getting to his feet, Ethan went to answer it. He opened the door to two men. Both of them wore uniforms. There was a cruiser behind them parked next to his rental car.

"You folks got trouble here?"

It was the elder of the two who addressed him. He had a paunch, a ruddy complexion and a full moustache that matched his red hair. Ethan stood back, permitting them to enter the room. Lauren had risen from the bed to anxiously face them.

"Sheriff Howell," the one in charge introduced himself. He tipped his head in the direction of the younger man, who wore a stoic look on his narrow face. "And this is Deputy Wicowski."

Neither of them offered to shake hands. The sheriff peered at Lauren. "I know you, don't I?"

She nodded. "I live in the area, out at Moon Lake." She told them her name.

"And yours?" the sheriff asked, turning to Ethan.

Ethan obliged him. The sheriff gazed at him, frowning. *He's trying to remember where he heard my name,* Ethan thought.

Before the lawman could pursue it, Lauren spoke up with a pleading, "Please, we're losing time."

"All right, Ms. McCrea, go ahead and tell us what this is all about."

"My daughter. She's been kidnapped."

Lauren repeated the story for them. To her credit, this time she related the episode with a minimum of emotion, although Ethan knew she was all torn up inside. The deputy took down the particulars in a notebook.

"This woman on the bicycle," the sheriff said. "Give us a description of her."

"I can't be accurate. She was wearing sunglasses and a bicycle helmet. From what little I could see of her hair, I think she was a bottle blond. Sort of anemic-looking and somewhere in her twenties, I'd guess."

"Build?"

"Thin, maybe just a little over five feet. I'm not sure."

"That the best you can do?"

Ethan was beginning to think he didn't care much for Sheriff Howell. Lauren's baby had just been abducted, and all this pompous jerk could do was bark at her.

"I'd say under the circumstances, Sheriff, that she gave you a pretty good description. Anyway, she was occupied with helping the woman, not with taking an inventory of her."

Ethan could see the sheriff didn't appreciate his observation, but he let it go. Turning to his deputy, he briskly instructed him, "Go over there, Eddy, and take a look at her car. Then see if you can find any witnesses who saw anything at all. Knock on a few doors along there. Could be somebody was looking out a window at the time."

Deputy Wicowski moved toward the door. When Ethan started to join him, the sheriff stopped him. "Where do you think *you're* going, mister?"

"With your deputy, that's where. I don't intend to just stand around doing nothing when—"

"You stay right here, I have some questions for you."

Ethan thought about telling the lawman to go to hell. But

when he glanced at Lauren, he reconsidered. He didn't want to leave her here at the mercy of this guy and his bullying tactics.

When the deputy had departed, Sheriff Howell directed his attention back to Lauren. "And you never saw or heard a thing?" He seemed to find that hard to believe.

"As I told you, I had my back to the car. And there was all this rock blaring from the music store down at the corner."

"Yeah, they've been warned about the volume there." The sheriff thought about it while he sucked at his teeth. "Woman down with her bike didn't have her back to the car, though. Sounds to me like it could have been a setup. Helmet and sunglasses to disguise her, and then she keeps you busy with her accident while a partner grabs the baby."

Ethan had already considered this strong possibility. He supposed it must have occurred to Lauren, too.

The sheriff was looking at him again. "How do you figure in this?"

Ethan had been wondering when he would get around to that. Before he could respond, Lauren spoke up. "He's Sara's father."

What did it cost her to reveal that precious secret? Probably a lot, if the strain in her voice was any indication.

"Which makes me want her back as much as her mother," he gruffly informed the sheriff.

"Ethan Brand, huh?"

He's remembered.

"You're the guy the state troopers arrested for murder over at Moon Lake last year, aren't you?"

"Jury decided I wasn't guilty, Sheriff. And if you're thinking I might have been involved in my daughter's abduction—"

"No need to get hot over it. Nobody's accusing you of any involvement. But parent abduction is always a possibility, and I've got to consider all the angles."

Yeah, I just bet you do.

The hell with his suspicions. They were wasting time. Ethan wanted action, and he didn't trust Howell to deliver it. "Kidnapping is a federal offense, isn't it? So why aren't we calling the FBI?"

"I'll notify them, but until an agent is able to be on the scene—and remember distances in Montana—my department will handle it."

Ethan could see it on his face. The sheriff didn't like the idea of the FBI being on his turf.

"How will you handle it?" Lauren pressed him.

"We're gonna do all we can to get your girl back to you, Ms. McCrea. We'll question anyone who might have been in the area, issue an Amber Alert."

Ethan knew that meant bulletins with Sara's description would be broadcast on radio and TV. They'd probably also appear on the Internet.

"Better give me all the details, Ms. McCrea." Howell took out his own notebook. "Start with what she was wearing."

"A yellow stretchie. Pale yellow, with white cuffs on the arms and legs."

A stretchie? What was a stretchie? Ethan wondered. He realized he knew next to nothing about babies or their needs. Yeah, he'd have a lot of catching up to do. He refused to so much as consider the possibility that such an education might not be necessary.

"That's it, then," the sheriff said, snapping the notebook shut after Lauren finished with a full description, as well as providing him with a photo of Sara she took from her purse.

Ethan wasn't satisfied. "What do you mean, 'that's it'? There must be more that can be done. A *lot* more."

Howell leveled a stern look at him. "We're a small department, Mr. Brand, and sometimes we get stretched pretty thin, especially in tourist season like this. I said we'd do our best for you, and we will, but you have to realize we've got other emergencies that come up."

Ethan knew he was probably being unreasonable, but he couldn't help it. This was *his* kid they were talking about, and he wanted her found. Was so frustrated by the need that, had it been in his power to demand it, he would have personally conducted a door-to-door search of every building in Elkton, stopped every vehicle leaving town. As it was—

Ethan had no chance to finish the thought. Deputy Wicowski reappeared.

"Learn anything, Eddy?" the sheriff asked him.

The younger man shook his head. "Nobody saw anything, and the woman on the bicycle seems to have vanished. Car looks clean, but maybe the lab boys will turn up something."

"Let's hope so," Sheriff Howell said, but he didn't sound encouraging about that. "You'll have to leave your vehicle with us while it's examined, Ms. McCrea. If you don't have any other transportation back to your cabin, then Deputy Wicowski will run you—"

"You expect me to go home? Just sit there and wait while Sara is missing?"

"That's just what I want you to do. If this is a kidnap-for-ransom, then whoever took your daughter will contact you with instructions. And seeing as how they left no ransom note in the car, could be they're counting on reaching you by phone. You need to be there for that."

"Lauren is going home with me in my car," Ethan informed them sharply. "I'm going to wait there with her."

Lauren looked like she wanted to challenge his decision, but she raised no objection. Maybe because she realized he was prepared to defeat any argument. Damn it, if there was nothing else he could do, then he was going to keep this vigil with her. Whatever their issues, they shared a daughter whose life was at risk.

LAUREN WAS SILENT on the way to the cabin. She hadn't spoken since they'd left the motel after the sheriff's instructions to immediately call his office should the kidnappers phone them. Ethan had expected her to question his intention when he'd grabbed his travel bag and thrown it into the car, but she'd said nothing.

The desolate look on her face when he glanced over at her in the passenger seat had his insides clenching on him again. He knew she was sick with worry. He wanted to stop the car, take her in his arms, tell her everything was going to be all right. But he had a feeling she wouldn't welcome his comfort.

They reached the cabin. The place looked forlorn without the baby that should have been arriving there with them. Ethan parked the car. They got out and went up the steps to the porch. Lauren took the key out of her purse and inserted it into the lock of the front door.

And that's when the telephone inside the cabin began to ring with an insistent shrill.

Chapter Five

It was just as well Lauren reached the phone before him, Ethan decided. With the rage that was simmering inside him, he would probably have recklessly promised the caller that, if his daughter was harmed in any way, he would tear her abductor apart piece by piece.

Heart in his throat, Ethan watched as Lauren plucked the phone off the wall. Listened tautly when she identified herself with a quick, breathless "Lauren McCrea."

There was a long silence after that. She held the receiver so tightly against her ear that, even though Ethan stood close enough to feel her breath mingling with his, he was unable to hear what the speaker was telling her.

Her face was explanation enough, however. He saw the eager expression on it fade into disappointment. This couldn't be the call they'd hoped for. His heart settled back into his chest, heavy with his own disappointment.

Lauren finally interrupted the caller. She said impatiently, "I'm sorry, but I'm not into that line of work anymore. Yes, I do appreciate your need, but I just wouldn't be interested in making an exception. No, I don't know of anyone else who might be available, and I really have to go now. I'm expecting another call."

Ethan watched her hook the receiver back in its cradle.

"You okay?" he asked her.

A dumb question. Neither of them was okay.

"It was someone wanting me to write a speech for him," she said, her voice lifeless.

"Yeah?"

"That was what I did when I lived in Helena. I wrote speeches for politicians."

Helena, Ethan thought. It was the state capital of Montana. He remembered it was where her ex-boyfriend lived. He wondered if the guy had also been connected with the political scene and if that was how Lauren had met him. Not that it mattered.

"But now…"

Her voice trailed away into silence. Unaware of her action, she lifted a hand to her head and dragged her fingers through her auburn hair. It was a habit he'd observed before when she was worried, upset. He knew she was fighting for her sanity.

She deserved to hear something reassuring from him, words that would bolster her courage. But all he could do was stand there, aware of the warmth of her body close to his while he inhaled her alluring fragrance.

Bastard.

How could he permit his senses to kick in on him at a time like this?

Suddenly conscious of his gaze, of the intimacy of their proximity, Lauren nervously moved away from him. There was a bar that separated the kitchen from the living room portion of the cabin. He had noticed the groceries on it this morning when he was here, but only now did he realize the structure hadn't existed last November.

She went around to the kitchen side of the bar, using it to put distance between them. Ethan didn't try to follow her, accepting the wisdom of a physical barrier. As for the issues that divided them emotionally… well, he hoped that for now they could set them aside. It was imperative they work together in harmony to recover Sara. She was all that mattered.

"If you're hungry, I can fix you something to eat," Lauren offered, dumping her purse on the countertop.

He had forgotten all about the late lunch he had promised himself on the way back to the motel. His appetite had vanished along with the promise, but he understood her need to occupy herself with an activity of some kind.

"A sandwich would be fine. Anything you've got."

Hands thrust into the pockets of his cords, he stood on his side of the bar while she removed sliced ham, cheese and a loaf of bread from the refrigerator. He was aware that both of them were resisting the urge to eye the telephone on the wall above the countertop. It didn't ring again.

"It's your turn," she said as she busied herself making his sandwich.

"For?"

"I told you just now what I worked at in Helena. The rest you learned last winter. You pretty much know everything about me worth knowing. But I know very little about you."

He was surprised she would care. "Does it make any difference?"

"It could."

"How?"

She put down the knife she was using to spread mayonnaise on the bread and solemnly met his gaze. "Has it occurred to you that Sara's disappearance might have a connection with her father?"

"In what way?"

"For one thing, there's your money."

"I told you—"

"That you aren't rich. Yes, I remember. But if *I* thought you'd inherited wealth, then others must have assumed it, too, and if Sara's disappearance *is* a kidnap-for-ransom…"

The media, Ethan thought. They hadn't bothered with his renouncement of his grandfather's fortune. Instead, they had emphasized how he came from money. Much more sensational that way.

"That would make sense if her abductors knew I was Sara's father. Pretty ironic, considering *I* didn't know it."

"I don't know how they could have learned it, if they did. But considering her resemblance to you and that you were here with me nine months before her birth, it's possible. And if your grandfather's money isn't the explanation, then something else associated with you or your past could be. I want to know everything, Ethan. I *need* to know."

She finished his sandwich, put a plate under it and set it on the countertop in front of him. There were stools under the bar. He dragged one out and straddled it.

"Starting with what?"

"All the way back." She took a carton out of the refrigerator. "Would you like a glass of milk?"

"Sure."

She poured the milk and placed it next to his plate. Then she perched on another stool on her side of the bar and looked at him expectantly.

All the way back. That wouldn't be easy. Not with his memories. He picked up the sandwich, bit into it and chewed slowly to give himself time to collect his thoughts. Then he began to relate the story Lauren waited to hear.

"My father had a taste for things that went fast. Cars, speedboats, motorcycles, planes. You name 'em, he had them. One of them ended up killing him, along with my mother and his younger brother, Mac. His Cessna went down in a storm over the Cascades."

"How awful for you!"

Ethan shrugged. "Kids that age can be pretty resilient. I was seven years old."

"And left an orphan."

He took another bite of the sandwich, washing it down

with the milk. "I could live with being an orphan. Getting sent to my grandfather was something else."

Ethan had few pleasant recollections of his existence in Jonathan Brand's vast Tudor mansion on the shore of Lake Washington.

"You'd think with all the rooms in that house of his, and just the two of us to rattle around in them, we could keep out of each other's way, but it didn't work like that."

"You had no brothers or sisters?" Lauren asked. "No cousins?"

"Nope. I was an only child, like my mother had been, and Uncle Mac had been a bachelor. The other grandparents died years before. That left just the old man and me as surviving members of the family. And you can stop looking at me like that."

"How?"

"Like you're feeling sorry for me." He took another long swig of the milk before adding, "Though come to think of it, maybe I deserved to be pitied. My grandfather could be a bastard."

"Difficult?"

"Oh, yeah, the old school of discipline, as severe as they made them. I hung on until I finished my education, and then I got out. Joined the Army, thinking I would make a career of it. What I really wanted was to get as far away as possible from Jonathan Brand and his damn money."

"Did you?"

"If you call a prison cell in North Korea getting away, then I did. Another man and I were captured on a reconnaissance mission that went wrong. Spent nearly four months in that hellhole before they were able to negotiate our release."

He saw Lauren look puzzled for a minute, and then her look shifted to an expression of understanding. "The nightmare," she said, and he knew she was remembering that evening when Sara had been conceived.

"Battle wounds heal and go away," he said. "The emotional

ones take longer, and they leave scars. That's why I needed to rebuild my life after the Army and I parted company."

"You came back to Seattle?"

Ethan nodded. "To civilian life and a new direction. Pop had left me this small company, a marine salvage operation. Except I couldn't touch it before I reached the age of twenty-five. One guess who had been authorized to handle it until then."

"Jonathan Brand."

"Who'd deliberately mismanaged it, wanting his grandson to be dependent on him. Only the outfit was mine now. He couldn't control it any longer. It just about killed him watching me fighting to turn the operation around and not asking for a thing from him while I did it."

"Did you succeed?"

"There were problems, but I was doing okay. Would have done better if the old man hadn't kept interfering. I put up with it until he used all that influence of his to lose me a contract."

"Was that when—"

"The day I went to his mansion, the one all the newspapers wrote about, yeah."

Ethan would never forget that morning and the angry scene in his grandfather's library. He briefly described it for Lauren and how he'd stormed out of the room afterwards. How Jonathan Brand had stood in the doorway shouting after him, warning his grandson he would disinherit him, cut him off without a penny.

"As if I cared."

"But the media said—"

"I know what they said. That I had a floundering company, which made me desperate to get my hands on funds. All bull. If I'd wanted the old man's fortune, I wouldn't have driven straight to his legal firm to renounce any claim to it."

"And did you?"

"I tried, but his lawyer was in court. With the state I was

in, though, I didn't want to wait. So I wrote up my own renouncement on the spot, had a secretary witness it and place it on file."

"Then what?"

"I went back to my office. The police turned up there a little later to bring me in for questioning. Seems Jonathan Brand's housekeeper found him in his library bludgeoned to death. I was released, but I knew it was only a matter of time before they arrested me and charged me with his murder."

"Why, if he was alive when you left him?"

Or wasn't he? That was the real question Lauren was asking. Ethan could see it in her eyes.

Not you, too, Lauren.

"Certainly he was alive. What's more, Hilary Johnson knew it. She was standing there on the staircase when I walked out of the library. She had to have heard the old man shouting after me, must have seen him in the doorway."

"So why—"

"Why did she lie in her deposition and on the stand? Swear she heard nothing but our rage behind the closed door of the library, and that when she went to check on her employer a little while later he was dead? They're good questions, Lauren. I've been asking them myself ever since that day."

Lauren went on gazing at him, sober, thoughtful. "I don't suppose she, herself…"

Ethan knew what she was suggesting. He gave her all the reasons why Hilary Johnson couldn't have killed his grandfather. She had no motive, never had a quarrel with Jonathan Brand and was incapable of wielding the murder weapon.

Ethan had been no stranger to the instrument of his grandfather's death. A stone replica of a Mayan god. He'd gotten in trouble as a kid when he'd knocked the piece over and damaged the table on which it always stood. It would have required real strength to lift that thing, much less open his grandfather's skull with it. And Hilary Johnson was a diminutive woman.

"Wasn't there any other staff in the house?"

"There were dailies who came in as they were needed, but none of them were there that day. No visitors, either, other than me. At least that's what Hilary testified. But someone had to have been there after I left."

"And robbery—"

"Ruled out. Absolutely no evidence of anyone breaking or entering. No prints on the murder weapon, either. It had been wiped clean, except for traces of blood."

"So it came back to you." Lauren was thoughtful again. "What about your renouncement of the inheritance? That wasn't enough to clear you?"

Ethan shook his head. "It worked for and against me at the trials. My defense claimed it left me without a motive. The prosecution said it was a worthless argument since it was written after I'd allegedly killed my grandfather. That meant I was using it as an alibi while knowing all along I'd still inherit, because the renouncement wouldn't be legally binding in the absence of the old man's lawyer."

"Was that true?"

"Questionable."

"So you could still inherit?"

"Uh-uh. Since then, I've officially relinquished all claim to any part of Jonathan Brand's estate. The only money I have now is what my marine salvage operation earns me."

"But Sara's kidnappers may not know that. If they *have* learned you're her father, they could think you capable of paying a huge ransom."

Then why haven't they contacted us by now? That's what Ethan wondered, but he didn't say it. It would imply his daughter's abductors had another agenda, one that would alarm Lauren, and she was already scared enough.

He glanced down at his plate and was surprised to discover

that he had finished the sandwich. The glass of milk was also empty. He had drained it without realizing it.

When he looked up again, Lauren was gazing at him in silent speculation. Why? Hadn't she believed what he'd told her? Or, like so many others, did she still doubt his innocence? The possibility depressed him. He could have asked her. He didn't. Maybe because he feared her answer.

Oh, hell, what good had reliving all of it been, anyway? It hadn't helped them to make sense out of the whole mess, brought them any closer to understanding just why Sara had been taken. Because if her kidnapping hadn't been for ransom, and with his gnawing uneasiness arguing it *wasn't,* then he couldn't imagine the explanation.

Lauren was no longer gazing at him. She had turned her head to stare out the window at a flock of ducks on the lake. The haunted look on her face chewed him up inside.

"Whenever anything bad happened to me," she said, her voice wooden and faraway, "I would try to think of it as a useful life experience, something I could store away to equip me for that novel I want to write one day. But this—"

She shuddered visibly.

"This," she went on, "I can only think of as something that should never happen to any mother, for any reason whatever."

Or a father, Ethan thought miserably.

WHAT WAS the point? Lauren asked herself. She had known when she'd undressed, climbed into bed and turned off her bedside lamp that sleep would elude her. Tired though she was, how could sleep be possible when she was so painfully aware of Sara's silent, empty crib sitting there in the shadows mocking her?

Could anything be worse than the exhaustion of long, cruel hours waiting for a telephone that never rang? Of fixing an evening meal that neither she nor Ethan wanted? Sitting in

front of a television watching a program you didn't care about
just so you could listen to the periodic bulletins that described
your missing daughter?

It was just after midnight when, having heard from neither
the kidnappers nor the sheriff's office, Lauren finally surrendered to that exhaustion and went to bed. Hoping maybe she
would sink into a few hours of merciful oblivion. But she
hadn't drifted off and knew now that she wouldn't. *Couldn't,*
even though Ethan had insisted she turn in.

Ethan. She thought about him in the other bedroom, wondered if he was as sleepless as she was. There was a solid wall
that separated them, but she could feel his closeness.

She had mixed emotions about his presence here. He offered a strength she valued, and perhaps without him this vigil
would be unbearable.

*But you relied on your own strength that morning when he
was arrested and all your illusions about him were shattered.
And you survived those months when you carried his baby,
bore her and cared for her without him. Whatever you suffered, you managed it alone.*

And now Ethan Brand was back in her life, and Lauren
wasn't sure she wanted him. He was capable of a fierce anger
that scared her. He'd demonstrated that anger with Sheriff
Howell back at the motel, impatient with the poor man who,
in all fairness, had probably been doing his best to help them.

Ethan had tried to exercise that same take-charge attitude
with her. She could see how he and his equally strong-willed
grandfather would have clashed. But to suppose…

*What, Lauren? Say it. That the last of those conflicts could
have ended in murder? Is that what you think? That Ethan
might actually be capable of so savage an act?*

No, certainly not! How could she entertain such a possibility when, from the beginning, she had perceived an innate
decency in him? She had trusted her instinct then about Ethan,
and she trusted it now.

All right, so he wasn't a killer, but she still had other issues of trust where he was concerned. Like his failure to be honest with her. She could understand it now, though if she were honest with *herself,* she had yet to forgive him for hurting her. Nor did she trust him yet not to try to take Sara away from her. Providing, that is—

Don't think it. You will *get her back. You* have *to get her back!*

This was absurd! Why was she lying here like this tormenting herself? Fear and grief were always so much more agonizing late at night when you were in bed and wide-awake. Better to get up and occupy yourself somehow. It wouldn't relieve the heartache, but it would make it more endurable.

Throwing back the quilt that covered her, Lauren sat up and swung her legs over the side of the bed. The fall weather had been so mild that she had yet to turn on the furnace. But the nights were cool, though there had been no hard frosts. Unusual for Montana in October.

Shivering without the quilt, she slid her feet into her slippers and groped for her robe on the chair beside the bed. She didn't bother with the lamp, didn't need it.

How many nights had she awakened in the dark and found her way straight to the side of the crib to feed or comfort her daughter? And what she wouldn't give to be doing that now.

Besides, the night was clear and the moon was up. The room was far from black. Bundling into her robe, she crossed to the door and eased it open, careful to make no sound that would alert Ethan in the next room.

The cabin was dim and silent. Wanting to keep it that way, she headed quietly toward the kitchen to get herself a glass of water. She was halfway across the unlighted living room when a movement from the alcove startled her.

Coming to a stop, she turned in that direction. Someone stood there at the side of her desk! She thought of the kidnappers and for a brief, wild moment she was convinced one of them had broken in, that he was here in the cabin!

Then the tall figure detached itself from the heavy shadows and stepped into the pool of moonlight that spilled through the windows. It was only Ethan, of course. She should have known.

Though he was not the sinister manifestation of her imagination, he was no less a riveting sight. Barefoot, wearing nothing but a pair of snug jeans riding low on his hips, he was just as he had looked on that morning eleven months ago when he'd emerged from the bathroom to find the two state troopers waiting for him.

But with a difference. This time, moonlight gleamed on the hard muscles of his arms and chest, carving out the angles and planes of his strong face. A breath-robbing sculpture. Except he wasn't marble. He was bone and flesh. *Dangerous* flesh.

"Sorry if I frightened you," he said, his voice low and late-night raspy.

"What were you doing there?" she challenged him.

"Looking out at the moonlight on the water. It's quite a sight, isn't it?"

Lauren joined him in the alcove where she was able to see the moon's silver path shimmering on the lake. Yes, it was very beautiful. Something she could have appreciated under other circumstances.

"You couldn't sleep, either, huh?" he asked quietly.

"No."

"Why did we think we could?"

"How long have you been out here?" she asked him, ignoring his question.

"A while. I just thought I'd feel better…"

He didn't finish. He seemed almost embarrassed. It struck her then. He had been keeping watch here in the gloom, guarding her. Doing what he was unable to do with his daughter, making sure she stayed safe.

Although she was tempted to tell him she didn't need his protection, that she had been successfully looking out for herself ever since she had turned eighteen, she didn't. It would have been mean-spirited somehow. Besides, she was touched by his concern.

There was an awkward silence between them. Lauren was conscious of how close they were standing. So close that she could feel the heat of his solid body. The darkness somehow made their nearness more intimate. And risky.

Feeling altogether too vulnerable, she moved away from him and reached for the switch on the wall. The lamp hanging over her desk bloomed with light. She felt safer with its glow.

If Ethan guessed her reason for the light, he didn't remark on it. Its illumination afforded him a different view of the lake. This one was hanging on the wall above the switch.

"Been a few changes in the cabin since last winter," he observed. "Like the bar between the kitchen and the living room. I noticed that before. But the picture here is new, too, isn't it?"

"Yes."

Thumbs hooked into the pockets of his jeans, he studied the watercolor. It depicted the lake just after sunup, with a layer of mist over its waters.

"I like it," he decided. "It's good."

"Thank you. It wasn't easy getting that light. I struggled with it."

He turned his head to stare at her, one of his heavy, dark eyebrows lifted in surprise. "*You* painted it?"

"Yes."

"What do you know. She's both a writer *and* an artist."

"The art is strictly amateur stuff," Lauren stressed, "and sometimes I'm not sure about the writing."

But his compliment pleased her. It also made her uncomfortable. Or was it the sight of his naked chest?

Needing to put a greater distance between them, she started for the kitchen again. "I was on my way to get a drink of water," she explained over her shoulder.

She hoped he would stay behind in the living room, but he followed her into the kitchen."

"Want one?" she asked, taking a clean glass out of the cupboard.

"I'm fine."

He was hovering behind her when she opened the refrigerator where she kept bottles of cold water.

"Is that baby formula in there?" he asked.

"Yes."

She helped herself to the water, closed the refrigerator. He watched her as she drank from the glass she'd filled.

"Then you don't, uh—"

She lowered the glass from her mouth. "Breast-feed Sara? No. Insufficient milk. I was heartbroken. I'd been looking forward to nursing her, but now with what's happened…"

"Yeah," he said gruffly, understanding.

Whoever had taken Sara would be able to easily obtain the formula she was accustomed to. Even if it wasn't the right one, Sara would accept it. That she was not being adequately fed and cared for was unthinkable.

In danger of choking, not on the water she'd swallowed, but on her emotions, Lauren hastily set the glass on the counter.

"I know it's tough," Ethan said, "but I'd like to hear about her."

Lauren hesitated. She could appreciate his interest in his daughter, and he did have a right to know. Except she wasn't sure she could bring herself to talk about Sara without losing her self-control.

"Please," he added.

"All right. What would you like to know?"

"Whatever you can tell me." He leaned against the bar behind him. "Though I guess at two months old, there isn't much personality yet."

"You couldn't be more wrong about that."

"Yeah?"

"She's a darling and was from the moment I brought her home. I think she was being patient with a nervous mother, because she hardly ever fussed. New babies aren't always alert, but almost from the beginning Sara noticed color and movement. The mobile over her crib. Did you notice it?"

"She liked it, huh?"

"Loved it. She'd wave her arms and legs and make cooing noises when I swung it for her. And when she smiled for the first time, smiled right up at me, I—"

Lauren's voice broke. The loss of self-control she had feared was very close. If she went on, she would end up sobbing raggedly.

"I'm sorry. I—I just can't do this."

Ethan shoved himself away from the counter, reaching her in one quick stride. Before she could stop him, or even decide if she wanted to stop him, he had hauled her into his arms.

"It's okay," he said, holding her close.

"Why do I have to be such a mess?"

"You're entitled."

His big hands slowly stroked her back. She ought to have pulled away from him. She knew that. But the comfort he offered her was too soothing to resist, too necessary.

All the same, she was afraid of it. Afraid of how secure the solid wall of his chest felt beneath her cheek pressed to his warm flesh. She could hear his heart beating, thundering in her ear. Could smell his skin, a scent that was clean and masculine.

Danger!

Dragging her head back, she searched his face looming above hers. His square jaw had tightened, making the cleft in his chin more pronounced. There was an intense expression in his blue-green eyes, something that was raw and demanding. Nothing to do with comfort now. It was pure desire.

In another moment, his mouth would swoop down over hers. She would more than feel him, hear him, smell him. She would taste him, welcome his lips on hers. And it would be a mistake.

"We can't," she whispered.

He tried to hang on to her when she made the effort to draw away from him, but then he let her go.

"Would it be so wrong?" he said.

"Yes. There's Sara. I can't forget Sara."

"Damn it, Lauren, do you think I'm not remembering and suffering, too? Okay, so I saw her for only a couple of minutes. But that's all it took to have her steal a big piece of my heart."

His words twisted her insides, making their daughter's loss worse than it had been, if that were possible. And her recovery even more urgent.

"What are we going to do, Ethan?" she implored. "I don't know how much more of this I can take."

LAUREN FELT GUILTY when they met over breakfast. Her plea of last night hadn't been fair to Ethan. How could she expect him to carry the burden of her anguish, even though he had rashly promised her he intended to do all in his power to restore Sara to her safely. But what could he possibly do that the sheriff and his department weren't already trying to accomplish?

"You get any sleep when you went back to bed?" he asked her, pouring himself a second mug of coffee. He had declined anything else but that and toast. She had no appetite, either.

"A little. I was afraid to fall asleep too hard in case the phone rang and I wouldn't hear it."

She needn't have worried. There had been no call yet from the kidnappers. Nor had the sheriff anything encouraging to report when they'd checked with his office the first thing that morning. Lauren's car had turned up nothing useful and, though he and his deputies would continue to investigate all possibilities, their efforts had yet to produce a result.

"You?" she asked Ethan, knowing he couldn't have slept much, either. He looked as worn as she felt.

"Some."

He was silent for a moment. Then he set his mug down on the table with a decisive bang.

"The hell with this," he growled. "I'm not going to sit around here any longer waiting for something to happen."

He was a man of action, frustrated by a vigil that had prevented him from doing anything but pacing restlessly. Lauren had known that eleven months ago when they'd been snowbound in the cabin. She'd known it yesterday at the motel when the sheriff had stopped him from joining Deputy Wicowski out on the street. And she had known it last night when she had watched him struggling to keep his impatience in check. Now he'd had enough.

"If this is about my desperation," she started to say, "then—"

"It's about my desperation, too, Lauren."

"Don't you think the sheriff and his people are already doing whatever needs to be done?"

"No, I don't trust that they are."

"But what can you do?"

"I can hunt on my own. I can drive back to Elkton and cover the area where Sara was taken, question everyone I can find. Have you got another photo of Sara I can show around?"

"Yes, I'll get it for you." She rose from the table. "I know you need to do this, Ethan, and I wish I could go with you, but I can't. If her kidnappers call—"

"Yeah, someone has to stay here by the phone." He frowned. "The thing is, I don't like leaving you on your own."

With the effort she should have made last night, Lauren restored the courage that had failed her since Sara's abduction. "I don't need protecting, Ethan. I can take care of myself."

"I know that," he said solemnly. "Your strength is something I've never doubted. Not since that night you hauled me out of a snowstorm and brought me here. But do me a favor, huh? Lock the doors behind me, and keep them locked. And something else…"

He gave her his cell phone number, and instructed her to call him if she heard anything from either the kidnappers or the sheriff.

Five minutes later, after pocketing the photograph she'd handed him, he was gone.

Chapter Six

The telephone remained maddeningly silent. There was no word from the kidnappers, the sheriff or Ethan as the morning hours crawled by.

Lauren was so weary from worry and lack of sleep that she stretched out on the sofa to rest. As anxious as she was, she didn't think she was capable of drifting off. But she wanted to be close to the phone in case she did.

As it turned out, her fatigue was enough to put her solidly to sleep for over an hour. She felt better when she awakened. In body, anyway, though certainly not in mind.

It didn't seem possible she could have missed the ring of the telephone. She'd been too alert for it, even as heavily as she'd slept. However, she immediately checked the answering machine. There were no messages.

Knowing it would be impossible for her to concentrate on any occupation, she turned on the TV. But the newscasts that reported Sara's abduction were so upsetting, hinting as they did at the possibility of a grave outcome, that Lauren turned off the set.

There was nothing for her to do after that but wander from room to room, repeatedly gaze out the windows and wonder what was happening with Ethan in town. All the while, her tension mounted.

It was past noon and her nerves raw when Ethan returned

to the cabin. She had the door unlocked and open by the time he arrived on the porch.

"Anything?" she asked. Not that it was necessary to inquire. She could see by the look on his face that he had nothing worthwhile to report.

He shook his head. "No one seems to have heard or seen anything. What about you?"

"A call from a friend offering her sympathy, and one other from a reporter asking questions I declined to answer. Otherwise…"

"Yeah."

"Can I fix you something to eat?"

"I grabbed a bite at a fast-food place in town, but you go ahead."

"I had a bowl of soup. It's all I want."

"Then let's sit down. I've got something to ask you."

There was a tautness in his voice that instantly told her his trip into Elkton hadn't been entirely uneventful.

"What is it?" she demanded, leaning toward him hopefully when they'd settled at the table.

"It came to me on the drive back here. Something obvious we ought to have thought of straight off, and would have if we hadn't been so broken up over Sara's kidnapping. But it shouldn't have been overlooked by the sheriff, and that it apparently has is one more reason why I don't trust—"

There was the sound of another car pulling into the driveway. The sheriff with news?

Whatever Ethan had started to tell her would have to wait. Getting to their feet, they hurried outside. But it wasn't one of the sheriff's vehicles that parked next to Ethan's rental car. This was a plain, unmarked sedan. The woman that emerged from it was equally unremarkable.

In her late forties or early fifties, with graying hair and wearing a warm smile as she approached them, she looked like someone's sweet-tempered mother.

Lauren was wary as she and Ethan came down from the porch to meet their visitor. For all she knew, the woman was someone else from the media looking for a story.

"Lauren McCrea and Ethan Brand. Am I correct?"

She addressed them in one of those little-girl voices that always struck Lauren as unexpected when it came from a mature woman. She and Ethan traded glances, and she knew he must be thinking the same thing. How did their visitor know their names?

"That's right," Lauren said, cautiously accepting the hand that was held out to her.

"I'm Marjorie Landry," she introduced herself.

She briefly, firmly shook Lauren's hand and then, in turn, Ethan's hand. Before they could question her, she opened her purse and produced her identification for their inspection. Lauren found herself looking down at an FBI shield.

Agent Landry, replacing the badge in her purse, looked up at the porch. "What a pleasant spot. Do you think we could sit there while we talk?"

There were rustic chairs ranged along the length of the porch. Lauren's grandfather had made them himself from wood he'd collected on the property. They turned two of the chairs to face each other. Ethan indicated he preferred to stand. When they were settled, with Lauren and the agent in the chairs and Ethan leaning against the porch railing, Marjorie Landry expressed her sorrow over the kidnapping of their daughter.

"If you've been wondering why I didn't get out here sooner," she went on, this time in a brisk tone, "it's because I've been on your case back in Elkton."

"So the sheriff's department filled you in?" Ethan wanted to know.

Agent Landry took a notebook out of her purse. "It's all in here. But I'll want further details. Have you had any contact yet from whoever took her?"

"None," Lauren said.

Agent Landry looked regretful. "I'm going to be honest with you, then. If you haven't heard from Sara's abductors by now, it's highly unlikely you ever will. Believe me, I'm speaking from long experience with the Bureau when I tell you this. That means this isn't a kidnap-for-ransom. It's about something else."

Lauren's heart plummeted.

"Like what?" Ethan asked.

"I think we can rule out perversion. There are none of the characteristics of that here. I'm sorry to bring up such an ugly thing, but if we can eliminate the worst scenario…"

Lauren should have been relieved. She wasn't.

"What else?" Ethan pressed the agent, his face looking grimmer by the moment.

"It could be an individual who wanted a child of their own and took this way to get one. It happens. Or there's another possibility."

"Such as?"

"Revenge, and they're using Sara to get it. People can have very twisted motives when it comes to this kind of thing. Do either of you have any enemies? Someone who'd go to excessive lengths to make you suffer?"

Neither Lauren nor Ethan could think of anyone who might want to use Sara to punish them. Marjorie Landry took a pen from her purse, opened the notebook, and began to question them at length, jotting down the particulars of their histories.

It was clear to Lauren by now that the woman was an efficient agent. That she was trying to cover all the possibilities, no matter how extreme. Lauren could appreciate that, but the whole thing seemed without explanation. A mystery that was growing more tangled by the hour.

She knew that Ethan was feeling equally dissatisfied by the lack of results. The sharpness in his tone when he spoke to the agent was evidence of that.

"Let me ask you something. Just what are the chances of the FBI recovering Sara for us?"

"All I can tell you," she answered him evasively, "is that we'll be using all of our resources to find and return your daughter to you."

"In other words, no guarantees."

Palms up, the woman spread the fingers of both her hands in a gesture that indicated a degree of helplessness. "Montana's population isn't a very large one."

"Meaning?"

"The Bureau is spread pretty thinly over a widespread territory, and with the caseload the district already has—"

"I get it. We're not the only priority."

"There is Sheriff Howell, remember. He and his department are also working on your behalf."

"And you'll be working with him, right?"

"Of course."

"Just how closely will you be working with him, Agent Landry?" Ethan probed.

"What are you saying, Mr. Brand?"

"That I got the feeling from the sheriff yesterday he isn't all that enthusiastic about the FBI."

"He'll cooperate with us." Marjorie Landry assured him.

But Lauren hadn't missed the woman's hesitation. *She isn't telling us, but it's obvious Sheriff Howell and the Bureau have clashed in the past, and that isn't in our favor.*

Closing her notebook, the agent tapped her pen against it. "I think I have everything I need for now, but if anything else should occur to you—"

"Yeah, there is one other thing," Ethan said.

But before he could tell her, a cell phone inside her purse began to trill. She removed the phone and got quickly to her feet.

"Excuse me. I have to take this."

She moved to the far end of the porch where her conver-

sation with the caller wouldn't be overheard. Lauren and
Ethan exchanged glances. They couldn't distinguish the brief
conversation that followed, but it was possible to detect an urgency in the agent's responses.

Is it about Sara?

Marjorie Landry ended her call and hurried back to the chair
where she had left her purse. Stuffing the phone and the notebook into the bag, she turned to them. "I'm sorry, but I have to
leave. We have another case going down and I need to be there."

Not about Sara.

The agent gave Lauren no chance to vent her disappointment. She thrust her business card at her.

"My number is on the card. Don't hesitate to call me. And
if you shouldn't be able to reach me, you can always contact
me through the sheriff's office. I'll be in touch."

And with that final, hasty promise, she was on her way to
her car.

Ethan drew away from the railing, scowling after the car
as it turned in the driveway and sped off through the trees.

"We've just been dismissed," he said after muttering an
angry obscenity under his breath.

"You don't think she's serious about our case?" Lauren
asked him anxiously.

"She's competent, but she's got too much to handle. The
sheriff, too. And if they aren't able to give us everything
they've got…"

Then we can't count on them. Ethan didn't say this, but
Lauren knew he must be thinking it.

"There's something else," she said. "When you tried to find
out how closely she would be working with Sheriff Howell
and his people—"

"Yeah, she didn't want to admit it, but it looks like the FBI
and the sheriff have issues. That's not good."

No, Lauren thought, it isn't. Because if the Bureau and the
local law enforcement were locked in some power struggle,

then they couldn't work effectively as a team to find and return Sara to her.

Worried, she looked out at the lake. Its restful waters had always soothed her in the past, and she needed that view now. Needed it to quell a desperation that threatened to turn into panic. Her hand was crushing the business card Agent Landry had given her. When she realized what was she doing, she tucked the card safely into the pocket of her slacks and went back to gazing at the lake. But the business card made her remember something.

"What you tried to tell Marjorie Landry before her phone rang," she said to Ethan, "was it what you started to tell me when—"

Lauren broke off. This time she herself was the cause of the interruption.

"There they go again!"

"What are you talking about?" Ethan asked, puzzled by whatever had suddenly distracted her.

"Those flashes of light from the other side of the lake."

He swung around and stared across the waters. The flashes—brief, rapid bursts of white light—were repeated.

"See them?"

"Yeah. What are they?"

"I don't know. Probably nothing, just sunlight reflecting off something. But they're odd. They remind me of when I was a kid and a friend and I would signal each other with pocket mirrors. Anyway, to get back to what I was asking…"

But Ethan refused to let her drop the subject. *"Again?"*

"What?"

"You said, 'There they go again.' That means you've noticed them before. When? How often?"

"I don't know. Several times over the past few days or so. What does it matter? It isn't important."

"The *same* kind of flashes?" he persisted.

"I suppose. Why are we bothering with this?"

"Let me tell you something, Lauren. When I was in the army, I was recruited to be trained for a special forces unit, operations like the one that landed me in North Korea."

Where was all this leading to? Lauren wondered impatiently.

"'Why me?' I asked my commanding officer. He told me it was because I had the kind of useful instinct that couldn't be learned. I don't know how true that is, but there are times when I sense stuff I can't explain."

"Are you saying you're sensing something now in connection with those flashes?"

"Well, there's something that wants me to find out about them, yeah."

"But what could they possibly have to do with us and Sara's kidnapping?"

"Maybe nothing. I just know I have this urge to investigate them, and it's an urge that needs to be satisfied. What's over there on that end of the lake?"

"There's a small cottage in the trees there. It's the only other place on the lake."

"Who owns it?"

"I don't know. It's a rental cottage, but I don't think it's occupied very often."

Ethan continued to look out at the lake, but this time his gaze was focused on her short pier at the bottom of the long slope below the cabin.

"You've got a boat down there at the pier," he said.

"Just a little one that belonged to my grandfather. I use it for fishing or painting, but I haven't been out in it since Sara's birth. If you're thinking of crossing the lake in it, forget it. The outboard motor is in for repair."

"There are oars, aren't there?"

"Yes, but why not go by car?"

"How far is it using the road?"

"It's not a direct route. Probably four miles or so."

"I can get there faster rowing across. And if there is some-one there, it won't look like a deliberate visit. Just a casual outing in the boat and along the way stopping by to say hello to the neighbor. Besides, I could use the action."

"Ethan, this is all so—"

"What? Crazy? Unlikely to have anything at all to do with Sara? That's true, but I can't go on doing nothing. If there's a chance to learn answers that could help us to find her—and I don't care how remote it is—then I mean to use it. Right now it's all we have, Lauren."

Yes, she could understand his need, because she shared it.

"All right, you've got to do this, but you still haven't told me what you were going to tell Marjorie Landry."

"I'll tell you in the boat."

"Ethan, I can't go with you. If the phone rings and I'm not here—"

"You heard what she told us. Sara's kidnappers aren't going to contact us."

Lauren turned her head, looking longingly at the cabin be-hind her, reluctant to leave it. "I do have call forwarding," she said, "and a cell phone I got after Sara's birth. So if I have my cell phone pick up any calls and take it with me…"

"Perfect," he said decisively.

SCARCELY A RIPPLE disturbed the waters of the lake. Its pol-ished surface reflected a perfect mirror image of the woods that rimmed the shoreline. The evergreens of that dense for-est, together with the mountains behind them, provided a dark contrast to the deciduous trees whose crowns flamed with the brilliant colors of October.

Lauren, seated in the stern of the rowboat facing Ethan, was oblivious to the scene. Under other circumstances, she would have been occupied with either admiring it or painting it. At this moment, however, her attention was focused entirely on Ethan.

The ease with which he handled the oars amazed her. His steady strokes sped their craft smoothly across the surface of the lake. But then she didn't know why she should be surprised. His strength was apparent.

The early afternoon had grown unseasonably warm. Ethan had peeled off his sweatshirt. The white T-shirt beneath it fitted him so snugly that Lauren was able to see the play of the muscles in his broad shoulders and strongly corded arms as he pulled at the oars. It was a tantalizing sight, summoning an unwanted image of the winter night when those powerful arms had been wrapped around her, melding them in a union that had resulted in Sara.

Considering the issues between them that hadn't been resolved, and perhaps never would be resolved, the memory wasn't a wise one. Lauren put it away and urged Ethan to tell her what he'd had no chance until now to relate either to her or Agent Landry.

"This thing that occurred to you on your way back from Elkton," she prompted him. "You said it was something obvious that shouldn't have been overlooked by any of us, and yet all of us did overlook it."

Lauren had supposed he'd been waiting until they were well under way before he rested on the oars long enough to explain himself. But he kept on rowing with a rhythm that seemed effortless.

"We all agreed, didn't we," he began, "the abduction was no random thing? That it wasn't just some impulsive act because Sara's kidnappers recognized an opportunity and seized it?"

"Yes, it was deliberate. Sheriff Howell said as much, that it had to be a setup."

"Which means it was planned in advance. How?"

"I don't see what you're—"

"Think about it. The woman on the bicycle shot out in front of you just as you were turning into the parking lot. An accident that was no accident, but it forced you out of the car long enough to let whoever else was in on it to snatch Sara. *How,* Lauren? How did they know you were going to be arriving in that place at that time?"

"They were waiting for me," she said slowly, understanding now what he was saying, "and that has to mean—"

"They knew in advance, yeah."

He's right. This is *something Ethan and I should have thought of immediately. And, as he said before, we* would *have thought of it if we hadn't been so upset over Sara's disappearance.*

But, as Ethan had also pointed out earlier, the sheriff himself ought to have considered it. That he apparently hadn't certainly brought his competence into question again. Perhaps Agent Landry's, as well.

"Wait a minute," Lauren said, a flaw in this whole assumption suddenly occurring to her. "There is no way they could have known I would be there when I was. *I* didn't know it myself until—"

"Until you made that appointment with the lawyer. Who did you speak to in his office, Lauren? The lawyer himself?"

She shook her head. "His receptionist."

"Someone you know, someone whose voice you were able to recognize?"

"I didn't think about it. I just asked for an appointment with him, and she gave me one for two o'clock. But you can't suppose—"

"That your lawyer's receptionist played a role in Sara's kidnapping? Maybe, maybe not. Is there anyone else who could have known about the appointment?"

"No, I didn't tell—" Lauren broke off as she remembered something. "Hold on. There was someone else who knew. The furniture store in town phoned just as I was fixing myself lunch. I'd been looking for a high chair for Sara, one of the old-fashioned wooden kind. And even though I knew it would be months before she was ready for a high chair, the store was able to order me just what I wanted. They called to say the chair was in and could they deliver it."

"And you told them what?"

"That I had a two o'clock with my lawyer, and since they were only two doors down from his office, I'd pick up the chair myself after my appointment."

"Man or woman?"

"It was another woman. And, no, I couldn't say who that was, either."

"So, both the lawyer's office and the furniture store knew where you would be at two o'clock."

"But not that Sara would be with me."

"Not for sure, but they could have assumed it if you were in the habit of bringing Sara with you whenever you came to town."

Ethan was silent for a moment. Throughout their conversation, he had continued to propel the rowboat across the lake, never once stopping to catch his breath. They were nearing their destination now, and he seemed in no way winded.

"One of those two women," he said thoughtfully.

"Or someone they could have mentioned it to."

"Yeah, people have a way of gossiping about the most trivial things."

That either of the two women could have been responsible in any way for Sara's abduction was an unpleasant idea. Far more chilling was the possibility that one of them was directly connected with the kidnapping. And if she was someone Lauren knew, even in a casual way, that was worse.

But why? she asked herself. If it *had* all been planned beforehand, what reason could these people have for taking Sara? It always came back to that maddening *why*.

"It will need checking into," Ethan said, as if he'd read her thoughts.

Lauren nodded and looked away from his steely gaze, finding it unsettling. The pair of trumpeter swans who had made the lake their home all summer, delighting her with their presence, were gliding serenely through the shallows off to her left. They would soon be on their way to a milder climate. That, too, was a sad realization.

"Is HE ANYONE you know?" Ethan asked her softly, joining her on the pier after he'd secured the rowboat.

"I don't recognize him," Lauren murmured, eyeing the lean figure who stood in the clearing below the wood-shingled cottage nestled among the pines behind him.

Whoever the man was, he had to be aware of their arrival. And yet he never paused in the work that occupied him.

There were storm windows stacked on the grass beside a bucket of soapy water. Sponge and squeegee in one hand, he managed with his other hand to hold each window upright as he methodically washed it. Whenever he turned a window from front to back, sunlight glittered off the panes of glass.

"So much for the mysterious flashes of light," Ethan said as they headed up the path from the lake.

"That accounts for today, but it doesn't explain the other times I noticed them."

"Maybe we can get him to tell us."

Lauren didn't know about that. The man looked none too friendly to her. "What are we supposed to say? That we're just paying a neighborly social call?"

"Leave it to me."

She had the urge to tell Ethan he could use a lesson in self-restraint regarding his habit of taking charge of every situation. Not that he would have listened to her. He was just that kind of man.

In any case, it was too late for her to say anything. They were within earshot now of their objective. Although the spare figure had seemed to show no interest in their approach, he straightened from his work when they reached him. A pair of piercing black eyes gazed pointedly at Ethan.

"Training for the Olympics?" he said.

Ethan was clearly as perplexed by the question as Lauren was. "I'm sorry?"

"Thought you might be, way you were going at that rowing out there."

He must have been watching them the whole time. And although he offered them no welcoming smile, it seemed the melancholy look on his face belied a dry wit. Maybe he was not so unfriendly, after all.

Ethan chuckled. "I'm afraid I've got a long way to go before I qualify."

"You could have fooled me. Hell, I can't even paddle a canoe, which would have appalled my ancestors."

A Native American, Lauren thought. She could see that now in his proud features and long, coarse black hair tied in a ponytail. She wondered if he was a descendant of the Flathead people who had once ruled this part of Montana.

"Name's Ethan Brand," Ethan introduced himself. "And this is Lauren McCrea, who has the cabin on the other end of the lake."

"Wondered who had that place." Dropping the sponge into the bucket and with one hand hanging on to the window he'd been washing, he tucked the squeegee under his arm to free his other hand long enough to shake their hands. "Rudy Lightfeather," he said.

His name confirmed his heritage.

"This is real work, getting all those windows ready for winter," Lauren remarked casually, indicating the enclosed porch stretched across the entire face of the cottage where the screens would be replaced by the storms. "Have you been working on them all week?"

If her question hadn't sounded quite as innocent as she intended it to be, and it probably hadn't, he didn't challenge it.

"Nope. First day on the job."

Not the explanation then for all those other bursts of light.

"Nice place," Ethan said, pretending to admire the cottage.

Rudy permitted himself a faint grin. "No need to be polite. I don't own it. I'm just hired to take care of it."

"Oh? Would you mind telling me who does own it? I heard it was a rental cottage. That's why we rowed across to take a look at it. I have some friends who'd love to spend a few weeks on the lake."

"You'd have to talk to Sloan Real Estate Agency about that. They manage this property, and another one somewhere in the hills on the other side of Elkton, for a woman named Hilary Johnson. I guess she inherited them from her parents along with her house in town."

Lauren was careful not to exchange glances with Ethan. She was afraid her surprise would be altogether evident to Rudy Lightfeather if she did.

Hilary Johnson. The ex-housekeeper who testified against Ethan. Is it just a coincidence she owns this place?

Ethan had to be equally surprised, and yet he didn't register it. "I'll do that," he said. "But it would be nice to see what the cottage looks like inside before I talk to them. I'd like to be able to tell my friends about it. I don't suppose…"

"You asking for a tour?"

"Could we?"

Rudy considered his request. "Guess nobody's going to object to that."

The caretaker lowered the storm window to the grass and, with the squeegee back in his hand, turned and led the way to the steps that mounted to the porch. Once inside the enclosure, he took a key out of his pocket and fitted it into the lock of the front door.

"I don't know what state the place is in," he said to them. "I haven't been inside since the last renters left. I'm responsible only for the outside. A cleaning service comes in to do the rooms, and I don't think they've been here yet. Gotta warn you, though. If you're looking for fancy accommodations, you won't find them here."

His caution was no exaggeration. The living room, kitchen, two bedrooms and a bath which Rudy escorted them through were cramped, their walls drab and their furnishings shabby. That might have been excused, Lauren decided, if the place had been clean and neat. It wasn't. Cupboard doors gaped, dirty dishes were piled in the sink and there was trash everywhere. As if the cottage had been vacated in a hurry.

"What a mess," Rudy muttered as he led them back into the living room, waving the squeegee like a conductor's baton at the clutter on all sides. "Glad I don't have to put it back to rights."

There was one item of interest in the disorder. Ethan spotted it first on the coffee table where it was half concealed by old magazines—a pair of binoculars. He picked up the glasses and trained them on the front window that overlooked the lake, as if nonchalantly testing them for their worth.

Lauren understood the message he was conveying to her. The polished lens on binoculars, if used out in the open, were capable of reflecting the sun's dazzling light. Like small mirrors.

Ethan put the binoculars back on the table. "So, Rudy, when did you say these last renters left the cottage?"

"I didn't say. But they had to have pulled out sometime yesterday. That's when Vi Appleton over at Sloan called to tell me the place was empty and I could start on the windows."

"You happen to know their names, Rudy? If I could contact them, maybe they'd be willing to recommend the cottage. I think my friends would appreciate that."

Rudy Lightfeather was no fool. He had to realize that any recommendation from people who would leave the cottage in this condition, no matter what their haste, would be of little value. But if the caretaker was suspicious of their motives, he didn't pursue it.

"Never heard their names," he said.

"Then I guess you didn't meet them."

"I wasn't introduced, no, but I had a glimpse of them when I was called out here a couple of days ago to repair the water pump. A young couple, but they weren't interested in socializing. He just complained about the pump and then disappeared inside with her."

Ethan turned to Lauren with an offhanded "I wonder if they could have been that couple we ran into in town. Didn't they say they were staying out at Moon Lake?"

Not waiting for her response, which Lauren knew was unnecessary, Ethan gave his attention again to the caretaker.

"What did they look like? You remember?"

Rudy hesitated, as if wondering whether to mind Ethan's probing, which by now had to be pretty obvious. He must have decided he didn't.

"She was a skinny blonde, no meat on her."

Lauren went rigid.

"And him?" Ethan asked, maintaining the careless tone in his voice.

Rudy looked amused. "Now that's kind of interesting."

"Why?"

"Because the only thing I really remember about him was his eyes. You don't see that color every day. A pure blue-green. Just like yours. Odd, huh?"

Chapter Seven

"Not now," Ethan said as they made their way back to the pier.

Lauren glanced at him, waiting for him to explain why he wasn't ready to talk about what they had learned from Rudy Lightfeather. It wasn't because the caretaker might overhear them. They had parted from him just outside the cottage. He had already disappeared around the corner of the building to fill another bucket with water for his windows.

But Ethan was silent after his brief request. Although she burned with a need to discuss that startling conversation in the cottage, Lauren didn't press him. She clambered down into the rowboat, seated herself in the stern, and managed to restrain herself while he seized the handles of the oars as if they were weapons in the hands of a warrior.

There was an urgency in his powerful strokes that drove them out over the waters of the lake. And a tautness in his square jaw that told her he was seething inside.

Lauren's own emotions were churning. When he continued to maintain his tense silence, she abandoned her patience.

"Enough!" she challenged him. "We have to talk."

Even if he was prepared now to examine Rudy Lightfeather's revelations with her, she expected him to go on rowing, just as he had when they'd crossed the lake before. But this time he lowered the oars in their locks, allowing the boat to drift. She watched his hard body slowly thaw.

"Sorry," he said, shaking his head. "I was just trying to sort it out."

"Whatever sense it makes, or doesn't make," she said, leaning toward him earnestly, "your instinct was on target. There *was* a reason for us to visit the cottage. A *good* reason."

"Lauren, we can't be sure the blonde he described was the same one who—"

"It *has* to be true! The couple who occupied that cottage took Sara! Whoever they are, and wherever they are now, they have Sara with them!"

"There's a strong argument for it, yeah."

Why was he being so cautious? "The binoculars! Don't forget the binoculars! That's the explanation for all the flashes of light I noticed! They must have been using them out in the clearing to spy on me! They planned to kidnap Sara, but they needed an opportunity and by watching me—"

"Lauren, take it easy. The binoculars could indicate that's what they were doing, that they were interested even before I turned up here, but it's not a certainty. None of it is a certainty."

"This is Sara we're talking about!" she cried. "How can you be so calm about it when just a minute ago—"

"Because I realized that being all worked up over it just stands in the way of getting her back. Either we help ourselves by examining all of this rationally or…well, we could lose her forever."

It was a harsh warning, one that Lauren didn't want to hear, but in the end she knew he was right. In her excitement, she had lost her self-control.

Turning her head, she gazed out across the waters toward the shallows where the trumpeter swans had been busy among the reeds. There was no sign of them now.

When she looked back at Ethan, she had regained her composure. Or as much of it as she was able to recover, considering her daughter was still missing.

"All right," she said, steadying her voice, "what did we learn that's true and not just wild speculation? Hilary Johnson owns the cottage. That much is the truth, isn't it?"

"There was no reason for Rudy Lightfeather to lie about it," Ethan agreed. "It might be just a coincidence that this couple happened to be renting her place, or—"

"She's involved with them somehow. And since you have a connection with her yourself…"

"Yeah, that's one too many coincidences."

"Then what does it all mean?" Lauren pleaded with him. "Suppose Hilary Johnson *did* put that couple in her cottage and that they *were* watching me, what were they waiting for? The chance to abduct Sara?"

Ethan looked unhappy. "I have a feeling it just might have been something else they were waiting for."

"What?"

"Me."

She stared at him. "I don't understand."

"Think about it, Lauren. Nothing happened until I arrived at your cabin yesterday morning. With those binoculars, they could have seen that from their end of the lake. And then in the afternoon Sara was taken."

"Because you turned up?" She shook her head, bewildered. "What sense does that make?"

"It could, if Sara's kidnapping has something to do with my being her father."

"We've been over that before. And, yes, as I said then, it's possible someone could have guessed you're Sara's father, even though I never shared her paternity with anyone. But is it likely?"

"It is if it was Hilary Johnson who figured it out. You pointed out to me yesterday it was no secret I was with you nine months before Sara's birth. The woman could have seen you around town with Sara on any number of occasions, and since she knows what I look like—"

"*Your* eyes."

"Those and a couple of other features my daughter inherited."

"No," she said slowly, "I don't mean Sara. The man in the cottage. Rudy said he had eyes like yours."

"The same color, Lauren. But a lot of people have blue-green eyes."

"One too many coincidences. You said it yourself. This man, Ethan—*could* he be related to you?"

"I don't see how. Like I told you, I'm the only surviving member of the family on both sides. Well, Sara now, too. And to suppose this guy—" He broke off, his frustration evident. "Hell, it's all too fantastic."

Yes, it was, Lauren thought. The whole thing was inconceivable. The couple who had stayed in the cottage. The possibility that Hilary Johnson was in some way associated with them. Sara's kidnapping that, if it was not for ransom, seemed to have no logical motive, particularly where Ethan was concerned.

There was a sober look on his face as he gazed at her in silence for a long moment, both of them at a loss for words.

"You could blame me, you know," he finally said, his voice as solemn as his expression.

"For?"

"Sara's kidnapping. Because if this whole thing *is* somehow connected with me, then in a way I'm responsible for it."

Lauren didn't know what to tell him. She supposed he had a good reason for wondering if she thought he was at fault for Sara's abduction. Why not, when yesterday she'd been convinced their daughter had been taken because of his alleged wealth. She had even angrily accused him of it in her grief.

"So, do you?" he asked. "Blame me?"

"No, of course I don't," she assured him.

He seemed relieved. But there was still a question in his

eyes. It had nothing to do with guilt this time. She wasn't sure she was able to adequately define it, but there was something intimate about it. As if he were asking: *Then where do you and I stand, Lauren? Exactly what are you feeling about me?*

She looked at him, at that strong, square-jawed face with its cleft chin and lethal blue-green eyes, and she remembered how completely she had fallen under his spell eleven months ago. It would be so easy to surrender again to this compelling man.

But everything had changed since last year. They were no longer the same people. They had a daughter now who, in one sense, had drawn them together and, in another, had pulled them apart. No, Lauren couldn't answer Ethan's silent plea. She didn't know what she felt for him now and wasn't prepared to hear what he might be feeling for her. Maybe just because the subject scared her.

"Anything else has to wait," she said softly.

He seemed to understand her. "You're right. All that matters is getting Sara back. And whatever it takes," he once again promised her fiercely, "I mean to see to it that we do."

Gripping the handles of the oars, he dipped the paddles into the water, sending the rowboat on its way again.

"The sheriff," Lauren said. "We've got to contact the sheriff with what we've learned. Agent Landry, too."

None of it was anything but conjecture, she knew. But solid or not, they had to make the sheriff and the FBI listen to them. Had to get both of them to seriously pursue it.

Ethan nodded. "But not by phone. I want a face-to-face meeting with Howell in his office."

LAUREN SLID A GLANCE in Ethan's direction. With hands clenched down at his sides and feet braced slightly apart, his long-limbed body had assumed the fighter's stance that had become familiar to her by now.

It was a reaction that didn't surprise her. Ethan's demand for action had met a stone wall.

"What do you mean he isn't available?" he said, a scowl on his face as he leaned toward the counter that separated them from the dispatcher on the other side.

The angular woman, who poked at the glasses that kept sliding down her nose, looked in no way troubled by Ethan's anger.

"Just what I said," she responded mildly, as if she had both heard it all and seen it all before and was by now immune to any but the most severe emergency. "Sheriff and his deputy are out dealing with a pileup on the four-lane. A real mess, so I can't say when they'll get back. But when he calls in, I'll let him know you're waiting."

That wasn't good enough for Ethan. "And that's supposed to satisfy us?"

The dispatcher thought about it for a few seconds. "There is one bit of encouraging news. The department is finished with Ms. McCrea's car. Sheriff said it can be released to her."

Ethan looked thoroughly disgusted. "That's your idea of *encouraging*? Come on," he said to Lauren, "we're getting out of here."

Before she could object, he had cupped her elbow and was firmly steering her in the direction of the door to the street. Lauren was just able to get out a fast request over her shoulder.

"Could you please contact FBI Agent Marjorie Landry and let her know everything we told you? We weren't able to raise her on her cell phone on the drive in. She said the sheriff's department could always reach her."

"What about your car?" the dispatcher called back.

"She'll collect it later," Ethan answered for her.

"And what do I tell Sheriff Howell?"

Ethan didn't bother with a reply this time, and Lauren was given no chance to express one for them. Ethan already had them through the door and out on the sidewalk.

Pulling her elbow away from the hand that grasped it, Lauren swung around to face a glowering Ethan. "Did anyone ever tell you you can be very overbearing?"

"Yeah, well, there are some occasions that call for it."

"You evidently regard this as one of them," she said dryly. "So now what do we do?"

"We're going to take charge of this thing ourselves."

"We're not detectives, Ethan."

"Maybe better ones than Howell and Landry are at the moment. Look," he reasoned, "we can't rely on them. Hell, they're never available when we need them. They're too busy chasing off on other cases to devote the full time and energy that Sara deserves. She's *our* kid, Lauren. There's no one who wants her back as much as we do, so let's try to find her."

It was an argument against which she had absolutely no defense. "Where do we begin?"

There was a look on his face that told her he was pleased with her decision. Silly of her to feel a sudden warmth just because of his approval, but she did.

"We'll start with Hilary Johnson."

There was no need for him to explain. If the woman *was* connected with the couple who had occupied her cottage at the lake, then his choice was a logical one.

Climbing back into Ethan's rental car, they headed for Hilary Johnson's address in the older residential section of town. When they pulled over to the curb in front of the frame house that Ethan had visited yesterday morning, he turned to her.

"Why don't you wait in the car while I see if she's here? I don't want her worried by the sight of both of us turning up at her door. She knows me, so there's a chance she'll talk to me if I'm on my own."

It's an excuse. He's just trying to make sure I stay safe if there should be trouble.

Lauren didn't need protecting, but she wasted no time arguing with him about it. In any case, his concern was unnecessary.

"No answer to my knocks," he reported when he slid back

behind the wheel a few minutes later. "I don't think she can be hiding in there, either. Both yesterday's newspaper and today's are on the doorstep. Looks to me like she hasn't been home at all for at least two days."

Then where is she? Lauren wondered. And what does she know? Anything that could help us to get Sara back? Or maybe everything.

Please, God, let us find our baby.

Keeping her emotions under control was getting more difficult, but Lauren managed an even-voiced "What now?"

"Don't know." He was silent for a moment, thinking about it. His fingers played a tattoo on the wheel. "All right," he decided, "since Hilary isn't available to answer our questions, then maybe someone at your lawyer's or the furniture store is."

"I don't understand."

"The women you talked to on the phone yesterday…one of them could have been Hilary."

Lauren was perplexed. "How is that possible?"

"I've remembered something, that's how."

"What?"

"When I was looking for Hilary yesterday, her neighbor told me she took temp jobs around Elkton filling in for people who had to be absent from work. I wasn't able to run her down at any of them, but maybe that's because I was hunting in the wrong places."

"You think it was *she* who either took my call at the lawyer's or phoned me about the high chair?"

"And learned you were coming into town yesterday afternoon and just where you would be and when, yeah. And if she passed on that information to whoever took Sara—"

"Then we'd be that much closer to establishing her involvement with the kidnappers."

"And maybe tracking her down."

Because if we're able to locate Hilary Johnson, she could lead us to Sara.

The furniture store was closer than the lawyer's office, so they went there first. Lauren remembered the stout woman who came forward to wait on them. She had placed her order with her for the high chair.

"I heard about your baby," she said, her round face puckered with sympathy. "I'm so very sorry."

Considering the circumstances, the woman had to be surprised by Lauren's appearance at the store.

Lauren thanked her and then quickly explained. "I'm not here about the chair. That has to wait. But can you tell me who phoned me yesterday?"

"Yes, it was me."

"Please, this could be very important. Did you happen to mention our conversation to anyone else?"

"I canceled delivery on the chair, but that's all."

"You're sure?"

"Yes."

The clerk was clearly puzzled by the earnest tone of her questions, but neither Lauren nor Ethan enlightened her. Thanking her, they left the furniture store and moved on to the lawyer's.

The young, Hispanic receptionist in the outer office was busy at her desk when they arrived. "Can I help you?" she asked, looking up from her computer screen.

Ethan again let Lauren handle it.

"I'm Lauren McCrea. I phoned yesterday morning to get an afternoon appointment with Mr. Garcia. Were you the woman I spoke to?"

The receptionist shook her head. "I was gone yesterday to attend a funeral. A temp was filling in for me."

Lauren exchanged glances with Ethan before asking hopefully, "Was it Hilory Johnson, by any chance?"

The receptionist hesitated, and then seemed to decide there was no reason why she shouldn't tell them. "That's right. But we're not going to use her again. She left the office for lunch and never came back. Didn't even bother to call in an excuse. Mr. Garcia wasn't happy about it."

The receptionist's dark eyes suddenly widened with understanding as she gazed up at Lauren. "Oh, you're the woman whose baby—"

"Thank you," Ethan cut her off before they could be delayed by an uncomfortable explanation. "We appreciate your help. Ms. McCrea will be in touch."

They swiftly left the office. Once back out on the sidewalk, Ethan turned to Lauren with a tight-voiced "Now we know."

Not for certain, Lauren thought, but there was the likelihood that Hilary *was* involved with the kidnappers and that she had passed on the content of her phone call to them. "What do we do about it?"

Ethan had already made up his mind. "She didn't come back to the lawyer's or return home. It has to mean she's hiding out somewhere, maybe with Sara's abductors."

"They could have disappeared from the area altogether, and if they have…"

Lauren couldn't bring herself to say it. That Hilary, together with Sara and the people who had taken her, might be out of reach by now, perhaps hundreds of miles away. If this were true, then it considerably lessened their chances of finding them.

"It's possible," Ethan agreed. "But to be on the run with a stolen baby, whose description is being circulated everywhere, is a big risk. I'd say it was much smarter to stay put for a while in a safe spot."

Lauren suddenly remembered what Rudy Lightfeather had told them back at the lake. "Hilary's other rental property! The one up in the hills! Do you suppose—"

"Exactly," Ethan said with a decisiveness that told her he had already considered this possibility. "It's worth checking out anyway. You remember the name of the agency Rudy said handles the place?"

"Sloan Real Estate. It's out on the north edge of town."

"Let's see what they can tell us."

"You'd better let me drive," Lauren urged when they reached the car. "It will be easier than giving you directions."

Ethan surrendered the wheel to her, and within minutes they arrived on the other side of Elkton at a storefront that had once been occupied by an antique shop and now contained the office of the real estate operation. When they got out of the car, Lauren hung back on the sidewalk.

She could see a desk just on the other side of the large plate-glass window. There was a woman seated there cradling a phone between her shoulder and her ear. She had red hair, a considerable amount of makeup and a predatory gleam in her gaze. That gaze was directed with interest at Ethan's tall, eye-appealing figure.

"Uh, look," Lauren suggested, "why don't you take this one? I somehow get the feeling you might have better luck in there on your own."

"Yeah?" His mouth quirked with humor, but he didn't expand on it. "And what will you be doing while I interrogate the redhead?"

"There's a gas station over there on the corner. I noticed the car could use a fill-up."

"All right." He started to reach for his wallet.

"I'll cover it," she insisted.

He didn't argue with her. In fact, when he parted from her, she wondered if he was just a little too eager to learn what Sloan Real Estate Agency had to offer him. Annoyed with that possibility, and herself for what she couldn't afford to feel, she climbed back into the car.

After all, she reasoned as she drove the half block to the corner, it was no surprise that other women would find Ethan attractive, or that he might respond to that. She could only hope it earned them results.

Since the station was in a section of town Lauren seldom

had a reason to visit, she wasn't familiar with it. But as she waited at the pump for the tank to fill, she could see it was a busy operation. There was a reason for that. The station was located just off the four-lane, making it convenient for all the traffic that traveled north toward the Canadian border.

When she left the sedan at the pump and went inside to pay, she saw that the place was more than the usual compact quick stop. Along with the customary basic groceries, there was an assortment of other wares, as well as a fast-food restaurant attached to one end.

There were also two counters, one at the front and another at the rear. The second desk was meant chiefly to serve the truckers, whose rigs arrived out back where the diesel fuel was presumably located.

All of this amounted to no more than a casual observation for Lauren as she waited for her turn at the front desk. Until, that is, she had paid for her gas, closed her purse and was starting to turn away from the counter. That's when her heart turned over at the sight of a figure just leaving the rear desk.

Lauren could so easily have overlooked her among all the other customers in the station. Probably would have, if the purchase tucked under the woman's arm hadn't captured her attention. It was an economy-sized box of disposable diapers. Even at this distance Lauren could tell that's what it was, maybe because it was a brand she'd always preferred.

Her heart more than just turned over when she took a second, harder look at the figure. It seemed to stop altogether. The woman wore a scarf over her head this time, not a bicycle helmet. But wisps of blond hair peeked out from under the scarf, and the sunglasses were the same, as was the excessively thin body.

When Lauren's heart started to beat again, rapidly now, she realized that the woman was hurrying toward the back door. There was a furtive quality about her haste, as if her errand had been dictated by a necessity that left her fearful of discovery.

She's getting away!

Lauren didn't hesitate long enough to consider the risk in pursuing the blonde. All that mattered was overtaking the woman and demanding the return of her daughter. Nor did she stop long enough to ask an attendant to phone the police. Afraid of losing her objective, she raced along the aisle toward the back door through which the blonde had fled.

As fast as Lauren was, by the time she emerged from the building no one was in sight. There was a sea of concrete here, large enough to accommodate the fleet of massive eighteen-wheelers parked at the back of the lot. Although several of the rigs were rumbling softly, an indication their engines had been left to idle, none of the cabs were occupied. Lauren guessed their drivers were either in the truckers' restrooms or the fast-food restaurant.

There was no one she could question, and the blonde had disappeared. Had she already sped away in a waiting car?

Refusing to give up, Lauren's head turned from side to side, her gaze sweeping the area.

There!

She caught a flash of movement between two of the trucks, a quick blur of burgundy. Was the blonde wearing burgundy slacks? Lauren thought she was.

Taking off after her, she flew across the yard. Reached the trucks and looked down the long aisle between them. Her target had vanished again. Where could she have gotten to?

There was a tall, board fence at the end of the aisle marking a division between the station and whatever lay on the other side. The fence was solid. Except for a gap where one of the vertical boards was missing. A gap wide enough to permit an adult to squeeze through it.

The woman must have escaped through this hole, and like Alice chasing the White Rabbit, Lauren went after her. Along the narrow canyon between the towering steel walls of the eighteen-wheelers she ran.

She never reached the gap in the fence. The blonde wasn't alone. Lauren should have known she wouldn't be on her own, that someone would have accompanied her, served as a lookout.

He must have been lurking at the tail of one of the two rigs. Lauren never glimpsed him, never heard him over the reverberation of the engines. She was nearing the fence when he struck with the speed of a viper, seizing her from behind as she passed the end of the truck.

A pair of arms went around her, stopping her, dragging her back, pinning her so tightly against his bulk that the wind was punched out of her.

Lauren's skin crawled with revulsion when she felt his hot breath near her ear. He issued his challenge in a rough, ugly growl.

"And just where do you think *you're* going?"

Chapter Eight

Lauren struggled in his grip, trying to break free. Her effort was useless. He was too strong for her, his arms locked around her like a vise.

When she started to twist her head around, attempting to get a look at his face, he prevented her action by freeing one of his hands just long enough to deliver a stinging slap to the side of her head. Lauren's ears rang from the blow.

"You try something like that again," he warned her cruelly, "and I'll really hurt you. Understand?"

Given no choice about it, she bobbed her head. He didn't want to be identified, but that didn't mean he wasn't prepared to listen to reason. Drawing air into her lungs, she pleaded with him.

"Look, just give my baby back to me. I'll give you anything you want. Whatever it is, I'll manage it somehow, I promise."

"I don't know what you're talking about," he sneered.

"At least tell me she's all right. Please, I have to know."

His laugh was low and as sour as his faint body odor. "You're crazy. What's in that head of yours? Anything at all?"

Lauren was frightened, but she was also angry. "If you harm her, harm her in any way, I swear I'll—"

His arms tightened around her, an iron band choking off her words. He was dangerous. Not just for her, but for Sara. Her threat had been a mistake.

"No, I didn't mean that," she quickly, breathlessly

amended her error. "I'm sorry I said it. Just be good to her, that's all I ask. If you'll only—"

"Lauren! You out here?"

She instantly recognized the voice that came from somewhere near the back door of the gas station. It was Ethan! She felt her captor go rigid.

"Don't try to follow us," he whispered, his alarm forcing him into an admission. "If you want your kid to stay safe, don't come anywhere near us again."

Muttering an obscenity, he flung Lauren away from him with such rage that she went sprawling down onto the ground, her purse flying out of her hand.

By the time she lifted her head from the oil-spattered pavement, all she could see was a fleeting glimpse of his back as he forced his way through the gap in the fence. And because he wore a sweat jacket with the hood pulled over his head, she couldn't tell even the color of his hair.

Ethan called to her again, a sharp, frantic edge to his shout this time. "Lauren, where are you?"

"Here!" she cried to him. "Over here between the trucks!"

She heard the sound of his feet striking against the concrete as he ran toward her. When he reached her, she was on her hands and knees and had managed to rescue her purse from beneath the wheels of the truck.

"What in sweet heaven are you doing down there? When I found the car out at the pump, I came inside looking for you, and the clerk at the counter said she saw you—" He broke off to help her to her feet. "Are you hurt?"

"I'm all right. Ethan, they're getting away!"

"Who?"

"The couple who took Sara! They were here! They went through the fence there!"

Ethan's face darkened with a savage look. Thankfully, he didn't stop to express doubt or to question her. "Stay put," he instructed her.

All she had time to do was call after him a cautionary, "He's a devil! Be careful!" And then he was gone, slipping through the opening in the fence.

Stay put.

She did for a long maddening minute, and then she realized she couldn't go on standing there doing nothing. Ethan was alone in there, and she was worried about him. She had to know what was going on, whether he might need her help.

Promising herself to be careful, Lauren went to the fence, ducked her head under the top rail to which the vertical boards had been nailed, and slid through the gap. When she stood erect on the other side, she was surprised to find herself in what amounted to an automobile graveyard.

The salvage lot was apparently an extensive one. Cars, or what were left of them anyway, stretched away on all sides. Every make and model was here in various stages of decay. There was no sign of either Ethan or the couple he was pursuing.

Lauren waited for a minute, listening for a sound that might provide her with a direction. But there were no footsteps. Nothing but the silence.

Although the cars had been packed tightly together in blocks, rows had been left open around the blocks. Lauren ventured up the first of these aisles, clutching her purse and pausing every few seconds to look and listen. Still nothing. Where were they?

As she wandered along the rows, she began to feel she was playing hide-and-seek in a vast maze. It was the perfect place to lose yourself. She figured that the blonde and her companion must have deliberately chosen the salvage yard to approach the gas station. It offered them the escape route they had needed.

Lauren wasn't sure at what point she realized that *she* was the one who was lost. Coming to a complete stop, she tried to get her bearings. It was hopeless. She couldn't distinguish one rusted wreck from another. By now, she had no idea how to find her way back to the gap in the fence.

It had been a mistake for her to come in here. Why hadn't she listened to Ethan and remained where he'd left her?

The urge to call out to him was strong, but she suddenly understood she couldn't do that. Whatever Ethan heard could also be heard by the enemy, and if she betrayed her presence, and they reached her first...

Trapped! She had trapped herself in here and was vulnerable!

This was ridiculous. She needed to help herself. Resisting the threat of panic, she turned around and started back the way she had come. She hadn't taken three steps when she heard it: the sound of someone approaching.

Lauren looked around for a place to conceal herself. She thought about diving down between the cars. Then she noticed that the vehicle just to her right was missing its back door. Hopping inside, she crouched low, hugging the rotted seat.

Seconds passed. When she could no longer bear the suspense, she risked lifting her head just high enough to peer through the cracked rear window. At that moment a tall figure came swinging around the corner and down the row in her direction.

The sight of Ethan filled her with relief.

She didn't blame him for being startled when she popped out of the car as he came toward her. "Lauren! What in the world were you doing in *there*? I thought I asked you to stay—"

"Don't scold me. I couldn't help it. I had to know what was going on, and then when I heard you coming, I thought it might be one of them, so I—"

She was trembling so badly she couldn't go on. He had come to a halt when she'd emerged from the car. But now, seeing how shaken she was, he reached her in three quick strides. She ought to have objected when he folded her into his arms. Instead, she welcomed his protective embrace, clung to him tightly.

"A devil," he muttered into her ear.

"What?"

"You called him a devil just before I went through the fence. And you're scared. Did he touch you?" he wanted to know, his voice rough with anger. "Because if the bastard touched you—"

"No," she lied, fearing if she didn't that Ethan might leave her to go tearing off again after her attacker. And she needed him here. Needed him to go on holding her.

Lauren wasn't entirely sure just when she began to realize she had traded one danger for another. She only knew that at some point she became aware that his embrace had become more intimate than protective. That he had molded himself so tightly against her body she could feel the hardness of his unmistakable arousal. That his strong hands on her back were no longer soothing her with comforting strokes but with slow caresses that could only be defined as desire.

In another moment, he would tip her head back, fasten his mouth on hers. To yield to that temptation would be so easy. And so wrong. Not just because this was neither the right time nor the right place. There was that, of course, but there was also the emotional turmoil that had been present from the beginning of their relationship. She knew that both of them continued to struggle with it. And there was their missing daughter.

"Sara," she reminded him softly.

Just the mention of Sara was enough. Ethan immediately released her.

"I'm sorry," she apologized for her momentary weakness. "I was behaving like a fool just because— Look, I'm okay now. Did you see any sign of either of them?"

Ethan gazed at her in sober silence for a few seconds, no

if wanting to be certain of her recovery. Or perhaps because he was disappointed in her resistance.

"No," he said, shaking his head, "they got away before I could catch up with them. I heard a car roaring off on the other side of the yard. I suppose that was them. What happened exactly? How did you run into them?"

Lauren related what had taken place back at the gas station, minimizing the episode that had occurred between the trucks to a verbal warning from the man who had challenged her. If Ethan wondered how she could have been threatened without managing to see his face, she gave him no opportunity to pursue it.

"Can we get out of here?" she urged. "If we don't get back to the car, the gas station is going to end up hauling it away for blocking their pumps. Providing, that is, you know the way. I'm thoroughly lost."

Ethan's sense of direction turned out to be far better than hers. He was able to confidently take them back to the gap in the fence.

"From what you told me," he said when they reached the car, "we know for certain now that this is the couple who took Sara."

"We know more than that. We know she's still with them. They wouldn't have risked stopping here for the diapers otherwise." For Lauren, this was the most vital knowledge. That her daughter was alive and receiving at least basic care.

"And they haven't left the area. They're out there somewhere within reach." The palm of his hand came down on the hood of the car with a frustrated smack. "But how do we find them?"

"Hilary Johnson's other house in the hills," she reminded him. "Unless they left Sara behind in their car while they sneaked through the salvage yard to get the diapers, and I don't think they would have risked having someone spot her in the parked car, then—"

"Yeah, someone else was looking after Sara back at their hideout, and that someone could be Hilary."

Lauren gazed at him, suddenly understanding his frustration. "You didn't have any luck at Sloan Real Estate."

Ethan shook his head. "Afraid I struck out. Oh, the redhead was friendly enough all right, but when it came to the subject of that house she wouldn't budge. Said there was no point in my going out to look at it because the owner had removed it from their rental listings. And since they hadn't kept the sheet on it, she couldn't provide me with directions anyway."

"If Hilary took it off the market, that's got to be where they're holed up."

"A strong likelihood, certainly," he agreed.

"There *has* to be a way of getting directions to the place."

His mind focused on the problem, Ethan didn't answer her. Lauren became aware of a man who had emerged from the front door of the gas station. From the way he stood there glaring at them pointedly, she guessed he was probably the manager.

"Uh, I think we're being asked to move the car away from the pumps."

Ethan didn't bother glancing in the direction of the station. His interest had been captured by another figure out on the sidewalk. A teenager had come whizzing by on a skateboard. He was now stopped on the corner waiting for the traffic light to change.

"The baseball cap!" Ethan said.

If this was a sudden revelation, Lauren didn't understand it. It was true the teenager wore a baseball cap, with its peak twisted around to the back and one of its seams parting from hard use. But what did this have to do with anything?

"I think I know how we might get those directions," Ethan said. "Let's get out of here."

Since the manager was headed now in their direction, his decision was a timely one. Lauren took the wheel again.

"Where are we going?" she asked as they reached the street, pausing for the traffic to clear.

"Back to Hilary's house here in town."

Lauren couldn't imagine why, but she waited until they

were under way before she questioned him. "Now what's this all about? What can we hope to learn when we've already been there."

"Plenty, I hope. It was that baseball cap. I remembered the old man next door was wearing one. Like the kid's, one of its seams was starting to split open."

He went on to explain how Hilary's neighbor had been in his yard raking leaves when Ethan had come looking for the ex-housekeeper yesterday morning.

"He knew about Hilary, knew about her family. There's a good chance he also knows about that place in the hills and how to get there."

The newspapers were still on the doorstep when they reached the Johnson house. Lauren pulled over to the curb and waited in the car while Ethan went to the neighbor's door.

An elderly man answered his knock. Presumably, this was the same one Ethan had referred to, although he wasn't wearing the baseball cap now. She watched hopefully as the two men conferred out on the stoop.

Her hands were clenching the wheel in suspense by the time Ethan returned and slid into the car. There was a look of triumph on his face when he turned to her.

"Got it!" he said. "The property used to be a farm Hilary's father let out to a tenant. The old guy would ride out there with him once in a while to collect the rent, so he remembered the place and how to get there."

Lauren exhaled in relief. "Bless him."

"Let's roll. I'll give you directions along the way."

Lauren hesitated. "Do you think it's time we brought the sheriff in on this?"

Ethan shook his head without pausing to consider her suggestion. "No more delays. These people have got to be worried that you ran into them like that. They could be ready to move on from a hideout they no longer consider safe. If we don't get to them now, we could lose them."

And Sara with them. The unspoken words hung in the air between them. His argument convinced her they couldn't afford to wait. At the same time, she was aware of the danger involved in their plan. But for the sake of her daughter, she was prepared to risk that and much more.

"THIS HAS GOT TO BE IT," Ethan said, indicating a pair of ancient wagon wheels that marked each side of the turn into the driveway.

Since there was no sign or a mailbox, only the wheels the neighbor had described, Lauren hoped he was right.

Either the old man's memory had been somewhat inaccurate or Ethan had been confused by his directions, because they'd lost valuable time backtracking on a labyrinth of unpaved country roads before arriving here.

It was late afternoon by now. There couldn't be more than an hour or so of daylight left. It was hard to tell, though. Clouds had moved in, obscuring the sun and making her wonder if it was going to rain.

"Doesn't look like any neighbors in the area," Ethan said as she swung the car into the narrow lane.

Which makes it the perfect hideout, she thought as she proceeded slowly along the rutted, weedy drive.

"You see any sign of a house?" he asked.

"Not yet."

"Me, either. But the minute we do, stop the car. We'll leave it behind and check out the place on foot. We don't want to alert them."

If they're even here, Lauren thought. There was no guarantee they ever had been. The property could be as deserted as it looked.

"Not much of a farm, huh?" Ethan observed.

He was right. The region was hilly, most of it in forest. It must have always been a struggle trying to farm it, and now the fields off on the right of the winding drive were abandoned and already shoulder-high with pines that had claimed them.

"You see it?" Ethan said, directing her attention to a roof peeking over the tops of those same pines.

"Yes." She rolled to a stop, nodding toward a grove of tall hemlocks on their left. "That looks as good a place as any to hide the car."

"Right."

She turned the wheel and edged forward, squeezing the sedan into the depths of the grove until it was tucked out of sight. There was a total silence when she cut the engine. Ethan lowered the window on his side, and for a moment they listened. Nothing. Not even the sound of birds. There was something almost eerie about the stillness.

"All right, here's the plan," he said. "You wait here while I—"

"Forget that. I'm coming with you."

"Lauren, let's not argue about this."

"I agree. We're wasting time, so let's go."

"I'd feel better if you stayed here."

"And I'd feel better going with you," she insisted. "Look, if you're worried I'm going to go all emotional on you again, like back at the salvage yard, I promise I won't."

"It isn't that. It's just—"

"You think I'd be safer staying here on my own. Well, I wouldn't be. It's much safer if I stick with you. For *both* of us."

He had no answer to that.

"Good," she said, unbuckling her seat belt and opening her door.

Seconds later, they moved cautiously on foot up the drive. The farmhouse, less than a hundred yards away, came into full view when they rounded a bend. Using the pines as a cover, they studied the setting.

In addition to the house itself, there were the remains of a barn that had collapsed into its fieldstone foundations, a rusted windmill that probably hadn't operated in decades and a machine shed. Though its roof was sagging, the weathered shed was still intact, its double doors hanging open.

There was a forlorn look about the whole place, including the house. As if it hadn't been inhabited in years.

"You see any sign of life?" Ethan asked her softly.

"No."

If Sara's kidnappers weren't here, then their effort to find this place had been for nothing.

Ethan, however, wasn't ready to be discouraged. "I want to check out that shed first."

Screening themselves behind all the vegetation that had gone wild, they worked their way around the perimeter of the clearing until they reached the gaping doors of the shed. From this angle, the house was no longer visible. If anyone was watching from one of its windows, they could not be seen.

Lauren followed Ethan into the gloom of the shed. It was empty except for a barrel of trash, an old croquet set with missing pieces and bales of rotting hay stacked against one wall. She didn't know what he expected to find here.

But Ethan, crouched down on the earthen floor of the shed, had already made a discovery. "Tire tracks here in the dust," he reported. "Somebody's been using the shed as a garage, and the tracks are recent enough to mean—"

He never finished. At that instant something hidden in the shadows launched itself from the top of the hay bales. As it hurtled past Lauren, almost brushing her face, she gasped in alarm. Recoiling, she collided with the barrel. It overturned, spilling its contents.

The cat—she realized that's what had startled her—landed on the floor and, without pause, streaked away through the woods. The animal had never made a sound, but the barrel had seemed like an explosion to Lauren. Had its crash been loud enough to be overheard at the house?

Ethan was worried enough by that possibility to go to the open doors of the shed where he stood listening. Left behind, Lauren righted the barrel, knelt and began to pick up the trash.

"I think we're okay," he decided, joining her back inside the shed. "As loud as the noise seemed to us, it couldn't have been heard as far away as the house. But let's not hang around in here. There's nothing more to be seen."

"That's not true," she said, coming to her feet.

The expression on her face when she looked at him must have revealed her excitement. "What is it?" he demanded. "What did you find?"

"This," she said, holding out an empty plastic bottle.

"Is that—"

"What you think it is, yes. A disposable baby bottle, with traces of wet formula still inside. And there were others like it in the trash barrel."

"That's it, then. Proof this is where they brought Sara."

Lauren didn't point out to him that the bottles weren't conclusive evidence, that their contents could have fed some other baby. How could she say it when she, too, wanted to believe their daughter could be within their reach?

"But what good does it do us?" she said, remembering the tire tracks and the absence of the vehicle that made them. "If this is where they kept their car, and it's not here, then they've cleared out."

"Not necessarily. They might still be off somewhere and intending to come back. And if Sara wasn't with them when they stopped at the gas station, then it could mean she's in the house right now with whoever is taking care of her." His jaw tightened. "It's time we tackled the house."

The need to investigate the house itself, and the risk it involved, awakened butterflies in Lauren's stomach. And when Ethan armed himself with a stout mallet from the croquet set, an action that said a weapon might be essential, those butterflies coalesced into a lump. Nerves or not, however, she had no intention of being left behind, not when she knew he was right.

With Ethan leading the way, they plunged back into the shrubbery outside. Silence was necessary now as they made their way toward the house. From time to time, she caught glimpses of the farmhouse through the lush growth that shielded them.

Typical of its kind and its era, it was a two-story, frame structure with a single-story kitchen wing off one end. Now that they were near it, she could see that, unlike the other buildings that had been allowed to deteriorate, the house itself had been kept in repair. But in the dwindling light, with the shades pulled down at all of the windows, it had a sinister look.

Nor, when they circled the house, keeping the overgrown shrubbery between themselves and its walls, did it look any less forbidding from the back side.

Ethan brought them to a halt behind a tangle of lilacs, where they spoke in undertones.

"I'm going to try to get inside," he said.

Lauren eyed the back door located off a porch that stretched across the kitchen wing. It looked solid. "What if the door and all the windows are locked?"

"They probably are."

"But if you break in, there's no way to cover the noise."

"I'm not going to do that unless I have to. See the cellar doors over there? That's how I'm going to get in. Maybe."

"You can't go in there on your own. I'm coming with you."

"Not until I signal you no one is waiting down in that cellar. You stay right here until then. Got your cell phone in your purse?"

"Yes."

"Then if I don't come out of there waving an all clear in three minutes, you get back to the car and out of here. You can call the sheriff when you're on the road, but not until then."

Lauren wasn't happy with his plan, but she was afraid if she objected to it, he wouldn't let her accompany him at all. She knew how much he didn't like her being here in the first place.

Mallet in hand and bent over in a half crouch, Ethan sprinted toward the house. Even though the drawn shades made the windows blind and the distance he had to travel wasn't far, she knew he was vulnerable out in the open like this. At any second, he could be challenged.

He wasn't. He reached his objective, the pair of old-fashioned wooden cellar doors. Would he find them locked? She watched as he tugged at a handle. The door lifted. He paused for a second, and she knew he was listening. Apparently satisfied, he eased the door higher until he was able to fold it all the way back. Then, still gripping the mallet, he vanished down into the dark cavity.

Keeping her solitary vigil in the lilac thicket, Lauren waited. It was the longest three minutes she had ever endured.

Not until his head appeared again in the opening was she able to draw a decent breath. When he beckoned to her, she quickly joined him.

"Careful of the steps," he whispered. "They're steep and wet."

He turned, and she followed him down into the stone-walled cellar. The few windows here were small and dirty, admitting only the weakest of light. Lauren was able to see very little in the deep gloom, but Ethan must have discovered an inside stairway or he wouldn't have summoned her.

He led the way across the earthen floor. The place was damp and smelled of mold and decay. They didn't speak and there was no sound from overhead.

Reaching the foot of a narrow stairway, they stopped to listen. The house wore the silence of desertion. But the stillness could be deceptive, cloaking a menace. For that reason, they crept up the stairs, Lauren close behind Ethan and fearing one of the old treads would squeak under their weight.

That didn't happen, but when he carefully spread the door open at the top of the stairway, it did creak softly. She caught her breath, but his action raised no alarm.

When they emerged from the cellar, they found themselves in the kitchen. Even in the murky light, Lauren could see all the evidence of a hasty departure. Cupboard doors yawned, food had been left uncovered on the table, unwashed dishes were piled on the counters.

It was a repeat of the scene in the cottage at the lake. And for the same reason. The occupants of the house had fled. It had all been for nothing, the effort she and Ethan had made to find this place, the caution they had so carefully exercised to get inside. Their silence wasn't necessary now.

"They're gone," she said, wondering how much more disappointment she could bear. "We've lost them again."

And Sara along with them.

"Looks like it," Ethan said, his frown registering his own disappointment. "Come on, let's have a look at the rest of the place."

"It's pretty obvious we're all alone here. What's the point?"

"If they got out because they panicked, they might have decided it was too dangerous now to take Sara with them. They could have left her behind."

That was possible, if not likely. She and Ethan could afford to overlook nothing, because if Sara *had* been ruthlessly abandoned, left here all on her own—

The thought was so horrifying that Lauren shuddered. Was her daughter somewhere in this house? It was both a hope and a fear.

"And if not that," Ethan added, "there's a chance of finding something that could tell us where they've gone."

Her anxiety mounting, Lauren accompanied him in the search. They moved rapidly from room to room, switching on lamps as they went. Dining room, parlor, bathroom, downstairs bedroom. In none of them was there either a sign of their daughter or an indication of where her abductors might have taken her. All they did find was further evidence of a quick escape.

They must have come straight back here after that business at the service station, Lauren thought, thrown their things together and gotten out. If only she and Ethan hadn't been delayed hunting for the place, they might have caught up with them.

But why had they been holed up here? Not because they were waiting for the delivery of a ransom. They'd never demanded one. Then what *had* they been waiting for? And why, *why* had they taken Sara in the first place?

Useless. They were all useless questions without answers, bringing her no closer to her desperate need to be reunited with her daughter. A need driven by her memory of the viciousness of the man who had held her between the high walls of the trucks. The thought of her baby in the hands of someone like that chilled her.

There was a door at one end of the parlor they had yet to investigate. Opening it, Lauren found herself gazing up into the dimness of an enclosed staircase.

"The stairway to the second floor," she reported to Ethan.

"Let me go first," he said, joining her at the bottom of the steep flight.

She started to move aside and then hesitated. "Did you hear something?"

"Like what?"

"I thought I heard a sound up there."

"I didn't hear anything."

"I guess it was nothing."

But she was glad he still had the mallet in his hand as he preceded her up through the shadows.

There was a small hallway at the head of the flight of stairs. It was occupied by nothing but a battered chimney cupboard that faced the stairs. Off one side of the hall was an open doorway. A glance inside revealed an unfurnished bedroom. It looked gray and hollow in October's early twilight.

At the other side of the hall was a narrow passageway. Lauren followed Ethan down its short length to the closed door at the end. When he closed his hand over the knob and turned, he met resistance.

"Locked?" she asked.

"Yes, and no key. Not on this side anyway."

It wasn't necessary for either of them to say what had to be obvious to both of them. That, if the door had been locked, there was a reason for it. Possibly a vital reason.

"Stand back," Ethan said. "I'm going to see what I can do about getting us inside."

She retreated a few steps, giving him the space he needed. Raising one foot, he delivered a powerful kick just below the knob. The lock was an ancient one, the door equally old. It crashed open, banging back against the wall on the other side.

Lauren came forward, looking over his shoulder into the room. It was another bedroom, but this one was furnished. A full-length mirror on the wall opposite the door reflected the last light of day that stole through the two windows.

The mirror also reflected something else. Catching her breath, and then releasing it in a rush, Lauren stared at the body of a woman stretched out on the floor between a pair of beds.

By the time she recovered from her initial shock, Ethan was inside the room and crouched beside the still figure. She swiftly followed him.

It wasn't until she rounded the foot of the first bed that she noticed the blood. It had pooled on the floor from an ugly wound on the side of the woman's turned head. She had either fallen and injured herself, or she'd been struck down. *Brutally* struck down, perhaps by whoever had locked that door.

"Is she—"

"I don't know." Ethan had his forefinger at the woman's throat, searching for a pulse.

She could still be alive. She could have made the sound I thought I heard at the bottom of the stairs. She could have heard us in the house and was trying to signal for—

Another thought suddenly occurred to her. "Ethan, this isn't the blonde. She's someone else, someone much older."

"I know."

He recognized the woman. The hardness in his voice told her that. "It's Hilary Johnson, isn't it?"

"Yeah."

She's so small, Lauren thought, gazing sadly at the slight figure below her. Much too small to have been something like a housekeeper, even if others had performed the heavy work in Jonathan Brand's mansion.

It was an oddly disconcerting thought, maybe because Lauren realized on another level that Hilary Johnson didn't deserve her sympathy. Not when her presence here was an almost certain indication now that the woman *had* played a role in Sara's abduction.

"I've got a pulse," Ethan said, "but it's a weak one."

"Then we've got to get help for her."

Lauren opened her purse and groped inside for her cell phone. She had no chance to use it.

During the course of the long afternoon, they had been subjected to a series of unexpected events. Those events had not ended. The last one was dealt to them in that second when, from the direction of the hallway behind them, came a loud *whump*. The blast was so strong it rocked the floor under Lauren's feet.

Chapter Nine

Ethan shouted something after her, but before he could get to his feet to stop her, Lauren had whipped out into the passageway. The sight that met her gaze down at its other end horrified her.

The chimney cupboard had exploded like a fragile eggshell with the force of whatever device must have been planted behind its door. That it was incendiary in nature was obvious since flames were rapidly engulfing the hall. She could hear their roar, feel the intense heat they generated, see tongues of fire licking toward her along the old, dry wood of the floor.

All this registered in her mind within the space of a few seconds. Then, pivoting, she fled back to the bedroom, colliding with Ethan in the doorway.

"The fire's already blocked the stairway!" she cried. "We can't get out that way!"

He drew her into the room, closing the door against the smoke billowing along the passageway. It refused to shut properly after his earlier abuse of it. Smoke began to curl in little wisps around its edges and under its bottom.

"Find whatever you can to stuff into the cracks while I see what I can do about getting us out of here," he directed her.

Lauren didn't question what that might be. Wouldn't permit herself to fear they might be hopelessly trapped. Panic was not an option. Urgency was.

Tearing the quilt off one of the beds, she hung it over the door, pressing its folds in and around the edges of the door as best she could. Then, stripping the sheets from the mattress, she knelt on the floor and bunched them along the bottom of the door. It helped, but it wasn't enough.

Smoke started to seep through the barrier, stinging her eyes as she worked, invading her lungs. She heard glass shattering behind her, and when she turned her head, she saw Ethan at one of the windows. His arm and hand wrapped with a pillowcase, he had smashed out the lower pane of the window and was now picking away the splintered fragments that still clung to the frame.

"Painted shut," he explained his action. "It wouldn't budge."

She got to her feet, started to join him at the window. "How far is it down to the—"

She broke off, coughing on the smoke she'd swallowed. But he understood what she had tried to ask.

"No need to worry about that. This window is over the kitchen roof. We'll crawl out on that and then it should be an easy drop to the ground. Come on, I'll help you through."

Lauren made her way swiftly to his side and then stopped again as memory seized her. "Hilary! We can't just—"

"I'm not going to leave her behind. Just get out there, and I'll lower her down to you."

Aided by Ethan, Lauren managed to scramble through the opening he'd cleared and onto the ridge several feet below her. By the time she'd secured her footing on the roof, which mercifully had a low pitch, he'd gone back for Hilary and was sliding her limp body feetfirst through the window.

Lauren braced herself to receive the weight. Had Hilary been a heavy woman, she probably wouldn't have been able to bear that unconscious load. As it was, she was able to wrap her arms around the ex-housekeeper's waist and, when Ethan released her, ease her down onto the slope.

When she straightened, her eyes just above the level of the window ledge, she could see the quilt over the door smoldering. The fire had reached the bedroom and was eating its way inside.

Ethan! Where was Ethan?

He appeared in the opening. "You forget your purse."

She took the purse from him as he reached out to hand it to her. She must have flung it down somewhere while she was trying to seal the door.

"Hurry!" she urged him.

There was a bad moment when Ethan tried to fit his broad shoulders through the frame. It was a tight squeeze that required his full strength before he was finally able to squirm his way into the open and join her on the ridge.

"Don't wait for me," he commanded her. "Get yourself down to the edge. I'll follow with Hilary."

Sinking to the shingles, she scooted herself on her backside down the slope until she arrived on the rim of the porch roof. When she turned her head and looked back, she saw smoke pouring from the window through which they'd escaped. Flames were leaping from the peak of the upper roof.

With Hilary in his arms, Ethan managed his own descent on his feet. He started to lower his burden to the shingles in order to help Lauren reach the ground.

"I can manage," she assured him.

She could, and she did. But the process of twisting over flat on her stomach, wriggling backward so that her lower half was dangling in space, and then pushing herself the rest of the way until her only contact with the roof were her hands clinging to the gutter, was an unnerving one.

She hung there for a few seconds before, summoning her courage, she released her hold and dropped to the ground.

When Ethan was certain she'd landed safely, he tossed her purse down to her, lowered Hilary into her waiting arms, and launched himself from the edge of the roof with maddening ease.

By the time they'd put distance between themselves and the house, and were crouched in the grass beside the inert figure of the ex-housekeeper, the building was an inferno.

"You okay?" Ethan wanted to know.

Lauren dragged in a mouthful of air that this time was not tainted by smoke and nodded. "You?"

"All in one piece."

For a moment they rested there in the deepening dusk, their gazes trained soberly on the raging conflagration that was rapidly consuming the old farmhouse. The blaze was instantly forgotten when a soft moan alerted them.

"She's coming around!" Lauren said.

They bent close over Hilary. The woman's eyes drifted open, her gaze slowly focusing on Ethan's face looming just above hers. The glow from the fire must have been strong enough for her to not only recognize him but to make out the color of his eyes.

"She has your eyes," she whispered.

Sara! Lauren thought. She has to be talking about Sara!

"The same as *his* eyes."

"Who?" Ethan demanded. "Tell us who he is."

Hilary frowned, looking dazed and then making another effort. "I thought I could manage him. Even after Seattle, I thought it would be all right. I was wrong. He's out of control now."

"Where has he gone?" Lauren pleaded with her. "Where did he and the woman with him take Sara?"

"Why, to Windrush, of course. They've gone back to Windrush."

Windrush. Lauren had heard the name before, but she couldn't remember what it meant. "Hilary, I *have* to know. Please, won't you—"

"Lauren, it's no good. She's out again. She needs an ambulance."

Lauren's conscience reminded her that, in her desperate

desire to learn answers, she had neglected to remember how serious Hilary's condition was. Nor could the woman have benefited from the less-than-gentle treatment that had been necessary in order to get her out of the house.

Through it all, Lauren had managed to hang on to her purse. She opened it now and took out her cell phone. Before she could punch in the number for emergency help, Ethan laid a hand on her arm.

"You don't have to bother," he said. "Listen."

She heard it then, too. The wail of sirens in the valley below the farm.

"A neighbor must have spotted the fire and reported it," Ethan decided. "Let's hope the paramedics are right behind the fire engines."

SHERIFF HOWELL was not happy with them.

"You two had no business playing cops. In case you've forgotten, I'm the law in this county."

"If we hadn't come out here when we did," Ethan angrily defended their actions, "Hilary Johnson would have burned up in that house. Or haven't you figured out by now what's got to be obvious? That the woman must have been left for dead and the fire meant to destroy her body and any evidence connected with the man who turned on her."

"There you go again, playing detective."

Which you should have been doing yourself, Lauren thought, wanting to say it but afraid if she did that Howell might charge them with obstructing the law.

"And I'll tell you something else," Ethan went on, ignoring the sheriff's warning. "The guy wasn't taking any chances on getting caught on the scene. That fire was set to go off after he took himself and his girlfriend out of the area."

And our baby is with them. So why are we sitting here arguing about it? Why aren't we going after them?

This further delay was maddening. But all Sheriff Howell

could rouse himself to do at the moment was gaze at them reproachfully from his side of the battered old picnic table, where they were seated a safe distance away from the activity at the house. That, and perform the annoying habit he had of sucking at his teeth.

The sky was dark now. Nor did the fire offer any glow. It had been nearly extinguished, leaving the farmhouse a smoking rubble. But Lauren had no trouble seeing the sheriff's ruddy face. There were all the lights from the fire engines, the other vehicles that had accompanied them and the two police cruisers parked in the grass at the side of the drive. The ambulance had already departed with Hilary.

"You got another interesting theory?" the sheriff asked Ethan, his tone dry with sarcasm.

"Yeah, I do. *Even after Seattle.* Those were Hilary's words. She figured she could manage him *even after Seattle,* only she was wrong. What she said didn't make sense to me at first, but now it does. I think what she meant was that this guy, whoever he is, killed my grandfather, and she lied about it to cover for him."

"Maybe," Sheriff Howell conceded. "Or maybe she was in such a bad way she didn't know what she was saying."

"Not so. She was coherent."

Deputy Wicowski, who had been monitoring the radio in his police cruiser, arrived at the picnic table. He leaned over to murmur something in the sheriff's ear. Howell listened and then relayed his message to Lauren and Ethan.

"My office just contacted us with a report from the paramedics. Hilary Johnson didn't make it. She died in the ambulance on the way to the hospital without ever regaining consciousness again. Looks like we'll never know exactly what she *did* mean by her last words to you."

There was a long silence at the picnic table, each of them sobered in their own way by the news of Hilary's death. It was the fire chief, a grizzled veteran known for his tough language, who ended the silence when he joined them a moment later.

"There was no way we could save any of it," he said, referring to the house. "But from the way you folks described what happened when we got here, I'd say it probably *was* an incendiary device. Something involving a timer, a fuse and highly combustible material. Arson investigation may be able to detect evidence when they sift through the remains. One thing's for sure—whoever set it is a cunning bastard."

"He's more than that," Ethan maintained, "because even if he didn't kill my grandfather, Hilary's death *does* make him a murderer now."

Lauren could no longer restrain her impatience over the sheriff's inaction. "A murderer who has my daughter!" she cried. "Why aren't you out there catching him, Sheriff?"

"If it's within my power, Ms. McCrea, I intend to do just that. But I was counting on Hilary Johnson explaining about this Windrush. Only, with her gone, it'll take some digging to learn what she was talking about when she told you—"

"You don't have to wait for that! I *know* what Windrush is and where it is!"

The four men around the table turned their gazes on her in surprise.

"Hell, Lauren," Ethan said, "if you knew all along, why didn't you—"

"But I didn't. It just sounded familiar, that's all. It's only now I've remembered I came across it in the research I was doing for one of the books I wrote last year."

Ethan leaned toward her earnestly. "And?"

"It's a hotel in the mountains. One of those big Edwardian resorts on the shore of a remote lake in British Columbia."

"Doesn't mean it's the same Windrush the Johnson woman was talking about," the sheriff pointed out.

"It must be," Lauren insisted. "It's an unusual name. I've never heard it in connection with any other place."

"It's worth checking out. But British Columbia?" Howell shook his head. "That's a problem." He turned to his deputy. "Eddy, radio the border. See if they can tell you whether a couple with a baby crossed over into Canada in the last few hours or so."

Wicowski headed for his cruiser. The fire chief trailed after him with the intention of rejoining the other firefighters, who were preparing to depart with their equipment.

Lauren glanced at Ethan. She could see he was restless, wanting action as much as she did and unable to hide it. She'd learned eleven months ago that he was one of those men who needed to be occupied. His long confinement in that Seattle jail, and before that in a North Korean cell, must have been a real hell for him.

He was starting to get to his feet when a dark sedan sped up the driveway. Another sightseer to add to the confusion, Lauren thought. There had already been several of them that the deputy had sent on their way.

But when the car rolled to a stop and its sole occupant emerged from behind the wheel, she could see this was no sightseer. Lauren recognized the woman at once. It was FBI Agent Marjorie Landry.

"Wicowski must have been awfully busy on that radio of his," Ethan observed as the agent hurried toward the picnic table.

When she was close enough for Lauren to see the expression on her face, she understood what Ethan meant. Marjorie Landry wasn't wearing this morning's sweet-tempered smile. She had a severe look that said she'd been informed of all that had been happening since she had last met with them and was no more happy about their activities than Sheriff Howell was.

The agent's little-girl voice lost no time in blistering them when she reached the table. "If what I've been told about the two of you is right, and I have no reason to think it isn't, then your actions are inexcusable."

"Yep, *real* busy," Ethan muttered.

If Agent Landry heard him, she wasn't interested in an explanation. She was much too intent on lecturing them.

"Irresponsible behavior is not the way to get your baby back."

"What is, Marjorie?" Ethan asked her with a deliberate familiarity. "Waiting while the FBI does nothing?"

"The Bureau will not tolerate unauthorized interference in their investigations," she went on, sidestepping his pointed question.

I never figured her for a by-the-book type, Lauren thought. *But I guess she is, which makes her no more effective than Sheriff Howell.*

When Agent Landry had finished venting her displeasure with them, she turned to the sheriff. "What's the latest? Anything?"

Howell shared with her what Lauren had told him about Windrush. The agent looked perplexed.

"British Columbia? That's a long way from here. Why would they be on their way to British Columbia, if in fact they are? What could they possibly want at this—what did you call it? Windrush?"

The sheriff shrugged his heavy shoulders. "Who knows. Could be anything."

"Well, if they are headed there, then—"

She was interrupted by the reappearance of Deputy Wicowski.

"What did you learn, Eddy?" the sheriff asked him.

The stoic deputy shook his head. "There's been a lot of traffic up at the border this afternoon. A number of couples were passed through the gates, a few of them with little kids. Being as how I could give them only a sketchy description and without names, they weren't able to tell me whether *our* couple went through their port of entry. 'Course, as they pointed out, the perps could have used another port of entry or managed to cross the border illegally. They did promise to study their videotapes and get back to us with their findings."

And how long will that take? Lauren wondered, her frustration deepening by the moment. The sheriff and Agent Landry proceeded to add to that frustration.

"If it turns out they did cross the border," Howell said, "that puts the case beyond my jurisdiction."

Marjorie Landry nodded. "And mine. The Bureau has no authority to operate in Canada."

"No U.S. law enforcement does," Howell said.

"Except by permission through the proper channels," the FBI agent said.

"Right," the sheriff said.

So much for their power struggle in the past, Lauren thought sourly. Because on this subject, Sheriff Howell and Marjorie Landry were in total agreement. Like a couple of parents who had mended their differences, at least temporarily, they took turns sternly addressing Lauren and Ethan.

"It's out of our hands."

"There's nothing we can do except contact the Canadian authorities and let them handle it."

"I hope you both understand that."

"We'll do everything in our power to help the agencies up there recover Sara for you, but from now on you two stay out of it."

"*Strictly* out of it."

"THE HELL we will!"

Ethan had answered Lauren's question before she could ask it. But at least he'd had the wisdom to wait until they were in the car and on their way back to Elkton before he voiced his explosive opinion of Agent Landry and Sheriff Howell's bombastic instructions.

Wanting to be sure she understood him, Lauren responded quietly, "Then we're going after Sara's kidnappers ourselves?"

"Do you want to just sit and wait while the authorities wade through a lot of red tape that could cost us our baby?"

"You know I don't."

"There's your answer, then. All right, this Windrush is a long shot, but it's the only chance we have of catching up with them."

She was relieved by his decision. Having long since overcome any qualms about recovering Sara on their own, it was exactly what she had hoped to hear.

Ethan, who was driving this time, tapped his fingers on the wheel as they stopped at a crossroad to let a pickup go through. "The only thing is…"

"What?"

"They have a head start on us, and they know where they're going and how to get there. We don't."

"I think I can help with that. Or at least I know someone who ought to be able to tell us exactly where Windrush is and the best way of getting there."

"Who is it?"

"You remember when I told you this morning that a friend called to offer her sympathy? Well, her name is Vicky Waller, and she operates a travel agency in Elkton."

"Sounds promising. Think you can reach her?"

Lauren already had her cell phone out of her purse. "It's after five. The agency won't be open. I'll have to try her at home and hope she's there."

Vicky was at home. Less than three minutes later, after Lauren had explained her need to her friend, she rang off and turned to Ethan.

"She's willing to help us in any way she can. We're going to meet her back at the agency."

"Why there?"

"Because she thinks she might be able to make arrangements for us to travel to Windrush, and she needs her office computer for that. Keep your fingers crossed, Ethan."

VICKY WALLER had a passion for travel, which was why she had opened an agency that catered to the desires of clients seeking the perfect vacation. She also relished the rich foods served in luxury hotels and on cruise ships. And, as she cheerfully admitted, she paid for it with a zaftig figure.

That figure was parked now in a swivel chair as she faced them across her desk. "Okay, here's the scoop," she said, leaning toward them earnestly. "Windrush is just what you figured it is, one of those colossal hotels built somewhere around the turn of the last century and still popular with travelers who can afford to be guests in something that looks like a French château."

Lauren wondered not for the first time why Sara's abductors would be on their way with her to such an unlikely destination. *Back to Windrush.* Those had been Hilary's words, indicating the couple was returning to…what? Something familiar? Something vital?

"Problem is," Vicky continued, "it's not one of those hey-let's-stop-and-take-a-look-at-it-while-we're-passing-through kind of places."

"Why is that?" Ethan asked.

"Because it's in the middle of nowhere, which makes it a destination unto itself. Folks, we're talking about a region of British Columbia hundreds of miles from here. Oh, the lake and the mountains are to die for all right, but it's still wilderness. You don't get there by a four-lane highway. The only road linking it to the outside is long and undependable. No commercial airline to service it, either."

Lauren was perplexed. "Then how—"

"Train," Vicky said. "Windrush was built by a railroad baron, and in his day that made it easily accessible. Still is the best way to reach the place. VIA Rail has regular scheduled stops at its station on one of its main lines to the coast."

"What are our chances of getting on one of those trains?" Ethan asked her.

"Let's find out."

Vicky swung away from them in her swivel chair and began tapping keys on her computer. They waited tensely while she consulted the screen.

"Okay, here's what we've got. The nearest station to us is Ida. The trains stop there to pick up passengers on their way west."

Lauren nodded. "I know it. It's a town straight north from Elkton on the other side of the border."

"Yep, and less than two hours from here by car." Vicky leaned toward the screen, frowning with concentration. "Too late for you to make the train that stops at Ida at seven-fifteen. But here's another one at ten-o-five. That should give you plenty of time. It would put you down at Windrush first thing in the morning. Oh, blast."

"What?" Lauren anxiously asked.

"It's fully booked. No space available, not even in coach. Wait. Here's a bedroom that was canceled. Just the one."

Lauren didn't let herself examine the treacherous prospect of sharing a compact bedroom overnight with Ethan. "Reserve it," she said without hesitation.

Ethan's own reaction was equally swift. "See if you can get us a room at Windrush while you're at it."

Minutes later, with accommodations on both the train and in the hotel secured for them, they thanked Vicky and got to their feet. Ethan spotted information on Windrush in the rack of travel folders just inside the front door.

"Can I?" he asked.

"Help yourself," Vicky invited him. "That's what they're there for."

The travel agent eyed his long-limbed figure with interest as he crossed the office to the rack. Turning to Lauren at her side, she murmured in an undertone, "I don't know what the current relationship is between the two of you, and since it's none of my business, I'm not about to ask. But, honey, he is *definitely* a keeper."

Lauren didn't know how to respond to that. She was saved from the necessity of a reply when Vicky must have suddenly decided that, with their situation as grave as it was, her observation had been inappropriate.

"Don't mind me," she hastily apologized. "And, uh, look, I'm going to be praying that you find Sara and bring her back where she belongs."

Lauren folded her friend in a quick embrace. Then, before either of them could surrender to their emotions, she headed for the door.

Once out on the street, she turned to Ethan, who had followed her from the office. "There's no time to go back to the cabin and pack, but I would like to make a fast stop at the discount center over in the next block. It's open all night, and I need to buy at least a change of clothing and some other essentials."

"Yeah, I'd better pick up a few things myself."

Lauren gazed down at herself under the glow of a street light. "I hate to get on board that train like this. I smell of smoke, and my outfit looks like…well, like it's been through a fire."

"We both could use a cleanup." He consulted his watch. "It's just after six. We've got enough time before we hit the highway for the discount center, as well as a shower at my motel. I should collect what I left there anyway and then check out."

Lauren welcomed his suggestion. Less than half an hour later, bearing their purchases, they arrived at Ethan's motel room.

"You take the bathroom first," he said, switching on the lights. "There's a phone call I've been wanting to make all afternoon, and this being the first opportunity for it…"

He left the rest unsaid. *Mysteriously* unsaid.

"Has that instinct of yours been talking to you again?" she asked him.

"Could be. I'll tell you about it when we're on the road."

Lauren knew she had to be satisfied with that.

By seven-fifteen they were back in the car, with Ethan at the wheel again, and traveling north toward the border. The traffic was light, enabling them to make up for any lost time. And although the time of year made the hour as dark as midnight, the weather remained unseasonably mild. Lauren regarded all of this as a positive omen, maybe just because she needed to remain hopeful or lose her mind in her longing for her daughter.

With Elkton behind them, she was unable to quell her curiosity any longer. "You were just hanging up the phone when I got out of the bathroom. Was that because…"

"I had a long conversation, yeah." He hesitated, and although she could sense his reluctance, he went on. "All right, I won't keep you in suspense any longer. I was talking to a man in Seattle by the name of Donald Patterson. He's a real workaholic, so I took a chance he'd still be in his office. Turns out he was. He usually does come back to his desk to clean up odds and ends after a day in court."

"A lawyer?"

"Not just any lawyer, Lauren. Donald was my grandfather's lawyer. He and his firm handled all of the old man's affairs, so I knew he could tell me what I wanted to know."

"About?"

Ethan, occupied with overtaking and passing an eighteen-wheeler, didn't immediately answer her. Not until they were safely back in their lane did he continue.

"Jonathan Brand's will. I wanted to know the exact contents of that will."

Lauren was puzzled. "But weren't you already familiar with what it contains?"

"You forget I didn't intend to benefit from it. So, beyond knowing I was supposed to inherit everything, I never bothered to learn its exact terms. Why would I, especially after I renounced my claim to the estate. But *now*…"

There was a tautness in his voice that made her uneasy. "What are you trying to tell me, Ethan? That there are surprises in that will, something connected with Sara's abduction?"

He shook his head. "I'm not sure. It doesn't make sense yet. Donald told me that he'd been urging my grandfather for years to rewrite his original will, but the old man never saw any reason to change it. So it still stands."

"Meaning what?"

"That two-thirds of the estate was to go to Jonathan Brand's eldest son. That was my father. The other third would go to his younger son, my Uncle Mac. If the sons failed to survive him, which they didn't, then the estate would pass to their issue with the same division of all properties."

"But *you* were the only issue."

"Exactly. I was the sole grandchild, which meant everything was to come to me. And if I didn't survive my grandfather or renounced my claim, which I have, then the whole thing would go to *my* issue."

Lauren stared at him in a slow, fearful comprehension. "Are you saying…"

He didn't turn his head to look at her. He kept his gaze on the road. "Yeah," he said, his voice tighter than ever, "Sara is an heiress."

"Dear God! And she's been kidnapped by people who must have learned not only of her paternity but that she's worth a fortune. Hilary Johnson could have discovered this and told them. It *had* to be her since she was in on—" Lauren broke off as another realization occurred to her. "But that can't be right. How can they benefit from her abduction if they aren't demanding a ransom?"

"No, that doesn't make sense, unless…"

Ethan didn't go on, as if he'd caught himself about to say something that he feared Lauren wouldn't be able to bear. What? And then she remembered.

"All afternoon," she said. "That's what you told me back
at the motel. "That all afternoon you'd been wanting to make
a phone call. It was because of what both Rudy Lightfeather
and Hilary Johnson said about your eyes, wasn't it? That they
were *his* eyes. You didn't just dismiss that, either. It's been
on your mind ever since."

She waited for Ethan's response, but he remained silent,
his gaze fixed on the highway.

"You have to tell me," she insisted. "Don't you see that
not knowing what you're thinking is worse than hearing
you tell me just how much Sara is at risk? It is what has
you worried, isn't it? That you and the man who took our
daughter might share more than just the color and shape of
your eyes."

"All right," he finally admitted. "There is a chance this bastard could somehow be a Brand, though where he came from
and how he could exist without my ever being aware of him
is beyond me."

"And that's why you needed to know the exact terms of
your grandfather's will. Because if he, himself, is a legitimate heir—"

A new understanding suddenly struck her. A horrible one.
"Ethan, you've renounced your claim, so that takes you out
of the running. And if Sara—" The necessity of putting it into
words made her sick, but it had to be said. "If Sara should be
removed from the succession before her paternity can be verified, then what becomes of your grandfather's fortune?"

"It gets divided among various charities. Providing there
is no other direct issue."

"And if another grandchild turns up and can prove his
identity? Someone no one knew existed?"

"Then the entire estate goes to him."

*And it's beginning to look like he has turned up and that
he could even have been responsible for Jonathan Brand's
death.* That's what Lauren thought, and she knew Ethan was

thinking it, as well. It was a staggering possibility, both incredible and real at the same time.

But as bad as the impact of it was, there was something worse. A chilling question that Lauren couldn't bring herself to ask aloud. Surely Ethan must also be silently asking himself that same terrible question:

If the plan was to remove Sara from the succession, then why hasn't she been eliminated altogether? Why is her abductor still keeping her alive?

Chapter Ten

Even in the dim glow of the car, she could see the concerned expression on Ethan's face when he turned his head to look at her.

"He must have a good reason for keeping our baby alive and well, Lauren," he tried to reassure her. "We have to hang on to that."

So the same question *had* been gnawing at him. What's more, he'd guessed without her having to tell him that it nagged at her, as well.

"Yes," she said, clinging to what was both a hope and a dread. It was all she had, a blind faith that Sara would survive, that her abductor wasn't going to sacrifice her because he had some vital need of her they had yet to learn.

"Anyway," Ethan said, "all of this is still only so much speculation waiting for answers that might tell an entirely different story."

"There isn't much chance of our getting those answers tonight, either, is there? With the head start they had on us, they must have been able to make that seven-fifteen train."

Providing, she thought, that Ida had been their destination. It was only logical to suppose it was, however, since Vicky Waller had indicated the train was the best method for reaching Windrush.

"There's always the possibility of catching up with them

before Windrush," Ethan said, "but, no, it isn't likely. Look, why don't you try to sleep? We've still got a lot of road ahead of us, and I may need you to take a turn at the wheel."

His suggestion was a sensible one. Lauren was exhausted after the long, eventful day and a nearly sleepless night before that. But, as worried as she was, she didn't think it was possible for her to rest.

She surprised herself by drifting off within seconds of snuggling into the corner. When Ethan awakened her, they were approaching the border.

They were admitted through the port of entry with speedy efficiency. Tempting though it was, they resisted asking any questions about the couple they were pursuing. Their interest might have aroused suspicion and a delay they couldn't afford. Nor were the Canadian officials apt to tell them anything she and Ethan hadn't already learned from Deputy Wicowski's inquiry.

Ethan surrendered the wheel to Lauren once the border was behind them and promptly went to sleep on the passenger side. Fresh from her nap, she drove on through the night.

Though on her own now in the silence, she was acutely aware of the man at her side. Against her better judgment, her gaze kept shooting in his direction, making her conscious of the power of that hard body sprawled in the seat, muscular legs stretched out in front of him, big hands locked across his trim waist.

His head was turned toward her so that she was able to see the cleft in the chin of his good-looking face and the way strands of his dark brown hair fell across his brow. Even relaxed like this in sleep, there was a strongly sensual quality about him. It was heightened by the whiffs she caught of his faintly spicy aftershave. That alone was a potent aphrodisiac.

She remembered what Vicky had said about Ethan. *He is definitely a keeper.* Her friend's opinion had been a playful one, but there was a truth in her words that haunted Lauren. She knew if she didn't watch herself she would be longing for something permanent with Ethan. And there was danger in that direction. She couldn't forget what she had suffered throughout those long weeks following his abrupt and painful departure last year. Weeks without a word from him.

It had taken her months to recover from him. She couldn't, *wouldn't* let herself fall in love with him all over again, risk a repeat of that awful anguish. Because, face it, she *had* fallen in love with Ethan during that brief, but emotional, interlude they had shared.

Now, because the rescue of their daughter dictated it, they had been thrown together once again. But this time there was a difference, because there was more than just a sexual attraction that was always possible to overcome.

There was something much deeper. Something that involved a slow, mesmerizing recognition of the worth of the man beneath all that alluring bone and muscle. A warmth and a masculine strength that tugged at her. It was irresistible, but at the same time she was afraid to trust it. Afraid of being hurt by a love from which, this time, she might be unable to recover.

IDA WAS LOCATED just east of the division between the two provinces of Alberta and British Columbia. There was little to see in the town, which was already asleep when they reached it. In any case, they were interested in nothing but the railroad station.

An attendant at an all-night quick stop at the edge of Ida directed them to the station, which turned out to be a gingerbread affair situated at the center of the town.

A sizable parking area adjoined the station. Ethan checked his watch when they pulled into the lot.

"We've cut it a little close, but we've still got a comfortable fifteen minutes or so."

Providing the train is on schedule, Lauren thought. She had been anxious about that on the long drive to Ida. Worried that, if they should miss it, they would lose this opportunity to reach Sara.

There was no agent to tell them if the train was on time. The station looked unoccupied as, locking the car and armed with their bags, they headed for the platform. Except for a lone figure who lay flat on a bench against the outside wall of the building, this, too, was deserted.

He was evidently asleep, with arms folded across his chest, although Lauren couldn't be sure of this since the black Outback hat he wore was pulled down over his face so that only his chin was visible.

Lauren set the bag she had acquired at the discount store, along with what it contained, under a pole lamp and went to the edge of the platform. She gazed up the tracks, but there was no sign or sound of an approaching train.

She was still watching for the train when she realized that Ethan was missing. Looking around, she saw that he had drifted toward the bench where he stood staring down at the man stretched on its length.

Puzzled, Lauren joined him. "What is it?"

"There's a green feather stuck into the band of that hat."

"What of it?"

"I know of only one guy who has a hat with a feather like that. It's practically his signature."

"Ethan, it's just a coincidence. Come away before we wake him."

"Too late," came a deep voice from under the hat. Lifting his head and tipping the hat back from his face, the figure on the bench squinted up at them. "Looks like a man can't even catch a snooze without some busybody discussing his hat."

"Buddy Foley!"

The man sat up, swung his booted feet to the platform and grinned at Ethan. "Hell, I thought that voice of yours was familiar."

Astonished, Lauren looked from Ethan to the man he had identified as Buddy Foley. "You know each other?"

"From Seattle," Ethan said. "Buddy is a cop there."

"Aw, you've gone and disillusioned her, Brand. She probably had me figured as a Canadian cowboy."

He certainly looked like one, Lauren thought, watching the lanky figure in jeans and a fringed, suede jacket shove himself to his feet. But a cop?

She must have registered her alarm because Ethan offered her a quick explanation. "It's all right. Buddy had nothing to do with the investigation of my grandfather's murder. In fact, he was probably one of the few officers on the force who believed I was innocent."

"Then how do you come to know—"

"We met each other through Donald Patterson. Buddy has done some detective work for the legal firm."

"And if you ever breathe a word to the department that I'm moonlighting on the side," he warned Lauren, the grin still hovering on his boyish face, "I'm gonna forget how much I'm standing here envying this lout. You gonna introduce me, Brand, or keep this goddess all to yourself?"

"Her name is Lauren McCrea, and that's all you're going to get."

Buddy stuck out a hand, and she shook it. She wasn't sure if the wink that followed was intended for her or Ethan. Buddy Foley was something of a scamp, but she found herself liking him. She sensed that Ethan felt the same, even if he did scowl at Buddy when he hung on to her hand a bit too long before finally releasing it.

"Now," he asked him, "you want to tell me what you're doing here in the middle of nowhere, Foley?"

"Heck, and here I am wondering the same about you."

"It's a long story."

"Mine is a short one. Had to escort a witness, who refused to fly, to Missoula. I'm heading back after delivering him."

"This is some detour."

"Yeah, well, the department owes me some R and R, so I figured I'd drive my van up here and give this rail trip through the Rockies a shot. I hear it's something pretty good. What about you two? On vacation yourselves?"

"Not exactly," Ethan said. "Look, how long have you been here?"

"*Too* long. I pulled in just before five o'clock hoping there'd be room on the seven-fifteen train. No such luck. It was booked full. The station agent was still here then, so he was able to give me the last bedroom on the ten-o-five. Guess these runs are that popular."

Buddy must have acquired his accommodation before the cancellation of the bedroom Vicky was able to obtain for us, Lauren decided.

"Have you been hanging around the station since then?" Ethan asked him.

"Yeah, except for stretching my legs with a walk along the main street. Town doesn't offer much."

"You happen to be here when the seven-fifteen arrived?"

"I was."

"Then maybe you can tell me something. Did you see a couple with a baby board the train? The woman would have had blond hair."

Buddy had looked only mildly curious up to this point. But now, clearly puzzled, he glanced from Ethan to Lauren. "What's this all about?"

"I'll explain later," Ethan said. "Did you see them?"

Buddy nodded. "I noticed them."

Then we didn't make a mistake, Lauren thought with relief. They *are* on their way to Windrush with Sara. She knew that Ethan must be equally satisfied by this validation of their decision that, until now, had been questionable.

"The man," he pressed Buddy. "What did the man look like?"

"I said I noticed them. I didn't say I paid any attention to them, so I can't tell you what either one of them looked like. It was just a couple with a baby, that's all."

It wasn't a certainty, then, that this was their couple, Lauren thought, although it must have been them. She longed to ask Buddy if he'd been able to tell whether Sara was being looked after properly, but she knew he couldn't give her that. He was a cop, yes, but a cop on vacation. He would have had no reason to suppose that her daughter's kidnappers were other than what they appeared to be, a couple of parents traveling with their baby.

"Now do I get that explanation?" Buddy asked.

He would have to wait for it, because at that moment the lights at the nearby crossing began to flash. They were followed by the descent of the gates. The ten-o-five was arriving in Ida.

Buddy reached for his bag where he had slid it under the bench and joined them at the edge of the platform as the silver-and-blue retro streamliner pulled into the station.

The conductor emerged when the door rolled back, checked their tickets, and directed them to the car they were assigned to. Buddy was to occupy not only the same car but a bedroom near theirs.

"Look, I have an idea," he said, stopping them in the vestibule after they had boarded. "Either of you hungry?"

It was only then that Lauren remembered she and Ethan had eaten nothing since noon, hours ago, and for her that had been no more than a bowl of soup. Neither of them had had either the time or the appetite, but now…

"I could use something," Ethan admitted. "Lauren?"

"Yes, but they wouldn't be serving in the dining car at this hour."

"There's a lounge car behind the dining car," Buddy said. "The folder I picked up says there are sandwiches and drinks available until eleven o'clock. I want to hear that explanation. How about it?"

Ethan nodded. "I guess we could meet there after we get settled in our rooms."

"Got a better plan. Why don't you two go ahead right now to the lounge and check out the menu? I'll get the attendant for our car started on making up our berths and join you there." He turned to the conductor, who had followed them into the vestibule. "All right to leave our bags here for the attendant to collect?"

The train was under way again when Ethan and Lauren arrived in the sleek, art deco–style lounge car. Late though the hour was, a party was in progress. It consisted entirely of a group of older women. From the snatches of conversation Lauren overheard between the whoops of frequent laughter, she learned the women were all longtime friends traveling together on an annual reunion.

She and Ethan chose a table at the quiet end of the car, to which they carried their soft drinks and sandwiches from the bar. Buddy joined them there minutes later.

Lauren let Ethan relate their story. Although she offered no objection, she did wonder how wise it was to confide in Buddy like this. He was, after all, a cop, and she and Ethan had disobeyed the police in their quest for the couple who had taken their daughter. But Ethan seemed to trust Buddy, and he did listen sympathetically.

The women continued to celebrate at the other end of the car while the train rocketed through the night, angling northwest into the heart of the Rocky Mountains toward its ultimate destination of Prince Rupert on the Pacific Coast.

Munching on her chips and chicken-salad sandwich, Lauren wished she could be as carefree as those women. Instead, she sat here in a helpless silence, able to do nothing but anxiously wait for their arrival tomorrow in Windrush.

Would they be able to overtake Sara's abductors in time to prevent…what? They had no clue, only a terrible certainty that something was to happen at Windrush that mustn't happen.

It was after eleven when Lauren and the two men found their way to their assigned car toward the front of the train. They parted in the corridor. Wishing them a good night, Buddy disappeared into his bedroom, which was one compartment removed from theirs.

The car attendant was nowhere in evidence, but he had prepared Lauren and Ethan's bedroom for them. Their bags were waiting for them side by side on the floor, both the wider lower berth and the narrower upper berth were made up, and the lights had been turned low.

Lauren stood just inside the door, feeling absurdly nervous. Maybe it was the setting itself, with the suggestive gleam of the sheets on the beds and the soft lights contributing to a mood that was definitely intimate.

Or maybe it was Ethan. She had never been so aware of him. His tall body seemed to fill the room, making it difficult for her to breathe.

In all fairness, with the space so confined, there was nowhere else for him to be but close beside her. He must have sensed she was awkward with the situation.

"Look," he said, "why don't I wait outside while you get ready for bed?"

She welcomed his offer and didn't argue with him when, just before slipping into the corridor, he insisted she have the lower berth and he would take the upper.

There had been no pajamas in her size back at the discount store in Elkton, so she had purchased a nightie. It hadn't seemed to matter at the time. But now, changing into the gown, she was conscious of how much it revealed.

She could see Ethan was conscious of that, too, when he returned a few moments later and found her kneeling on the berth to lower the shade at the window. Those heart stopping blue-green eyes of his darkened at the sight of her in the thigh-length nightie. She could read his candid desire as their gazes meshed.

"Uh, I'll just take my turn in here," he said. To her relief, he vanished into the tiny water closet.

She was still struggling with the shade when she heard him emerge after a couple of minutes. "This thing doesn't want to stay down," she complained, turning her head in his direction. "I don't know what's wrong with—"

She got no further than that. Her discovery of his long body clad in nothing but a pair of snug briefs robbed her of speech. He was all muscle and lean flesh. Tantalizing flesh.

Though in no way self-conscious about himself, he was aware of her dismay. "Sorry," he apologized. "I don't own a pair of pajamas. I usually sleep in the raw."

If he had meant the briefs to be a concession to modesty, then he had failed. They left nothing to the imagination.

"Trouble?" he asked.

"What?"

"The shade. Here, let me do it."

Before she could prevent it, he had squeezed onto the berth beside her. She could feel the heat of his big body as he leaned across her, reaching for the catch on the black shade.

"You have to lock it in place," he explained. "By turning the catch like this. Okay?"

No, it wasn't okay. With the shade secured, he sought an acknowledgment of her understanding by turning his head to look at her. Their gazes collided again. There was a long moment of silence, nothing but the muted sound of the train wheels clacking over the rails beneath them.

Ethan ended the silence between them with a husky "Lauren?" It was a simple, direct question of her willingness.

Either he read her long, trembling sigh as a form of assent or he was too impatient to wait. He reached for her then, arms wrapping around her to draw her up against his hardness.

With the blood beating in her ears, its roar drowning out the sound of the wheels on the rails, she lifted her face to meet his mouth as it settled over hers.

It had been eleven months since she had felt his lips on hers. She had forgotten how they could be both gentle and demanding as he kissed her thoroughly, deeply. Had forgotten how absolutely right those lips were, as if they belonged nowhere else.

What Lauren hadn't forgotten was the way her traitorous senses clamored for more of him. But had she been this hungry for him on that winter night in the cabin? And had he complied this eagerly, inhaling her, tasting her with his tongue?

Even when he tore his mouth away from hers, he went on assaulting her. This time with words.

"The fire," he said gruffly.

What was he trying to tell her?

"This afternoon in the farmhouse," he went on. "One or both of us could have perished in the fire. I haven't been able to stop thinking of that. We might have lost each other."

"But we didn't die."

"We *could* have," he insisted.

"What are you saying, Ethan?"

"That time is too precious to waste. Let's not throw tonight away, Lauren."

She understood him then. He was asking for more than kisses. He was asking her to let him demonstrate her value to him with his entire body, perhaps even his soul.

She needed him. She admitted that. But her need conflicted with the memory of the despair she had experienced that cold morning when he had been taken away from her. Of all the despair she had gone on suffering in the long weeks that followed.

"Ethan," she pleaded with him, "I don't think I could bear to repeat—"

"Don't," he said, silencing her objection by placing his forefinger against her mouth. "Don't let this push-pull thing between us matter. We'll worry about all the complications when we have to, but not tonight."

Because there may not be another night for us. Was that what he was saying?

"Nothing is real," he said, "but what we're feeling here and now."

If it was an irresponsible argument, she no longer cared. She wanted what he wanted. And, yes, the rest could wait.

"I think," she murmured, "that upper berth isn't going to be occupied tonight."

Ethan needed no other invitation. Fitting his mouth over hers, he kissed her again. She responded with her own kisses, helped him to dispose of her gown. Parted from him briefly but reluctantly in order to permit him to shed his briefs, to clad himself with a feverish haste in a condom he removed from his bag.

There were no barriers between them now. Nothing but the urgency they answered when his body joined with hers. The train sped on through the night, its swaying movements in concert with their own rhythms, heightening their pleasure in each other.

And then, afterward, there was only the train, rocking them with the gentleness of a cradle. Snug in the cocoon of Ethan's arms, Lauren listened to the steady clip-clip of its wheels on the rails.

Ethan's even breathing told her he was asleep. She wasn't ready to close her own eyes just yet. Her mind was too active with remembering the endearments he had crooned into her ear, of the way his body had cherished hers as they'd celebrated each other in a blaze of joy.

He had told her not to worry, that tonight was all they needed and they would deal with the rest later. She couldn't help it. She *was* concerned, because there was something else she remembered.

In the car on the way to Ida, she had told herself she couldn't afford to risk falling in love with him again. But it was too late for denials. She knew she *was* in love with him again. Or maybe she had never been out of love with him.

But was it enough? When all this was over and done with, would anything remain that was substantial enough to build something lasting for them? Or was Sara all they really shared?

AT FIRST, Ethan thought it was a stretch of rough track that was shaking him out of his deep sleep. Then he realized it wasn't the train. It was a hand on his shoulder rocking him back and forth in an insistent effort to rouse him.

"Ethan, you have to wake up!"

Lauren's voice. Struggling to full awareness, he opened his eyes and lifted his head from the pillow. They hadn't bothered to turn off the lamps. He could see her beside him, propped up on one elbow.

"What time is it?" he muttered, trying to clear his head.

"I don't know. Late. A little after five, I think."

Which meant they were nowhere near their destination. So why had she awakened him in the middle of the night?

"There's something I have to tell you!" she said.

This time he could hear it in her tone. Excitement mingled with urgency. Throwing off the last of his drowsiness, he sat up in the berth, almost bumping his head on the underside of the upper berth.

"What is it? What's wrong?"

"Keep your voice down," she cautioned him. "I don't want them hearing us."

"Who?"

In answer, she sat up beside him and placed her hand on the paneling at the head of their berth. *"Them,"* she said, indicating their neighbors on the other side of the wall that divided the bedrooms. "Ethan, they're in there!"

He stared at her, wondering if she was lucid.

"Don't look at me like that!" she whispered, "I'm not crazy, and I'm not imagining things! I heard her! I heard Sara crying in there!"

Ethan tried to be patient with her. "I don't know what you heard, but it couldn't have been Sara. Lauren, they're not on this train. They can't be. You heard Buddy. He saw them board the seven-fifteen."

"I don't know how it's possible, but they're here! Not only on this train, but right next door to us!"

Ethan leaned back, pressing his ear against the paneling. Silence. "I don't hear anything. Are you sure you weren't—"

"Don't say it! I wasn't having a dream! I was awake, and I did hear Sara!"

"All right, I believe you. You heard a baby crying in there, but it has to be someone else's baby."

She shook her head in a wild denial. "I tell you it *is* Sara! Why are we sitting here like this? We have to do something! We have to go after her!"

Ethan attempted to reason with her. "Lauren, with a wall between us and that next bedroom, there's no way you could know Sara's cries from another's baby's cries."

He watched her drag her fingers through her auburn hair, an action that he recognized. It meant she was in an intense emotional state. He was concerned about her, thinking she was so desperate by now to recover her baby that she was confusing her longing with reality.

"I can't, huh?" she challenged him.

He saw her take a deep breath to steady herself. When she continued, it was in a calm but no less vital tone, as if she realized how essential a sane argument would be to convince him that she knew just what she was talking about.

"After all the nights I woke up and went to her, do you think I wouldn't know my own daughter's cries anywhere, anytime, whatever the circumstances? A man may not relate to this, Ethan, but it's a—a kind of primal thing, I guess. Mothers able to identify their young among all the others in a herd. It's true."

"Lauren, I—"

"You have that gut instinct of yours that we've both been trusting, haven't you? Well, this is mine."

That was good enough for Ethan. If Lauren believed beyond a doubt that Sara was only a few feet away from them, then her certainty deserved his immediate action.

Swinging out of the berth, he surged to his feet. He wasted no time looking for the pair of briefs he had tossed somewhere on the floor hours earlier. Nor did he bother with shoes or a shirt. All he needed were his jeans hanging on a hook just outside the water closet.

Seconds later, barefoot and bare-chested, wearing nothing but the jeans he'd hurriedly donned, he unlocked the door and slipped into the narrow corridor. Ethan's objective was the door immediately on the right. The bedroom behind it separated their own room from Buddy Foley's compartment.

His fist was in the air, ready to bang on the door, when he checked himself. How smart was this? Not smart at all, he suddenly realized. He couldn't go pounding on the door, demanding to be admitted.

If the bastard was armed, and Ethan had no way of knowing that he wasn't, then this whole thing could end badly. He had Sara's safety to think about, providing of course she and her kidnappers were even in there.

On the other hand, what choice did he have except to knock and hope that one of the bedroom's occupants would open the door? He had to get in there!

So, all right, if he didn't identify himself, they would have no reason to suppose he was anyone but the conductor or the car attendant. And once this door was cracked, he would force his way into the compartment and, if it proved necessary, manage somehow to disarm his opponent. Why not, when his special army training had equipped him with the skills to defeat an enemy?

Okay, so it wasn't much of a plan. But it was better than

just barging in there without at least anticipating trouble and being ready to deal with it.

"What are we waiting for?" Lauren whispered impatiently.

Ethan turned his head to see her hovering just behind him. He might have guessed she wouldn't sensibly wait in their bedroom.

"Get back out of sight," he instructed her in a low voice. "They know what you look like, and if they catch a glimpse of you out here, they'll have that door shut and locked before I have a chance to act. There's no reason to suppose they'll recognize me, at least not before I manage to get inside."

To his relief, Lauren bought his excuse to remove her from any immediate harm. Once he had satisfied himself that she had backed off several paces down the corridor, he rapped his knuckles against the door. Not with the kind of angry force that had been his first impulsive intention, and which would have resulted in instantly alarming them, but with a firmness that he hoped would sound like someone official at the door.

His knocking brought no response. He repeated his effort, a little louder now. Nothing. When he laid his ear against the door, he heard only silence. No noise of anyone stirring inside, no evidence of some hasty scrambling that would tell him they had been alerted to his presence.

Ethan risked trying the door. The knob refused to yield. Locked of course. He should have known it wouldn't be easy. He'd have to get tough about it.

This time, he hammered on the door, calling out insistently, "Conductor out here. Open up, please."

There was no reaction from inside the bedroom, but there was plenty of it out in the corridor. Doors had opened along the length of the car, and heads were poking out. He could see they belonged mostly to the women who had been celebrating in the lounge car. From the frowns on their faces, he knew they were more than just curious about the disturbance. They were annoyed by it, as well.

Buddy Foley's door also opened. He emerged from it with hair tousled and wearing his suede jacket over a pair of loud pajamas.

"Hell, Ethan, what's going on out here?"

Ethan hesitated. Then, deciding that he could use the support of a man he'd already shared their story with anyway, he rapidly explained the situation to Buddy, keeping his voice low so the spectators along the corridor wouldn't overhear him.

The cop looked at Lauren, and Ethan could guess by his expression what he was thinking, even though he didn't say it. What's more, Lauren guessed it, too.

"I'm not delusional," she swiftly defended herself. "I heard her. My daughter *is* in that room."

"What about through the wall on your side?" Ethan asked Foley. "You hear anything at all?"

Buddy shook his head. "I was dead to the world. I didn't hear anything until your knocking. But I suppose," he conceded, "that it could have been some other couple with a baby that I saw boarding the seven-fifteen. But if that's so, how did your couple get aboard *this* train? There were only the three of us there on the platform at Ida."

"I've been thinking about that," Lauren said. "They could have been hiding until the train pulled in and then boarded while Ethan and I were on our way to the lounge car."

Buddy nodded. "And managed to avoid me while I was headed in the other direction. Yeah, I guess that's possible. Look," he suggested, "why don't I go find the car attendant and get him to let us into that compartment with his key?"

Ethan was skeptical. "You think he could be convinced to open the door?"

Buddy's boyish face wore a conspiratorial grin. "A cop's badge can be very persuasive, even if it isn't a Canadian one. And, uh, while you're waiting, you two need to go back inside and get some clothes on. You go on standing out here like that and one of these bystanders is apt to go running to a conductor with a complaint."

Ethan, aware that he was in nothing but his jeans, glanced at Lauren. She was in no better state. For the first time he realized she was wearing his shirt she must have snagged from the hook in her haste. And that's *all* she had on. What's more, he didn't like the way Foley was eyeing her provocative flesh exposed below the tails of the shirt.

"We need to try to keep a lid on this," Buddy added, "until we know what's what."

"Okay, but make it fast."

"Right." The cop turned and started along the corridor, calling to the spectators, "Show's over, folks. Nothing to worry about."

Muttering, they began to drift back into their compartments. While Lauren kept a vigil outside the locked door, Ethan hurried into their own bedroom to throw on some clothes. Within two minutes, he was back outside to relieve Lauren. The corridor was empty now and silent. Nor was there any sound of movement behind the locked door.

Lauren rejoined him in the corridor a short while later, pulling a sweater in place over her blouse. They waited without talking. Where was Foley? What was taking him so long?

It seemed to take forever before the cop finally reappeared at the end of the sleeper. He was accompanied by the car attendant in his dark blue slacks and matching vest. The man looked none too happy and didn't hesitate to express his irritation when he reached them.

"This makes no sense," he said in a slight accent that Ethan thought was probably French-Canadian. "I told the gentleman here when he roused me out of the crew quarters that this bedroom is not occupied."

"What do you mean it isn't occupied?" Ethan challenged him. "We were told the train was fully booked and that we got the last available accommodation."

"True, but this bedroom has a plumbing problem, so it couldn't be offered. But your friend insists you won't be satisfied until I open it for you."

"So, humor us."

Shrugging, the attendant produced a key, unlocked the door, spread it inward, and stepped back. "There, see for yourselves."

Chapter Eleven

The bedroom was empty, including the water closet and the tiny clothes closet. Ethan was certain of that because he insisted on checking all of them while the car attendant hovered in the doorway, watching him with disapproval. Nor was there any sign that the compartment had been recently occupied.

He retreated from the bedroom in defeat, joining Lauren and Buddy waiting in the corridor. Meeting Lauren's gaze, he shook his head, even though he knew she must already be aware of the verdict.

He was prepared to see despair in her eyes, or at least disappointment. The expectation had him feeling miserable, because he would have given anything in that moment to be able to place Sara in her eager arms. But to his surprise, her expression registered nothing but acceptance.

"It looks like I made a mistake," she apologized to the car attendant as he relocked the door. "I'm sorry we put you to all this bother."

Mollified, the attendant faced her. "That's all right. Is there anything else I can do for you?"

"I don't think so. Our next stop *is* Windrush, isn't it?"

"It's our only stop after Ida. The train will get in at six thirty-five."

Lauren thanked him, and the attendant went off down the corridor jangling his keys.

Ethan was anxious about her. She was too calm. "Lauren, are you okay?"

"Aside from feeling like a fool, you mean?"

"There's no reason for you to feel that way."

"I don't." There was defiance on her face now. "Because I'm not wrong. They *were* in that compartment."

"Lauren, be reasonable. You can't go on believing that when you saw for yourself that the bedroom is empty. They couldn't have just vanished."

"They didn't, but they could have slipped away while I was trying to convince you earlier that it was Sara I heard crying."

"Even if I admit that's possible, you heard the attendant. The bedroom was never occupied."

"I don't care what he said," she maintained stubbornly. "They were there."

"And where are they now?"

"Somewhere on this train. They have to be since we haven't stopped, and at the speed we're moving there's no way they could have gotten off."

"So what are you saying? That we should search the train?"

Ethan wasn't serious, but when he saw the earnest plea in those brown eyes gazing up at him, he knew that Lauren was. He felt helpless. What could he do when she refused to give up?

Buddy had remained silent during their exchange. Ethan slid a glance in his direction. "What do you think?"

The cop lifted his shoulders in a little shrug. "I guess it couldn't hurt to look."

Ethan sensed, however, that Buddy thought it would be a waste of time, even if he did add agreeably, "Give me a minute to get out of these pajamas, and I'll go with you."

Foley is probably right, Ethan thought as he and Lauren waited in the corridor while the cop went into his bedroom to change. *This whole thing is a waste of time.* But he couldn't bear to destroy the certainty which Lauren clung to so tenaciously. And, if he were honest with himself, he continued to have a hope of his own, illogical though it was.

"How about we start up front in the baggage car?" Buddy suggested when, fully dressed, he rejoined them.

Weaving slightly with the movement of the train, the three of them went forward to the baggage car, which was just across the connecting vestibule from the sleeper. The door to the baggage car was unlocked, probably in order to give passengers a ready access to their larger luggage that was stored there. They discovered when they entered the car that any valuables the train carried were securely locked inside a steel cage.

"No place in here for two adults and a baby to hide," Buddy observed.

Still, Lauren wasn't satisfied until they checked the entire length of the baggage car, including the contents of several crates and an old trunk.

"From the sound of it, the engine must be just in front of us," Buddy surmised. "That makes this the first car."

And without any way to reach the engine from here, Ethan concluded. He'd noticed the only doors other than the one by which they had entered were two pairs of wide, sliding doors at the side of the car. That meant the baggage car was a dead end.

Leaving the baggage car, they began to work their way back toward the rear of the train.

The temptation to knock on the doors of the other compartments in their own car, which was the only sleeper on the train, had to be resisted. Any unofficial request to search those compartments was certain to be resented when they had already disturbed their occupants. And since those occupants had behaved in no furtive manner earlier, it seemed highly unlikely Sara's abductors would have sought refuge with any of them.

The crew's quarters in a portion of the next car were also off-limits, although their open doors were an indication that none of the service staff had anything to hide.

The dining car was dim and silent. It would be another hour or so before breakfast preparations would bring it to life again. The lounge was also deserted except for the conductor and his two assistants, who were resting at one end. None of those relaxed figures challenged them as they passed with a studied innocence through the car. Although they could have tried to enlist the help of the conductor, they feared he might prevent them from continuing their search.

Systematically, the three of them moved from car to car, looking into the sleeping faces of the passengers in the coaches, checking restrooms and observation decks. Nowhere did they find anyone resembling the couple they sought traveling with a baby.

Except for the hypnotic rattle of the wheels on the rails, there was an early morning stillness throughout the length of the train that seemed to emphasize their failure. Ethan could feel Lauren's mounting discouragement by the time they crossed the vestibule and arrived at the door to the last car.

Aching for Lauren, he reached for the knob. It refused to turn. "Locked," he said, puzzled by the discreet No Admittance sign on the door.

"And no way to see what's on the other side," Lauren said, indicating the shirred curtain behind the glass of the window.

Buddy looked regretful but resigned. "Looks like we have no choice but to turn back."

But Ethan wasn't ready to give up. "The hell with that." Lifting his hand, he rapped sharply on the door.

"Jeez, man," Buddy muttered, "think of the hour. If there is anyone in there, they're not going to thank you for this."

"Too bad."

There was no answer to his knock. Ethan tried again. When

there was still no response, he hammered on the door with a loud, "We're not going away until you open up!"

This time, to his satisfaction, his demand was not ignored. There was a snapping sound of the lock being turned on the other side. The door was pulled back just wide enough to reveal a man in the narrow opening.

Ethan figured he was somewhere in his late twenties, well dressed and wearing glasses on a face he would have described as pompous. The light in the vestibule was not strong, but it was sufficient enough for Ethan to tell that the eyes glaring at him were not blue-green. Unless he was wearing tinted contacts, this couldn't be Sara's abductor. Nor did he fit the image in any other respect, though there was something about him…

"Didn't you see the sign on the door?" he challenged them coldly. "Who are you? What do you want?"

Ethan explained their need as briefly as possible. His request was met by an immediate denial.

"In case you haven't realized it by now, this is a private car. What makes you imagine the people you want would be in here? They couldn't possibly have gotten by this door. We keep it locked at all times."

"Still, we'd appreciate it if you'd let us have a fast look around. There's always the chance that—"

"Absolutely not. Mrs. Sterling, whose husband owns this car, was feeling unwell when she went to bed. I won't have her disturbed by something so preposterous."

"Maybe this will change your mind," Buddy said, displaying his badge.

The pale eyes behind the glasses glanced down at the shield. "Very impressive," he said as he continued to block the door. "Except it identifies you as a member of the Seattle Police Force. You have no authority here, and if you did, I would be asking to see a search warrant. Now, either you go away or I call the conductor."

Ethan was in a mood where he would have forced his way

into the car, and damn the consequences, if Lauren hadn't placed her hand on his arm, restraining him. Before he could argue about it, the door was shut in their faces. They heard the sound of the lock being shot on the other side.

There was a moment of silence. Then Lauren, her voice dull with defeat, murmured, "A private car. He was right. They can't be hiding in there, and since they're nowhere else on the train…" She drew a deep breath and released it slowly. "It looks like I was wrong, after all, and they were never in that compartment."

Ethan wanted to take her in his arms, comfort her, but he didn't think she would welcome that. Not in this moment when he could see she was struggling valiantly to hang onto her self-control, to accept her mistake.

"It was worth checking out, anyway," Buddy said. "You two ready to head back to our rooms?"

Ethan looked at the locked door to the private car before he turned away. "There was something funny about that officious jerk."

"Yeah, I know," Buddy agreed. "He was wearing a business suit, tie and all. It is funny he should be dressed like that at this time of the night, but it isn't suspicious."

"I suppose that's it." *What else could it be?* Ethan thought.

Returning to the sleeper, Buddy parted from them outside his door. "I'm sorry we didn't have better luck," he said. "You going to be okay, Lauren?"

"Yes," she assured him.

But Ethan didn't think she was okay at all. She looked drained. He waited until they were inside their bedroom, and then he took her in his arms.

"We'll catch up with them at Windrush," he promised her, holding her close.

"I want to believe that. I've *got* to believe it," she added fiercely, threading her fingers through her hair.

"You're exhausted. There's plenty of time yet before we get there. Why don't you go back to bed?"

He thought she might resist his suggestion, but she didn't. When he released her, she kicked off her shoes and crawled onto the berth without bothering to get out of her clothes. He perched on the edge of the berth beside her.

"Aren't you going to stretch out, too?" she asked him, lifting her head from the pillow.

"In a bit."

Her head sank onto the pillow again. She closed her eyes on a long sigh. Within seconds, her breasts were rising and falling with the slow, rhythmic action of a woman sleeping soundly.

Ethan was mesmerized by the sight of those lush breasts, by the memory they evoked of the fantastic sex he and Lauren had shared earlier. He felt his groin tighten and knew that, if he weren't careful, he would be fully aroused again.

Bad timing, Brand.

It was safer to shift his attention to another area. He settled his gaze on her upraised arm where her hand was curled around her head. Her fingers were in her hair. She had fallen asleep that way, tugging unconsciously at the silky, auburn strands.

It made him smile to remember how she was forever abusing her hair, raking her hands through it, winding it around her fingers, brushing at it without worrying about its tumbled state. He had never known a woman to treat her hair like that. It was exceptional. But then, she was an exceptional woman, without vanity as far as he could tell.

It was one of the things, among others, that Ethan had learned about her in these past two frantic days. Things the brief interlude in her cabin last winter hadn't permitted him to learn. And the more he discovered, the more he liked and admired just who and what Lauren McCrea was.

The mother of your child.

It was with a jolt that he reminded himself of that. A jolt that had a sudden tenderness welling up inside him. And with

it came a ferocious urge to protect her, as he'd been unable
to protect their baby. Hell, she looked so vulnerable like this,
so damn defenseless lying there that—

What are you doing?

He was frustrating himself with emotions he had yet to understand, that's what he was doing. Emotions he wasn't ready
to deal with. Not when his daughter, whom he had failed to
protect—and never mind that it made no sense to blame himself for that—demanded his concentration.

Was that why he was unable to rest? Why he sat here with
the need to get her back gnawing at him? Or was it something
else, which probably had no connection at all with the need,
that kept nagging at him?

The man who had answered the door of the private car.
Ethan continued to feel there was something not right about
that meeting. Something in the back of his mind…

Lulled by the cadence of the train, he must have dozed. He
didn't know for how long. But suddenly, fully alert, his head
jerked up from where his chin had dropped to his chest.

It was not the way he'd been dressed.

When Ethan had complained there was something funny
about the guy, Buddy had pointed out the peculiarity of the
business suit he'd been wearing at an hour when he should
have been in a robe or pajamas. Ethan had agreed. But, as he
now realized, this had nothing whatever to do with what had
been bothering him.

Familiar. That was it. There had been something vaguely
familiar about the guy. Not a recognition with an actual identity but some kind of connection that had eluded him. Until
now.

He thought he knew where he might have seen him, but he
couldn't be sure. He needed a verification. Buddy. He had to
check it out with Buddy. The cop ought to be able to tell him

Getting to his feet, he covered Lauren with a blanket. She
didn't stir. He left her sleeping and went along the corridor

to Buddy's door. Foley probably wouldn't thank him for rousing him again, but this couldn't wait.

The cop answered his knock without hesitation. To Ethan's surprise, he was still dressed.

"You didn't turn in again?"

Buddy chuckled. "No, I've been waiting for you. I could see you weren't satisfied when we got back here. I kind of figured you'd want to talk about it. Come on in."

He stood aside, inviting Ethan to enter the bedroom.

"Lauren asleep?" Buddy asked.

"Yeah."

"That's good. Have a seat."

Ethan settled in one corner of the berth and Buddy in another, both men turned to face each other.

"So what's bothering you?" Buddy asked.

"The guy in the private car. I'm not sure about this, but I think I've seen him before."

"You have any idea where?"

"Not until a minute ago, and then it came to me where I might have caught a glimpse of him. My grandfather's legal firm back in Seattle. I had only a minimum of contact with the outfit, Donald Patterson mostly. But you've done work for a lot of the lawyers there. Could he be connected somehow with their offices? Maybe even be one of the junior lawyers?"

Buddy didn't answer him for a moment. He sat there watching him. "If he is," he finally said, "then I'd be certain to know that, wouldn't I?"

"You would, yes, and you'd have said something straight off. Which I guess makes me wrong about the whole thing, except—"

He didn't finish. It wasn't Buddy's evasiveness that stopped him but the cool smile on his deceptively boyish face. That's when the truth struck Ethan with all the impact of a fist in his gut.

Sweet lord, he's in on it with them.

Ethan could see that Buddy was aware of his sudden cognition. What's more, he must have been anticipating this possibility and was ready for him. That's why he had remained in his clothes, why he had waited here vigilantly in case Ethan turned up.

Before Ethan could act, the cop whipped his service revolver from beneath the pillow where he had concealed it and trained it on him.

"You couldn't just let it go, could you, Ethan? You had to chip away at it until it was out in the open."

He and Buddy Foley had never actually been friends. Ethan had known him only casually. Now he realized he'd never known him at all.

He should have been worried about the gun, but he was too angry for that. "It's no coincidence you turned up here on this train, is it? None of it is a coincidence. So where did you hide the bastard and the blonde who stole my kid until they were able to sneak on board while you kept us busy? In your van parked somewhere near the station back in Ida, maybe?"

"Something like that."

"Rotten luck though, huh, that Lauren and I ended up in the bedroom right next door to theirs?"

"You could say that."

"And even worse luck that my daughter, bless her, should start crying in the night. You'd have heard her through your own wall on this side. And if you heard her, you must have figured either her mother or I could hear her from our own bedroom on the other side."

You were right all along, Lauren. Forgive me for doubting you.

"That meant the three of them had to be moved out of there immediately. They must have left while Lauren was trying to convince me she wasn't imagining things. It happened just like she said. Right, Foley?"

"You're doing just fine, Ethan. Got all the answers, haven't you?"

Buddy was still smiling at him. Ethan wanted to smack that smile off his traitorous mouth. And would have, if Foley wasn't holding the gun on him.

"You sent them back to the private car where the lawyer—he is a lawyer, isn't he?—took them in. Probably didn't want to hide them there, but he wouldn't have had a choice about it if he's one of you. And he must be."

"Smart guy."

Buddy had been smart, too. Smart in a cunning way when he had offered to join Lauren and him in their search of the train in order to make certain they didn't find Sara. A friend who was on their side, offering his services, flashing his badge. Sidetracking Ethan with that bit about the lawyer in his suit.

"The car attendant," Ethan remembered. "Don't tell me he—"

"Knows nothing about any of it. Dumb, if you ask me, or he wouldn't have accepted my bribe to lie about the compartment not being occupied. I mean, think of the risk he was taking." He shrugged. "But then, look at all the risks I've been taking."

"Why, Foley?"

"Come on, Ethan. You know why. Money, of course. Hell, a cop's salary doesn't go very far. Not when you want all the extras and a chance comes along for you to get them."

The whole thing stank. He knew that much, even if he had yet to fully understand this conspiracy or exactly how involved it was. It had to be pretty complicated if so many people were a part of it. Hilary Johnson, the couple whose identities he and Lauren still didn't know, the lawyer and Buddy Foley. All after what?

"Jonathan Brand's fortune, of course," he said aloud. "Only now the plan's all gone wrong, hasn't it?"

"Maybe not. Maybe it could be revived by eliminating the one major obstacle. That would be you, Ethan."

Foley was going to kill him. He had no other choice.

He can try, anyway, but I'll be damned if I just sit here and let him shoot me.

He had to get the gun away from Foley. And until he could determine just how to manage that, he needed to stall him.

"You'll never get your hands on that money, Foley. You and the others have made too many mistakes."

The cop didn't answer him. Keeping both his gaze and the revolver fixed on Ethan, he groped for the shade at the window. It lifted with a whoosh. The sky outside was no longer black. There was the glimmer of daybreak over the mountains massed on the horizon. The train couldn't be very far now from Windrush. Ethan could see Buddy was worried by that.

"We're finished here," he said.

"What now?" Ethan challenged him. "If you kill me, there's a good chance someone on the car will hear the shot. And even if they don't, a body in your compartment is going to be a bit awkward."

"There's a better way to get rid of you. No muss and no fuss." He rose from the berth and moved toward the door. When Ethan started to get to his feet, he waved him back with the gun. "Just stay where you are."

Foley cracked the door open wide enough to check the corridor outside with a quick glance in either direction. Satisfied, he stood back, motioning with the revolver for Ethan to precede him into the corridor. All the while, he was careful to keep enough distance between them to prevent Ethan from lunging for the gun.

The corridor was silent and deserted when they emerged from the bedroom. No help there.

Ethan had a bad moment when Foley's gaze rested briefly on the closed door to the bedroom he and Lauren shared. Did he intend to force Lauren to accompany them?

The cop must have sensed his concern. "Don't worry about her," he taunted Ethan. "I'll take good care of her. She's going to need me when she finds out her boyfriend has mysteriously disappeared along with her baby. I can be very comforting."

"You bastard! If you—"

"Move or you get it here and now. Not that way. Up front to the baggage car."

As long as he had that gun, Ethan had to obey him while looking for the opportunity to jump the cop. If only one of the occupants of the other compartments would appear just long enough to provide a distraction…

But they met no one along the length of the swaying car or in the vestibule when they crossed it and entered the baggage car.

"Unlock that door and roll it back," Foley commanded him, gesturing toward the outside door closest to the engine.

"Open it yourself." He might be going to hell, but he wasn't going to help Foley send him there.

"Don't be stupid. I couldn't risk that. I'd have to put a bullet in you first. But doing what I tell you buys you time. That many more seconds to live. And hope." He chuckled. "Not that you have any."

Though he wanted to shove that gun down Foley's throat, Ethan recognized the wisdom of his advice. He went to the door, lifted the lever that locked it and slid the door back in its tracks. The cold morning air rushed into the baggage car.

Taking a deep breath of that air, knowing it probably would be his last, Ethan turned around. If he had to die, it wasn't going to be with a bullet in his back. He'd go down facing his killer, defying him to the end.

He tensed, waiting for a burst of fire from the revolver, the heat of the bullet as it entered his flesh. But Foley had something else in mind.

"You get a choice," he said, lifting his voice above the roar of the engine that invaded the car. "Either I shoot you and throw you out, or you jump."

For a few seconds, Ethan was perplexed. What kind of trick was this? And then he understood. Yeah, Foley wanted him to take his own life. That way, when and if they found his body, there would be no bullet in it that could be traced to the cop's revolver. It would look like a tragic accident.

"I'm not going to make your dirty job easy for you. Go to hell."

"Hey, you never know, Ethan. You might just survive the whole thing."

Foley wouldn't be offering him this choice if he thought that was remotely possible. At the speed the train was racing along the tracks, Ethan would be leaping to his death. And if by some miracle he did survive the fall, his body would be so broken that he'd end up perishing alone and helpless in the wilderness.

Buddy moved toward him, squeezing him back until he was teetering on the edge, his hands clinging to either side of the opening. "What are you waiting for?" he urged. "Do it."

Ethan hung on stubbornly while knowing that at any instant now the cop would lose his patience. That a bullet from his gun would do what Ethan refused to do, tear him into him with such force that he would be punched out of the baggage car.

It was then, leaning so far backward out of the gap that his arms ached with the strain of his grip, that he saw them from the corner of his eye. Steel rungs attached to the outside wall of the car within inches of the open door. They composed a service ladder that mounted to the roof of the car.

An image of Lauren and what could happen to her without him fueled Ethan with a rage to live. With a swiftness born of desperation, and a skill that would never have been possible without his special forces training, Ethan released one of his hands and reached for the nearest rung. It eluded him until he stretched out his arm to its fullest extent.

When the cold metal was within his grasp, he removed his other hand from the doorway and launched himself into space. For a few seconds he swung there above the rail bed that passed under him in a blur. Heard the bark of the revolver behind him as Foley realized he was losing his target.

The bullet struck metal, not flesh and bone. By the time the cop fired again, Ethan had managed to exert enough strength to get both his other hand and his scrabbling feet on the rungs. Out of range of the gun now, at least temporarily, and with a solid surface under him, he swarmed up the ladder.

Gaining the roof of the baggage car, he gave himself no time to regain his wind before he pushed himself to his feet. Only then, steadying himself in a half crouch and with feet braced apart, did he permit himself to consider his situation.

He wasn't sure what Foley would do. If he was athletic enough, he would try to follow him up the ladder. And if he didn't trust himself to risk that—

Lauren! The bastard might go after Lauren in the sleeper! Use her as a hostage to force Ethan into surrendering himself!

In the rapidly strengthening light, Ethan was able to see the entire train stretched out behind the engine. What were his chances of finding another ladder on one of those cars, of somehow getting himself back down inside the train and reaching Lauren before Foley intercepted him?

Not great, he knew, but if he was to safeguard Lauren, it was his only option.

In the taut moments that followed, Ethan learned that speeding on foot along the length of a train while enclosed by walls and ceilings was no challenge. Undertaking it on the open roof of a racing train, with an icy wind blasting at you and the metal surface rocking under you, threatening to tumble you into space, was a treacherous business.

He swiftly discovered that the only way to keep his footing, especially crossing from one car to another, was to adopt a crablike gait. Every few yards, he would pause briefly to search for metal rungs over the side of the train and to look back over his shoulder for any sign of Foley.

There were no rungs, but there was Foley. Ethan was on the third car when, turning his head, he saw that the cop had managed to ascend the baggage car's ladder and was in pursuit.

Deafened by the roar of the train, Ethan wasn't able to hear the ping of the bullet from the cop's revolver. But it sparked a warning when it struck metal near his foot. A hail of other bullets followed, ricocheting off the rooftop. Ethan was able to avoid them by dodging and weaving, keeping enough distance between himself and Foley to prevent the cop from getting a close shot at him. Until, that is, he started to leap across the joint between the fourth and fifth cars.

It was in this second that the train swept around a curve, the cars angling with it so sharply and suddenly that Ethan was robbed of his balance and thrown down flat on the roof. Before he could scramble to his feet, Foley had overtaken him.

The cop approached him slowly, his mouth twisted with a smile of triumph. He was wasting no more bullets now on a target that was impossible to hit at any distance on a rolling rooftop. Only when he was within a few feet of Ethan did he raise the revolver again and aim.

Ethan was on his knees by then and aware of what Buddy was unable to see behind him. Not until the train rocketed into the tunnel and was swallowed by blackness did the cop realize, too late, what was happening.

Ethan smashed into him with all the determination of a linebacker, dragging him onto the rooftop. When the train shot out into the light again, both men were down and struggling for possession of the gun clutched in Foley's hand.

Though pinned under the cop, by exerting all his strength on the wrist he gripped, Ethan succeeded in smacking that hand hard enough against the steel roof that Foley released the gun. Before either man could recover it, the weapon went skittering across the roof and over the edge.

The revolver was no longer a threat to Ethan, but Foley was. Heaving against his weight, he threw the cop over on his back. Buddy sprang to his feet, a murderous rage on his face. Even down as he still was, Ethan was ready for his attack, his hands clenched into fists.

At that instant, the train lurched sharply as it thundered across a trestle spanning a deep river gorge. The jolt threw Foley down with such force that he went sliding over the curve of the roof. The cop tried to save himself, clawing frantically at the metal. But there was nothing for him to grab, and in the end gravity pulled him over the edge and sent him plummeting into the gorge far below.

Chapter Twelve

Ethan watched, stunned and helpless. He'd wanted to see the cop defeated, only not this way. No man deserved to die like that.

But there was no time to regret Buddy Foley. A glance at his watch told Ethan that the train would be arriving at Windrush in less than half an hour. He had to act swiftly or they would lose Sara again.

Climbing to his feet, he made his way rapidly back to the baggage car. Descending the ladder cost him little effort, but swinging back through the opening was a perilous business that required both strength and care.

Managing to land safely inside the car, he slid the door shut and locked it. The conductor was on his rounds when Ethan encountered him as he entered the sleeper.

"Is the train on time for Windrush?"

"We'll be stopping there on schedule at six thirty-five," the conductor assured him.

Ethan made a fast decision. "You're able to call or radio ahead, aren't you?"

"I can contact the station there if necessary, yes."

"It is necessary. Get them to have the police waiting when we pull in."

The conductor looked reluctant. "Is this an emergency, sir?"

"I promise you it is, and I'll explain everything to the police when we arrive."

Ethan couldn't afford the delay of an explanation now, especially about Foley's death. The conductor might believe him, even help him and Lauren to get inside that private car. Or maybe he wouldn't believe him and, instead, arrange to have Ethan held by the police, enabling Sara's abductors to escape before the whole thing could be sorted out.

Ethan couldn't take that chance. He and Lauren had to remain unhindered, at least until they convinced the police of the presence of the kidnappers on this train.

The conductor was still hesitant.

"Please, this is vital."

"All right."

With the conductor's promise secured, Ethan rushed on to the bedroom he and Lauren shared. She was still asleep when he entered. Hunkering down beside the berth, he put his hand on her arm. She was instantly awake. And alarmed.

"What is it? Are we—"

"Don't ask me any questions, Lauren. Just listen to me. You were right all along. Sara's abductors are on this train, hiding with her in that private car."

She sat up in the berth, her eyes wide and anxious as she searched his face.

"There's no time to explain how I know that. I just do. We'll be pulling into Windrush soon. The police will be waiting there, but until then you and I—"

"We can't just sit here!" she cried.

"We're not going to do that. We're going back to that private car. No, there's no way we can get inside until the police order it to be unlocked. Whoever is inside is alerted now. They could be barricaded in there, maybe even armed."

"Then, what—"

"We'll stand watch outside the door to the car to make sure no one leaves it until we reach Windrush."

Ethan had been thinking about this. He would have preferred to guard the door on his own and not risk Lauren. But
the job needed both of them. He'd save his explanation for
that when they got there. Right now, they had to hurry.

Trusting him, Lauren asked for no details. Swinging her
legs over the side of the berth, she scrambled into her shoes
and followed him out of the bedroom. Her gaze slid in the direction of Foley's door.

"What about Buddy?"

"We don't need him," Ethan replied briefly. That was a
story that would have to wait for a better time.

The train was no longer asleep. Passengers were stirring,
some on their way to the showers, others who were getting
off at Windrush placing their luggage outside their doors.
The corridor was crowded, making Lauren and Ethan's
progress along its length a problem.

The day coaches were even worse, the aisles so busy that
they had to squeeze through the traffic with hasty apologies.
The dining car involved another maddening delay. Atten-
dants, occupied with readying the tables to serve breakfast,
were slow to let them through.

Although the lounge, when they reached it, should have
been deserted at this hour, they found themselves blocked by
a couple engaged in a heated argument and in no hurry to let
them by.

All the while, precious minutes were slipping away.
Frustrated by the time they were losing, Ethan kept checking his watch.

They had three more cars to go when the train slowed and
eased to a stop. Ethan was frantic.

"What the hell! It isn't six thirty-five yet! We should have had
at least seven more minutes! Either the train is in early, or—"

"It's all right," Lauren said, glancing out the windows on
both sides. "There's no sign of a platform or station out there.
We must have just paused to let another train go by."

Ethan hoped so. Determined not to lose their target, he increased their pace. As they raced along the length of the next car, he related his plan to Lauren over his shoulder.

"When we get there, we'll open the outside doors on both sides of the vestibule. You get out on the platform side and I'll take the other side. That private car is bound to have more than just the door off the vestibule. If the police shouldn't be waiting, I don't want them slipping away from us out one of the sides or through the back end."

Ethan didn't know what he was going to do if the kidnappers emerged before the police arrived. He just knew he had to be there to prevent them from leaving with his daughter.

They were one car away from the private car when, to his relief, the train began to crawl forward again. Urgency driving him, he sped toward the last vestibule.

"Made it!" he said as, a moment later, the train slid into the station and rolled to a stop.

Jerking open the car door, he started to step through it, then froze in disbelief. Where the private car should have been, there was nothing but the tracks stretching away into emptiness behind them.

The private car was gone!

"Where is it?" Lauren cried in dismay, joining him at the open door. "What happened to it?"

One of the assistant conductors, who had arrived at the rear door to assist passengers on and off the train, overheard Lauren and misunderstood her expression of distress.

"Are you missing a piece of luggage, ma'am?"

"What we're missing," Ethan said quickly, "is the last car on the train."

"Oh, you mean the private car that belongs to the Sterlings. It was uncoupled from the train."

That was why they had stopped several minutes ago, Ethan realized. Not to let another train go by, but to detach the private car.

"Where is it now?" he asked.

"On a siding behind the old freight depot a few hundred yards behind us. It's always parked there when one or both of the Sterlings visit Windrush. Mr. Sterling has an interest in the hotel. And just about every other enterprise in Canada," he added with a chuckle. "Excuse me, sir."

The assistant conductor moved by them in order to post himself on the platform. Ethan drew Lauren off to one side.

"I'm going after that car," he instructed her rapidly. "The police should be out there at the station. If they're not, wait for them, and as soon as they arrive bring them on to the Sterling car."

Not waiting for her response, Ethan swung himself off the train and raced along the tracks. As his long legs carried him in the direction of the freight depot, he prayed he wasn't too late and that the couple hadn't already fled from the private car, taking Sara with them.

He could see the long building in front of him. Like the passenger station behind him, it was built in the style of a Swiss chalet. Probably to appeal to those guests of Windrush on a quest for the picturesque, and who expected to find it from the moment of their arrival.

Not that this mattered to Ethan. All he cared about was that private railroad car. He had to round the back side of the freight depot before he spotted it parked on the siding. It looked deserted, the curtains at its windows drawn.

Ethan mounted the steps without hesitation and hammered on the rear door. Unlike last night, there was only a brief delay until he heard the lock being turned on the other side. Either this meant nothing or it was a bad sign that indicated the car's occupants had nothing to fear.

The door was pulled back, disclosing the reedy figure of the young lawyer. His supercilious face expressed exasperation at the sight of Ethan.

"Not *you* again."

Ethan was ready for him this time. "Where are they? And don't lie to me again, because I know now for certain that you took them in last night and hid them. And if you don't produce them—"

He was interrupted by the cultured voice of a woman somewhere inside the car. "Charlie, who's out there?"

The lawyer turned his head. He started to call out a reply when a figure emerged from a room just behind him. She was slim, elegant had raven hair, and was in the act of belting a quilted satin robe that Ethan knew hadn't been purchased in any discount store.

"I'm sorry you were disturbed, Mrs. Sterling," the lawyer apologized in a tone of voice that was altogether different from the one he had used with Ethan.

"You should know by now, Charlie, that I'm never disturbed unless I choose to be." Despite her regal attitude, Ethan read a note of humor in her voice. "Now what's this all about?"

"Nothing you need to worry about, Mrs. Sterling."

"Thank you for your concern, Charlie, but I prefer to be the judge of that." She turned to Ethan and said briskly, "I'm Claudia Sterling. What is it you want?"

"Name's Ethan Brand, and I want my kid," he answered her with equal briskness.

One of Claudia Sterling's carefully groomed eyebrows elevated in surprise. "Are you telling me you have a child who's missing?"

"That's right, and you have her." *Or did,* he added to himself, hoping he was wrong about that and they were still here.

"You see?" the lawyer said, his pale eyes glaring at Ethan from behind his glasses. "The whole thing is absurd. Why he should think we're hiding—"

Claudia held up a hand, silencing him. "Why don't we let Mr. Brand explain himself."

Before Ethan could do that, a police car arrived. Lauren

emerged from the vehicle and hurried to the rail car, joining Ethan on the platform outside the rear door. She was followed up the steps by an officer who wore one of those patches of beard on his chin so small that Ethan wondered why the young men his age bothered to grow them.

The insignia on his cap identified him as a member of the Royal Canadian Mounted Police. Although these days, Ethan knew, they were neither mounted nor, except for ceremonial occasions, garbed in scarlet tunics. Like any other cop, he was dressed in a blue uniform.

None of this concerned Ethan. The fact that he was alone did. The officer must have been aware of his concern when Ethan cast a hopeful gaze in the direction of the police car.

"Sorry," he apologized. "I'm all there is. The RCMP depot down in Kingstown posts only one of us here, and that's just in the season when the hotel is open. Not much action in a place as tiny as Windrush, and what there is is usually covered by the security people at the hotel. Name's Dick Frazier."

This could be a problem, Ethan thought, shaking the hand that was extended to him. While the young officer seemed willing enough, he also struck Ethan as inexperienced. And with the main force of the law located in Kingstown, and who knew how distant that was, then what were their chances of—

"I've filled him in on the essentials," Lauren said, looking at Ethan as though she sensed his concern.

"Perhaps one of you," Claudia Sterling said dryly from where she continued to stand in the open doorway, "would be good enough to fill *me* in."

Frazier glanced at Ethan. "Uh, maybe you and Ms. Mc-Crea ought to do the honors. I'm not sure I'm clear yet about the whole thing myself."

Lauren nodded at Ethan, indicating she chose to have him handle the explanation. As briefly as possible, he rapidly gave them the particulars, starting with Sara's abduction back in Elkton.

The lawyer looked at him with scorn when he was through. "And just where is this Buddy Foley you claim confessed to you I gave refuge to the kidnappers?"

It was a tricky moment. If Ethan told them the truth, that Buddy was dead, they would demand to know exactly how his death had occurred. Maybe the young Mountie would believe him. But even an accidental death was suspicious until evidence verified it.

Dick Frazier would have no choice but to take him in for questioning. And when he learned that Ethan had been arrested last year on suspicion of murder—and the lawyer would waste no time in informing him of that—then Ethan might end up being held.

He couldn't risk it. He had to make sure he stayed free until Sara was found and returned to Lauren. And only then would it be safe for him to explain about Foley.

They were all watching him, waiting for his response, including Lauren.

"I wish I could produce Foley for you. But he gave me the slip after I got the truth out of him," Ethan lied, "and I wasn't going to waste time looking for him. For all I know, he's still somewhere on the train."

"Which has already gone on its way," the lawyer sneered. "How convenient for you."

Ethan turned on him. "I wouldn't be so smug about it, Charlie, because it looks like he's run out on you and left you to take the heat."

"I'm not going to stand here and listen to any more of these wild accusations!"

The Mountie must have decided it was time to calm the lawyer. "Easy. Let's all try to take it easy, Mr...."

"Heath, Charles Heath," Claudia Sterling supplied the name for him, then went on to explain, "Charlie did some legal work for me when I lived in Seattle before my marriage. That's why he's here. He's handling a difficult property transaction for me, and it all needed to be explained to me before I signed the papers he brought."

"Who else besides the two of you are occupying the, uh…" He nodded toward the interior of the private car.

Claudia seemed amused by the young Mountie's sudden awkwardness with a situation that could be defined as suggestive. "No one. My husband is joining me later, and we travel with staff only when guests are on board with us."

"Right. About last night then…"

"You want to know what Charlie and I were doing when he was supposed to have admitted this couple and the baby into the car. Nothing very compromising, I'm afraid. I had a terrible sinus headache. I took something for it and went to bed in my room. Charlie stayed up to work on the papers he'd brought. I wasn't satisfied with them."

"And this medicine you took?"

"Knocked me out. I was sound asleep until Mr. Brand showed up at the door."

"So, it's conceivable—"

"That Charlie did admit them while I unaware of what was happening?" She stood aside in the doorway. "Look, this is easily settled. Come inside, all of you, and search the car. See for yourselves that they aren't here."

Ethan glanced at the lawyer, waiting for him to object. Heath was still fuming, but he said nothing. His silence wasn't encouraging.

"If you don't mind," the Mountie said, "we will have a look."

Ethan knew by then what they would find. Nothing. Heath would have sent the kidnappers and Sara on their way the moment the car had been left on the siding. And now the bastard had nothing to worry about except preserving his innocence by expressing his outrage. But they had to make certain. The car had to be searched.

Even though Ethan had been raised in sumptuous surroundings, the private car's accommodations turned out to be more impressive than he could have imagined. It consisted of four bedrooms, two bathrooms with gold-plated fittings, a galley, a dining alcove and a sitting room with museum-quality paintings on its paneled walls.

They looked carefully in every area, but what Ethan had feared even before they began the search was true. There was no sign of the kidnappers or Sara, nor any evidence they had ever been here.

The satisfied smirk on the lawyer's face infuriated him, although he was more troubled by Lauren's expression. She looked sick with disappointment by the time they ended up in the sitting room. He started to put an arm around her to steady her, but she shook her head, indicating she would rely on her own strength.

Claudia Sterling also looked concerned by Lauren's grief. The handsome brunette might be pampered by every luxury her husband's wealth could buy her, but she was capable of a genuine compassion.

"I'm deeply sorry about your baby, and I pray that you get her back. But as you can see, she isn't here and never was." She turned regretfully to Ethan. "I'm afraid you were misinformed about that, Mr. Brand."

The Mountie cleared his throat. "It looks like we should be moving along. Sorry if we inconvenienced you, Mrs. Sterling."

Claudia and the lawyer, together with Ethan and the Mountie, started toward the door. Ethan hadn't taken two steps when he realized that Lauren wasn't joining them. She remained standing by the sofa, her head lowered in silence.

Seriously worried about her now, he turned back and touched her arm. "Come on," he said gently, "we have to go."

She didn't answer him.

"Lauren?"

Still no response. She was dazed. That's what he thought,

until he realized she wasn't staring down at nothing. Her attention was focused on the contents of the wastebasket squeezed against the side of the sofa.

Before he could question her, she bent down over the wastebasket, her fingers closing around the edge of something that peeked from beneath a discarded newspaper. The others now were as puzzled as Ethan as they turned to watch her.

Lauren straightened and held out what she had retrieved for all of them to see. It was a portion of a plastic wrapper, not much more than a torn scrap, but its label was clearly evident.

"It's the same brand as the one around the package I saw the blonde carrying out of the quick stop back in Elkton," she said, her voice calm and sure. "I recognized it then, just as I recognized it now, because it's the brand I use myself. In case you're wondering what that product is, you can see it's identified right here under the brand name. Disposable diapers. Now do you want to tell me Sara was never here?"

There was a moment of silence in the room. Then Claudia turned to the lawyer, her gaze no longer registering her trust in him as she asked a slow, shocked, "Charlie?"

Ethan had been wondering whether to hug Lauren for her sharp observation that had yielded her discovery or whether to remove with his fist the pompous expression the lawyer had worn throughout their search of the car. But there was no longer a need for that. Charles Heath's bravado had collapsed. Fear had replaced it as he stood there visibly trembling. His guilt was as apparent as if he had already confessed it.

"I guess you won't object, Mrs. Sterling," the Mountie said, "if we all sit down and talk about this. Because it looks like Mr. Heath here has a lot to tell us."

If CHARLIE HEATH did have a lot to tell them, he was in no hurry to divulge it. He huddled in a leather wing chair situated beneath an abstract painting, looking like a trapped animal confronted by his captors. Four pairs of accusing eyes, including Ethan's from where he was seated beside Lauren on the sofa, stared at Heath, waiting for him to begin.

But as deflated as Charlie was, as useless as he must have realized it would be at this stage to deny his role in the whole dirty conspiracy, he was still a lawyer. He knew better than to incriminate himself, at least not before he paved the way for his defense.

Ethan watched him run his tongue nervously across his lips that must have been dry with fear. "All right," he finally said, "I'll tell you everything I know, but I want it on record that I'm cooperating in order to help Brand and Ms. McCrea to recover their daughter."

"Understood," Dick Frazier agreed, pencil poised above the open notebook on his lap.

"There's something else," Heath cautioned the Mountie. "I'm an American citizen, and this is Canada. Anything I tell you here about what happened in the States can't be used against me back there."

Was that true, or was the lawyer simply going to any lengths to protect himself? Looking for confirmation, Ethan's gaze met Dick Frazier's where he sat near the door, but the Mountie shrugged.

Claudia Sterling spoke up sharply from her own chair on the other side of the room. "Stop stalling, Charlie, and get on with it."

"Seattle," the lawyer began. "It started in Seattle about fifteen months ago when Hilary Johnson—she was Jonathan Brand's housekeeper—came to me about…well, she wanted my advice."

Yeah, Ethan thought sourly, *if it was something shady, she* would *go to you and not one of the other lawyers in the firm.* Because if it was connected with his grandfather's estate— and Ethan realized by now that it was—then Heath, for the right price, could be counted on to supply her with information. There had been rumors about Heath's questionable practices, and Hilary could have heard about them. Talk, too, about the firm letting him go. That talk might have triggered the young lawyer's greed.

"Advice about what?" the Mountie asked.

"Her nephew, Anthony Johnson."

This is it, Ethan thought, leaning forward with anticipation, sensing he was about to hear a major revelation.

"Anthony was Hilary's only living family," the lawyer explained. "The son of her sister, Louise, who died several years ago. Louise never told either Hilary or her son who Anthony's father was. Said it was no one's business but hers."

"Hilary never said anything about a nephew," Ethan said.

"And no one we talked to in Elkton mentioned him, either," Lauren added. "As far as they knew, Hilary had no surviving family."

"I don't think she saw much of him while he was growing up," the lawyer said. "Anyway, the woman was as close-mouthed about her affairs as her sister must have been."

"But not on the day she came to see you, was she, Mr. Heath?" the Mountie said.

"No," Charlie admitted. "She told me that her employer had asked her to get rid of some things cluttering up a closet. She could sort through them to make sure nothing valuable was thrown out by mistake, but she wasn't to bother him about them unless she came across something important. There was a box of old photographs at the back of this closet. One of them—and it was labeled—was a picture of the old man's youngest son, Mackenzie Brand, who had died years ago in a plane crash."

Along with my father and mother, Ethan thought, beginning to understand where this reference to his uncle Mac was going and impatient for the lawyer to get there.

"'People can resemble each other, and it doesn't mean beans,'" Heath continued. "That's what Hilary said to me that day. How she'd been aware of her nephew's likeness to the Brands but had never thought anything about it. Until she came across that photo of MacKenzie Brand. 'The spitting image of Anthony,' she swore."

Ethan had no reliable memory of his uncle and, as far as he could recall, had never seen a picture of him, not one that had stayed with him, anyway. But the eyes! Hadn't he been told that he and MacKenzie shared those distinctive blue-green eyes that were a Brand family trait? Sara's eyes. The same eyes as—yeah, it had to be.

Ethan's insides tightened with the certainty of it even before the lawyer could tell them it was true. What's more, he knew that Lauren also understood what they were about to hear. She had turned her head and was gazing at him, her warm, brown eyes registering her concern for him.

But Dick Frazier was still very puzzled. "And?" the Mountie probed.

"Hilary wanted me to find out if Anthony could be the old man's grandson," the lawyer said. "I told her I didn't have any experience with that kind of investigating, but I knew someone who did."

I'll just bet you did. Buddy Foley, of course. The two of them must have put their heads together, Ethan thought, and decided there was a real opportunity here for big money.

"Who was this?" the Mountie asked.

"Buddy Foley," Heath said. "He agreed to look into it by going up to Windrush and—"

"Here?" Frazier interrupted him. "Why here in Windrush?"

"Because Hilary's sister, Louise, was a maid at the hotel. She'd worked in this place for years. This was where Anthony was conceived and born. Actually, he pretty much grew up here, according to Hilary."

"Go on," the Mountie urged.

Heath nervously licked his lips again. "Could I have some water?"

Claudia Sterling rose from her chair, went into the galley and returned with a glass of water that she handed wordlessly to the lawyer. There was a long, taut silence in the sitting room while they all watched Charlie gulp from the glass.

Ethan was rigid with impatience. The couple who had his daughter had a head start on them, and every minute they sat here meant they were getting farther away. Lauren, close beside him, had to have sensed his restlessness and understood it. She put a restraining hand on his arm. He knew what she was silently telling him. That she, too, wanted action, but hearing everything the lawyer had to say could be vital to their recovery of Sara. She was right.

"Are you ready now to go on, Mr. Heath?" the Mountie asked.

Charlie nodded. Cradling the glass in his lap between both hands, he continued. "Buddy learned at the hotel that MacKenzie Brand had been a guest there before his death. They couldn't tell him anything else, but he managed to find a woman in Kingstown who had worked with Louise at Windrush. She'd promised Louise never to share her secret with anyone, but he finally got her to admit that Louise and MacKenzie Brand had had an affair."

Dick Frazier, who had been taking all of it down, looked up from his notebook. "And Anthony Johnson was the result?"

It was unlikely that the young Mountie had ever handled anything of this magnitude before. But Ethan had to admire how thorough he was being, which said a lot about the RCMP's training of its recruits.

"Yes, Buddy was convinced by the time he came back to Seattle that MacKenzie Brand had been Anthony's father. I was ready to give Hilary his information and charge her for our services, but Buddy said no. This was too big, and why shouldn't we get a cut of the fortune her nephew was bound to inherit when we turned up a second grandson for Jonathan Brand?"

"And Hilary Johnson agreed to this?"

"I—yes. I convinced her it was a delicate business, and she needed us to handle it. We would arrange for a blood test, a DNA if necessary, to verify her nephew's claim. Only we needed to be patient. There was talk around the firm that the old man might cut Ethan out of his will altogether, or that Ethan himself was ready to renounce any claim to the estate, and if either of those happened—"

"Anthony Johnson would get it all," the Mountie said.

"That was part of it, yes. But it was also true that Jonathan Brand had an unpredictable nature. He would need to be approached with care if we were to persuade him to acknowledge Anthony as his grandson. I cautioned Hilary about this, thought she understood the risk, but…"

The lawyer's gaze shifted from the Mountie to Ethan. Meeting Ethan's cold stare, he seemed to shrink into the wing chair.

"What?" Dick Frazier pressed him.

"She made a mistake. She didn't wait for us to prepare her nephew. She told him who he was. He turned up at the Brand mansion, demanding to be recognized. Ethan had just stormed out of the place, and the old man was in no mood for Anthony. There was an ugly scene in the library, and…"

Reluctant to go on, Heath lifted the glass to his mouth again. It struck Ethan then as he watched the lawyer drink. Not the realization that it was Anthony Johnson who had murdered his grandfather in some blind rage or that he had ended up stealing Ethan's kid. These he had already accepted, even before he knew they were a certainty.

What hadn't registered with Ethan until now, probably because he'd been unwilling to admit it, was that Anthony Johnson was his cousin, connected to him by blood. Family. Somehow that made everything even worse.

Lauren must have known what he was feeling. That's why she found his hand and squeezed it. Curling his fingers around her own, he squeezed back, letting her know how much he appreciated her understanding.

"Go on, counselor," Ethan prompted Heath, unable to help the bitterness in his raspy voice, "tell us the rest. How Hilary covered for her nephew and how, along with her, you and Buddy Foley let me take the blame for my grandfather's murder."

"I didn't want you to go to prison!" he cried. "I was ready to speak out, but Buddy said you'd be all right. That, without better evidence, they would never convict you."

Ethan gazed at Charlie Heath, disgusted by his desperate pleas to look less guilty than he was. The man was weak and contemptible, deserving no sympathy. And Foley had been no better. No wonder the cop had believed in his innocence and had so falsely befriended him when he'd known all along who the real killer was.

"And, of course, the money had nothing to do with your silence, did it, Charlie?"

"There was all that wealth, and you didn't want it."

"That's right. Why shouldn't another heir turn up after all the smoke had cleared? Anthony could still make a claim on the estate, only now he'd get all of it. Plenty for him to share with you and Foley and his aunt. All the four of you had to do was wait a reasonable time. Except you didn't figure on my daughter, did you? She must have been a big surprise."

"It would have been all right, if…"

"What? If her paternity had remained unknown? But it didn't, did it? I discovered her existence. A real blow after all your watching and waiting, huh?"

"I wanted to abandon the whole thing then and there. I *did*," Charlie insisted. "But Buddy said no. That it could still work out."

"Yeah, we know how. By removing Sara from the scene before it could be proved that she was a legitimate heir to two-thirds of the Brand fortune."

"Kidnapping the baby was Buddy and Hilary's idea, not mine, I swear."

"And then what?" It made Ethan sick to ask it, but he had to know. "Exactly how was she supposed to be eliminated?"

"Not what you're thinking. Hilary and I would never have stood for the baby being harmed in any way. And she hasn't been. She was meant to…just disappear."

"By what means?" the Mountie solemnly asked.

The lawyer cast his gaze around the room, but if he expected help from any of them, he got none. Ethan, watching his Adam's apple bobbing nervously as he swallowed, resisted an urge to put his hands around that skinny throat.

"It—it was Buddy who arranged for it," Charlie said in a small voice, still trying to pile all the blame on Foley.

The Mountie aimed the point of his pencil at the lawyer. "Arranged for what, Mr. Heath?"

"Sara is to be sold to a baby broker."

Chapter Thirteen

Lauren felt Ethan's fingers around hers stiffen with rage. In the next second, he snatched his hand away, tightening it into a fist as he surged to his feet.

She was equally appalled and angry and didn't blame him when he started across the room toward the lawyer, shouting lividly, "You son of a—"

"No, Mr. Brand, bad idea." The Mountie came swiftly out of his chair to stop him. "We need to hear the rest if we're going to get your daughter back."

Watching Ethan, Lauren realized just how difficult it was for him to restrain himself. But to her relief he did manage to control his fury, because Dick Frazier was right. They needed to hear all of it.

The lawyer, cowering in the depths of the wing chair, babbled rapidly, "It isn't as awful as it sounds."

Not awful? Lauren wondered how he could say such a thing when trafficking in stolen babies was a despicable practice. One of the worst she could imagine. Just the thought of Sara being handed over to an illegal baby broker sickened her.

Heath, fearing that Ethan might still attack him, tried to soften the whole thing. "She would have been adopted by a wealthy couple. Raised with love and given every advantage."

Yes, Lauren thought, *because only a wealthy couple des-*

perate for a baby, and either not qualifying for one lawfully or unwilling to wait, could afford to buy one with no questions asked. Sara would be placed with people who were not only rich but who lived so far away from the place of her birth that it would be impossible to trace her. And though she would be raised with love and care, her true parentage would never be revealed to her.

Lauren couldn't stand it. The thought of losing Sara forever, of never seeing her again was unendurable. They had to find her, get her back before she could be turned over to that baby broker.

"Why?" the Mountie asked the lawyer. "Why were all of you going ahead with this thing? From what Ms. McCrea was able to tell me on the way over and from what I've learned here, you and Foley, along with Anthony Johnson and his aunt, must have realized it could no longer work. That Ms. McCrea and Brand were beginning to understand what was happening back in Elkton and that Anthony Johnson no longer stood a chance of claiming any part of that estate. So, instead of just pulling out while you could, why risk selling their baby?"

"We had to," Charlie said. "Anthony was giving us no choice. He promised not to involve Buddy and me, providing he got enough money to disappear. And if he couldn't get his hands on the Brand fortune…well, top prices are paid for healthy Caucasian babies."

"You miserable—"

Ethan started to go for him again, but the Mountie held him back.

"I didn't want to have anything to do with it, not after it started to come apart." The lawyer was practically whimpering by now. "But Buddy insisted that I be on the train with him. That we both had to see to it that Anthony was able to deliver the baby to the broker as planned, because if anything went wrong and he was caught, he would bring all of us down."

Claudia Sterling spoke then for the first time, contempt in her voice. "Resourceful, aren't you, Charlie? I understand it now. You used me to plant yourself here. Because the business of explaining the property transaction in person was just an excuse, something that could have waited."

There was something that Lauren needed to understand, too. "Why here at Windrush? Why come all this way to deliver Sara to this—" the words were loathsome, but she made herself say them "—this broker?"

"The broker asked for a remote spot to make the exchange," the lawyer said "Somewhere safe. But it was mostly because Anthony wanted it that way. It's familiar ground, and that seems to matter to him. Him and that girlfriend of his, Molly something or other. He met her while she was working here at the hotel."

The blond companion who helped him to kidnap my daughter, Lauren thought.

"Where are they now?" Ethan demanded.

The lawyer shook his head. "I don't know. Hiding somewhere out there until it's time for them to meet the broker, I suppose." He cringed when Ethan looked threatening again. "They didn't tell me, I swear."

"What about this rendezvous with the broker?" the Mountie asked him. "Just when and exactly where is this to occur?"

"Buddy handled all of that."

"He must have told you something."

"Nothing specific, only that Anthony and his girlfriend were to meet the broker sometime late this afternoon—I don't know where—and that he was to fly in."

"This had better be the truth," Ethan warned him, "because if you're lying—"

"It *is* the truth. Please, I don't have anything more to tell you. That's all I know."

Sometime late this afternoon, Lauren thought, her hands clenched in her lap. That gave them only hours to find Anthony Johnson and his girlfriend. Because if they didn't find them, if they were unable to prevent them from handing Sara over to the broker—

No! That mustn't happen!

With a nod of his head in the direction of the passage that led to the other rooms in the car, Dick Frazier indicated his wish to speak privately to Lauren and Ethan. They followed him to the end of the sitting room, stopping just inside the passage where the Mountie could keep an eye on the lawyer in case he tried to bolt.

Not that he would, Lauren thought. Charlie Heath continued to huddle in the wing chair, looking sad and beaten.

The three of them conferred in low tones.

"I wish there were other RCMP officers here to conduct a search for those two and your baby," the Mountie said, "but as I told you before, I'm it."

"What about bringing in other officers from this depot in Kingstown?" Ethan asked.

Frazier shook his head. "Too far away for them to get here in time to do us any good. Kingstown is eighty miles away over a bad road."

"Couldn't they fly in?" Lauren wanted to know.

"Kingstown is too small a depot to have any aircraft available. Besides, there's no airfield here."

"Then how can this broker fly in?"

"Has to be coming by floatplane. They do sometimes deliver guests that way by landing on the lake out in front of the hotel. But, look," the Mountie promised them, "it's not hopeless. Like I said earlier, there's a security force at the hotel. They're very efficient."

"You think they'd help?" Ethan asked.

"I'm sure of it. I know the manager over there, Donna Cardoni. She won't hesitate to offer her people."

"Could we please hurry?" Lauren appealed to the Mountie, anxiously aware of the minutes they were losing that could be critical to them.

Dick Frazier glanced in the direction of the wing chair. "I need to take Heath into custody and contact Kingstown so my superiors there can tell me what to do about him. I'll phone Donna on the way and explain everything to her. Then as soon as I get Heath secured in the lockup, I'll join you at the hotel."

"How do we get there?" Ethan asked.

"You could walk, but it's much quicker to take one of the trolleys. They make regular runs between the village and the hotel. You can catch one over at the train station. They swing by there every few minutes."

THE STATION AGENT was out on the platform when Ethan and Lauren arrived back at the train station. He had their luggage at his feet.

"The attendant in your car left it with me," he explained. "Hope everything is here. He said he had to gather it up pretty fast when he realized you'd gotten off the train without it."

"He mention anything about anyone else's things left behind?" Ethan asked him.

"I wouldn't know about that," the agent said.

There was a tautness in Ethan's voice that made Lauren glance at him. She was puzzled by his question, wondering if he could be referring to Buddy Foley. Maybe Ethan was thinking Foley hadn't remained on the train, that he, too, could have gotten off here in Windrush.

Before she could ask him about it, one of the shuttle buses in the guise of an old-time trolley appeared. It was empty when they boarded it, but after it turned out of the station yard, it collected other passengers bound for the hotel at its regular stops along the village's single street.

Lauren could see that it was not an actual village. There were no houses. The buildings, all in an alpine style meant to be as quaint and picturesque as the trolleys, contained nothing but boutiques that catered to the hotel's guests. As early as the hour was, the street was already busy with shoppers.

Lauren's impatience with their frequent stops had to be as evident as her reason for it. Ethan covered her hand with his own.

"I know it's not easy," he said, "but try to remember that, as long as Sara has value to them, they're going to take care of her. And until they get that payment from the broker, Anthony and his girlfriend aren't going anywhere. They're somewhere out there, and we're going to find them."

She appreciated both Ethan's determination and his words of reassurance. But hearing her daughter spoken of as a kind of commodity, even if this was how her kidnappers regarded her, was hard to bear.

Leaving the village behind, the trolley passed through a belt of trees and began to descend a long slope. At its bottom, looming in front of them like a vast French château, was the hotel itself, situated close to the shore of a large lake. Against a backdrop of spectacular mountains and with manicured lawns embracing it on all sides, it was an impressive structure.

Had the circumstances been otherwise, Lauren could have appreciated all this sprawling splendor. As it was, she was interested in nothing but the woman with a name tag on her lapel who was waiting for them on the front steps when the trolley looped around the drive and stopped at the main entrance.

She came down the wide steps to greet them as Lauren and Ethan stepped off the shuttle, the bags they carried identifying them as new arrivals.

"It's Ms. McCrea and Mr. Brand, isn't it?" They nodded. "Dick Frazier called to tell me you were on your way and to explain the situation to me. I'm Donna Cardoni."

The manager of the hotel was an attractive, smartly dressed brunette with an intelligent face and a pair of dark, concerned eyes. She solemnly shook their hands.

"I'm sorry this has to be your introduction to Windrush," she said, referring to the reason for their presence, "but we're going to do everything we can to help you."

Thanking her, they followed her up the steps and into a lofty lobby. Lauren could see from its elegance that cost had meant nothing to the railroad baron who had built Windrush.

"I've called a meeting of my security people—" Donna checked her watch "—forty minutes from now. It will take that long before Dick Frazier can join us, and I think he should be here for the meeting. Would you like to go to your room until then?"

Lauren shook her head. "I feel we should be doing something instead of just waiting. There ought to be something we can do."

"Of course. How about listening to some things that you'd probably like to know? Why don't we sit down, and I'll try to fill you in."

Lauren and Ethan exchanged glances. That Donna Cardoni had information to share was unexpected, but if it was at all useful, they wanted to hear it.

"We could go out on the terrace," the manager offered, indicating a range of French doors on the other end of the lobby. "We can talk there. I have to check with the desk, and then I'll be with you. Leave your bags here. I'll have someone take them up to your room."

She hurried away. Lauren and Ethan crossed the lobby and let themselves out through one of the French doors onto the stone-paved terrace that stretched across the length of the hotel.

Lauren could see why Donna Cardoni had suggested it. At this hour, the terrace was unoccupied. They would be able to talk here in privacy.

Standing at the elaborate, wrought-iron railing that edged the elevated terrace, Lauren looked out over the lake below. Her own lake back home was not exactly a pond, but this lake was immense by comparison. It was not only incredibly blue, but breathtaking with the high mountains rimming it on all sides, their lower slopes glowing with forests of aspen that had turned to pure gold with the season.

It wasn't the beauty of the scene, however, that occupied Lauren's thoughts. It was the enormity of the whole thing, not just the lake and the forests but the daunting size of the hotel itself.

"How can we ever hope to locate them in all this bigness?" she asked Ethan, who stood silently beside her. "They could be anywhere."

"It won't be easy," said a voice behind them, "but I don't think it's as much of a challenge as you might suppose."

They turned away from the railing to see that Donna Cardoni had joined them. She led them to a table and chairs situated in the warmth of the sun. Although the weather remained mild, the air off the lake was too bracing to seat themselves in the shade of one of the awnings.

When they were settled around the table, Ethan leaned toward the manager. "What you said just now…what did you mean?"

"Only that we don't need to concentrate our search anywhere but in the hotel itself and on its grounds. Anthony wouldn't try to hide out there in the wilderness."

"How can you be certain of that?"

"I'm not, but knowing him as I do—"

"You're familiar with this guy?"

"Familiar enough."

This was what she had meant back in the lobby by offering to fill us in, Lauren thought.

Donna began to explain it to them. "Anthony would think of Windrush as coming home. Probably the only home he's ever really known. He's familiar with every inch of it. Therefore—"

"He'd feel secure here as he wouldn't anywhere else," Lauren guessed.

"Not just that, but in control. And that's important to Anthony."

"How do you come to know so much about him?" Ethan asked.

"Because he was one of my employees."

This was news.

"We learned his mother had been a maid here years ago," Lauren said, "but we had no idea he stayed on after her death."

Actually, it wasn't so surprising since the lawyer had told them Anthony had met his girlfriend at Windrush, and that must have happened while both of them were working here.

"He not only stayed on," Donna said, "he was a regular fixture at Windrush. I got to know him fairly well. Or as much as anyone could get to know Anthony. He was always a strange young man. He'd never let anyone get close to him, except for his girlfriend, Molly Janek."

"Why would you have someone like that working for you?" Ethan wanted to know.

"Well, he never had any contact with the guests and, until Dick Frazier told me, I had no idea he could be dangerous. In any case, I had no choice about it. The owners insisted we keep him on. They had good reasons for their decision. Anthony has no training as an engineer, but he's amazingly skilled with mechanics. There was no machinery on the place he couldn't repair."

And that, Lauren realized, would have made him capable of creating an incendiary device like the one that destroyed the farmhouse back in Elkton.

"But there are experienced people who could have replaced him," Ethan said.

"Yes," Donna agreed, "and I hired two of them after Anthony left. But, you see, Anthony was valuable in another way."

"How?" Ethan wanted to know.

"Windrush is a seasonal operation. It shuts down in October. All of us are out of here by the end of the month. Everyone except a caretaker."

"And that was Anthony," Lauren surmised.

"Exactly. He never minded that Windrush is completely cut off all through the winter except for a weekly train when the weather permits. In fact, I think the loneliness suited him. Now you can see why I said he's familiar with every inch of the place and isn't likely to try to hide out somewhere in the forests."

Ethan, looking grim, nodded in understanding. "Because he wouldn't have to. He must know any number of places right here to conceal the three of them."

"The old hotel is a regular labyrinth," Donna admitted, "but my people are familiar with it, too. If they're here, or anywhere on the grounds, we'll locate them."

A young man, wearing the uniform of a bellhop, appeared on the terrace with a message for Donna. She got to her feet.

"I'm wanted at the desk. I'll see you at the meeting."

She left them sitting at the table. Lauren thought about the manager's promise to them and tried to believe she was right. That they would find Anthony Johnson and succeed in getting Sara safely away from him before it was too late. There were hours to go, but the time was already slipping away from them.

She was frightened, and Ethan knew that. "It's not going to help for us to go on sitting here until that meeting," he said. "Neither of us has eaten anything since last night. I noticed a coffee shop off the lobby."

Lauren shook her head, knowing she couldn't eat breakfast and manage to keep it down. "I could use some coffee, though." Coffee would keep her going.

They left the terrace. There was a large-screen TV in one corner of the lobby. They had to pass it on their way to the coffee shop. Although no one was watching it, the set was on and tuned to a newscast.

Lauren was oblivious to the program. Until a scene that suddenly filled the screen caught her eye. Coming to a stop, she stared at it, then slowly approached the set. Why was it so familiar?

Of course. The camera, obviously originating from a news helicopter, looked down on a train snaking through the mountains below. It was a train very much like the one that had brought them to Windrush through a similar terrain. Or were they the same mountains?

And why should this capture her attention? She had no reason to be interested. Unless the curse that Ethan muttered under his breath behind her…

Grabbing the remote from where it had been left beside the set, Lauren boosted the volume in time to hear the newscaster's startling report.

"It was along this same stretch of track, and from a train resembling the one you see, that the two railroad inspectors checking a trestle earlier this morning witnessed the man hurtling to his death. Although identification on the body has established that he was a police officer from Seattle, Washington, his name is being withheld pending notification of family. Whether his death was the result of an accident or foul play has yet to be determined."

Shocked by what she had heard, Lauren turned away from the set to face Ethan. His expression was as hard as stone.

"It must have been Buddy Foley," she said. "He was talking about Buddy Foley. I don't understand. You told all of us that he managed to slip away from you. How could he have—"

Lauren had no need to go on. She realized by now that something was wrong. *Very* wrong.

"You had some kind of showdown with him," she whispered. "That's what really happened, didn't it?" She ought to have guessed earlier, when Ethan had been so vague about Buddy's disappearance, that his explanation wasn't right.

Ethan remained silent. It didn't matter. His eyes said it all. She felt sick.

"You lied to all of us. You lied to *me*."

"All right, so I withheld the truth. But only long enough to make sure I stayed free until Sara was recovered. What other choice did I have? You tell me, Lauren. Just what else *could* I do?"

"You could have told me."

"When? There was no time. Anyway, I didn't want to involve you until I had a chance to…well, I never dreamt Foley's death would be discovered this soon."

"What? A chance to what?" A terrible thought occurred to her then. "Dear God, you and Foley! Did you—"

She caught herself, but it was too late. The damage was already done. Ethan understood what she had been on the edge of so impulsively accusing him of.

"Did I murder him, Lauren?" he said bitterly. "That what you want to know?"

"I'm sorry. I wasn't thinking. I just—"

"Yeah, I know. My innocence is still in question, even with you. Hell, I stood trial for killing my grandfather, didn't I? Doesn't matter that I've been vindicated, because where there's smoke…"

"Ethan, no! I know you're not capable of murder."

"Do you? So why have I got this lingering feeling that, if it hadn't been for Sara's abduction, we wouldn't be together at all? That you wouldn't have let me anywhere near her or you again?"

"That's not true!"

"Then you should have trusted me. But that's the problem with us, isn't it, Lauren? Even after all we've been through, you never could bring yourself to completely trust me. And without that, we have nothing."

Turning abruptly on his heel, his long legs carried him swiftly away from her. Lauren knew it would be useless to go after him. He was in no mood to listen to her.

She stood there, stricken with guilt. How could she have thought that he might have murdered Buddy Foley? It was hearing of Foley's death like that, and for a fleeting second... But that second of doubt was all it had taken to convince Ethan there was a yawning gulf between them.

Returning the TV remote to the place where she had found it, Lauren wandered back across the lobby. She stood by one of the French doors, gazing out at the shimmering waters of the lake and feeling miserable.

Although she knew that her stupid error could be resolved once Ethan had a chance to get over his anger and forgive her, there was no denying the larger issue it had triggered. One that could not be mended simply by communication. She could still hear his biting words on the subject.

If it hadn't been for Sara's abduction, we wouldn't be together at all.

They had bonded over Sara out of necessity, that was true. But if their daughter was all they had in common, if they shared nothing else, then their relationship was hopeless. Because even though Lauren was in love with him, Ethan had never indicated he was prepared to return that love. Nor had she any right to expect it.

Once Sara was back in her arms—and it was unthinkable to consider she might not be returned to them—there was every likelihood that, except for visits to his daughter, Ethan would be out of her life. She had to learn to accept that.

But standing there at the glass, she already felt the unbearable ache of his loss.

THEY MET in one of the hotel's conference rooms. Lauren was encouraged by the size of the security force. There were eight men and women who gathered around the table. Together with Dick Frazier and Lauren, who had every intention of participating in the search, the team was large enough to cover all areas of Windrush.

They were already assembled by the time Ethan arrived. Lauren experienced a bad moment when he strode into the room. What if one of the others, the Mountie in particular, had learned of Buddy Foley's suspicious death?

But apparently none of them had caught the newscast, because he wasn't challenged. Probably the police investigating Foley's death had had no chance yet to connect him with either Ethan or Windrush, which meant Dick Frazier hadn't been alerted.

If Ethan was worried about that eventuality, he showed no signs of his concern. His face was a taut mask without emotion when he joined them.

Lauren had no idea where he'd been after leaving her. Nor did she have any opportunity to ask him. He sat down the table away from her, avoiding all contact.

She put aside her distress about him with a fierce determination. All that mattered right now was Sara. And that meant giving her full attention to Donna Cardoni, who conducted the meeting with a brisk efficiency that emphasized the importance of locating Anthony Johnson, Molly Janek and the baby in their possession as quickly as possible.

The manager began by briefly filling in her security force about why they were there and then moved on to the particulars. "All right, people, this is how we're going to handle it."

She proceeded to organize the search by dividing the areas, then appointing two people to each section.

"Stick with your partners," she went on to instruct them, "and keep in touch on your two-ways. I want each team reporting in every half hour to the command center. That will be my office, where either I or Officer Frazier will be available at all times."

"Donna told me," the Mountie added, "that most of you would recognize Johnson and his girlfriend, and I know you're trained for emergencies. But if you spot either of them, approach them only if necessary and with every caution. They could be armed."

"One more thing," Donna said. "The entire staff has been alerted to be on the lookout for them. We'll also be watching for any sign of that float plane. Trouble is, with the lake as big as it is and with so many streams feeding it, that plane could land anywhere. It's much better if we find Anthony and Molly before the plane ever arrives. But we need to avoid alarming any of the guests, so keep all of this among yourselves."

With a scraping of chairs, they got to their feet. Before Lauren could leave the room with the partner that had been assigned to her, Ethan stopped her.

"I don't think your being a part of this is a good idea."

She knew his concern for her safety was genuine. She just wished it hadn't been expressed so coolly.

"They would prefer that neither one of us be involved in the search," she pointed out to him, "but since you refused to listen to that suggestion for yourself…"

"All right, so both of us insist on joining the search. I can't stop you, Lauren, but how about coming along with—"

"Who? You? I have my partner, Ethan, and you have yours. Let's leave it by agreeing that both of us will be careful."

She didn't need his protection, and didn't want it, not with him feeling as he did. Before he could argue about it, she hurried away to catch up with the young woman she had been paired with.

THIS IS A WASTE of time, Lauren thought, her frustration mounting as the minutes slipped away.

She and her partner had begun by looking through the staff quarters located in the attics of the hotel, all without result. Nor had the other teams reported any success yet.

Now she and the young woman, Barbara something or other, were out on the grounds where they had just checked the tennis courts and the cabana beside the outdoor pool. Useless. What next? Poking under shrubs?

It was long past midmorning. Even though the rendezvous with the baby broker was scheduled for late afternoon, there weren't that many hours left to them. Not with the days as short as they were in this season at this latitude. And the thought of losing Sara...

They were on their way to a gazebo on the other side of the lawns when Lauren's desperation could stand no more. Anthony Johnson might be all that was vile, but she didn't think he could be a fool. Surely he would have anticipated a careful search of the entire hotel and avoided concealing himself on its premises. But if they weren't here, then where? She had an idea.

"Look," she said, stopping her partner. "You go on. I'm going to catch the next trolley to the alpine village."

"What for? One of the teams already covered the village."

"I know, but I'd just like to look around up there."

The young woman was doubtful. "I don't know. We're supposed to stay together. What if something happens to you?"

"It won't. There are lots of people up there. I'll be perfectly safe."

Before the woman could raise any further objections, Lauren was on her way across the lawn to one of the shuttles that had just pulled up to the front steps of the hotel.

When she reached the village a few moments later, she saw that her argument about the large presence of people had been no exaggeration. Every boutique along the street was running an end-of-the-season sale, and the guests from the hotel were out in force to take advantage of all the bargains.

Wandering in and out of the shops through the crowds, Lauren began to wonder what she'd hoped to achieve by coming here. The team that visited the village earlier must have been thorough with their search. What could they have overlooked?

Nothing, apparently, although the garrets of the alpine buildings seemed a possibility. Until, that is, a clerk informed her that all of them were open lofts where stock was stored. And since the personnel of every store were kept busy chasing in and out of the lofts to supply the demands of their customers, it was highly unlikely that two adults and a baby could be hiding in any of them.

But Lauren stubbornly persisted in her search, trying as she moved from shop to shop not to think about Ethan. Not that she was entirely successful. She couldn't shake the unhappy realization that, once this was all over and done with, he would go back to his life in Seattle, while she—

Enough. Concentrate on Sara. Right now Sara is all that matters.

With that reminder firmly in mind, she arrived at the last shop at the end of the street. It was somewhat larger than the others, a kind of general store offering a variety of merchandise.

Pointless. There's nothing for you to discover here.

Lauren was on her way out of the shop, with the intention of catching a trolley back to the hotel, when she overheard one of the clerks tell another clerk, "I sold the last baby formula on the shelf to that woman who was just in here, and there's no more in stock."

"Well, we're certainly not going to order replacements with the end of the season staring us in the face."

Lauren came to a halt. Was it possible? Heart hammering against her ribs, she turned to the clerk and asked breathlessly, "The woman you were talking about…please, did you see where she went?"

"Out the back way, but—"

Not waiting for her to finish, Lauren flew through the store to the back door. Had someone else purchased that baby formula, or could it have been Molly Janek?

There was no one in sight when Lauren emerged from the

rear of the shop where the forest crowded almost to the walls of the buildings. Where could she have gone? The path that wound through the trees? It was her only choice, and Lauren didn't hesitate to pursue it.

The trail was carpeted in needles and shredded bark, permitting her to travel it in swift silence. On either side rose giant cedars, hemlocks and spruce. At first that was all she saw, and then through the evergreens ahead of her she caught a glimpse of a figure. A thin woman with blond hair and carrying a plastic sack.

Lauren's breath quickened at the sight of her. It had to be Molly Janek!

She was careful not to get too close and to use the cover of the trees as she followed her. But Molly couldn't have been worried about the possibility of pursuit. She never once betrayed any nervousness by checking over her shoulder.

This is dangerous, Lauren thought. *I should have asked the clerk to phone the hotel. But there had been no time. I would have lost her if I had hesitated.* Nor, reckless or not, did she consider turning back now. She had to learn where Molly was going, and only then—

She arrived at a fork in the path, the left branch descending in the direction of the lake, the one on the right continuing in a route roughly parallel with the shore. Which way?

There! She caught a movement through the trees. Molly was on the right branch. Lauren sped along the path after her.

Within yards, the trees thinned and then fell away altogether. Lauren hung back behind a fir, carefully peering through its concealing boughs into a clearing within sight of the lake. Molly was on her way across that clearing.

Lauren watched the woman as she waded through the high weeds, and then suddenly Molly vanished. In one second she was there out in the open, and in the next she was gone. As if the earth had swallowed her.

Intent on the mystery of Molly's disappearance, Lauren

failed to hear any sound behind her. Never knew he was there until his arms went around her like a pair of steel bands, his voice at her ear whispering harshly, "Making a regular habit of this, aren't you?"

Chapter Fourteen

Ethan's partner was a heavy, balding fellow who complained about his aching feet.

He's in the wrong occupation, Ethan thought, trying not to be irritated with the lumbering slowness of the security man as they searched the maze of storerooms in the basement of the hotel.

Finding nothing, they emerged from the back of the hotel at ground level. The slips where motorboats and sailboats were moored for the pleasure of the hotel's guests were just below them.

Ethan turned to his partner, Fred Griggs, and was about to ask him what area they were scheduled to check next when a young man down on the landing hailed them.

"That's Ted," the security man said. "He's in charge of the boats."

"He's upset about something," Ethan said as the young man charged up the slope toward them.

"One of the boats is missing," Ted reported when he reached them.

"You sure about that, Teddy?" The security man gazed out at the lake where several craft were on the open waters. "It's a fine morning, and if you've been busy supplying boats, maybe—"

"I know my boats," Ted cut him off, "and I know when one isn't accounted for."

"How could that happen if you were there the whole time?" Ethan wanted to know.

"Well, I wasn't. I locked up my office, that little building there at the foot of the dock, and came up to the kitchen to get a thermos of coffee. I couldn't have been away more than fifteen minutes, but when I got back the door was unlocked and one of the motorboat keys was gone from the board."

The explanation was immediately apparent to Ethan, who damned himself for not thinking of this at the start.

"Anthony Johnson," he said to his partner. "If he was a caretaker for the place, he would have known where to lay his hands on keys to everything, including a spare one for that office."

"I don't get it," the security man said, slow to understand.

"He grabbed that boat. That's where they're hiding, somewhere on the lake. It makes sense. They're out there waiting in the boat to rendezvous with the floatplane. How well do you know the lake?"

"Well enough," Griggs answered him. "But I gotta tell you, there's all kinds of little bays and inlets. They could be tucked out of sight in any one of them."

"We're going to cover them all." Ethan turned to the young man. "What does the missing boat look like?"

"A twelve-footer, white with a green canvas top and matching side curtains."

"Gas up your fastest boat for us," Ethan instructed him. To Fred Griggs he said, "Better use your two-way to tell them at the command center what we're doing."

Within minutes, he and the security man were speeding away from the dock. Ethan's sense of urgency gave him no chance to wonder about Lauren. It was just as well. She already had him tied in so many knots that he'd been unable to think clearly. And he needed his mind clear for what was ahead of him.

"YOU LIKE FOLLOWING people, huh, just like back in Elkton," he growled at her ear, referring to the episode behind the quick stop.

This was a sickeningly familiar repetition of that encounter. Lauren could smell the same faintly sour body odor on him, feel his fearful grip that she struggled to resist.

"Only this time, you don't get away," he said, shifting his hold with such lightning swiftness that, before she could prevent it, he had one of her arms pinned behind her back.

"Keep on fighting me, and I'll break it," he warned her.

Remembering that he had killed both Jonathan Brand and probably his aunt, Lauren knew that he wouldn't hesitate to kill her if she provoked him. She stopped struggling.

"That's better. I'm gonna give you what you want. I'm gonna show you where Molly went. Move."

With her arm still painfully locked behind her, he shoved her forward. They left the trees and started across the weedy clearing. Too late, Lauren realized what a terrible mistake she had made in following Molly Janek without telling anyone what she was doing and where she was going. All she'd been able to think about was her baby. She was still thinking about her.

"Sara," she said anxiously. "Is she—"

"Save it."

With the high weeds and from where she had stood behind the fir, Lauren hadn't been able to tell that the clearing wasn't entirely level. She could see now as they approached the center of it that it swelled here into a low, grass-covered mound a short distance from the shore of the lake.

Then, without warning, a shallow flight of stone steps appeared, descending from the edge of the mound to a stout door below. He forced her ahead of him down the steps, ordered her to open the door with her free hand and pushed her inside.

Lauren stumbled over an uneven floor. He jerked her up and then mercifully released her. Ignoring the soreness in her arm, she tried to see where they were.

There were no windows and he had closed the door behind them, shutting off the daylight. It would have been completely dark if there hadn't been several oil lamps burning, one of them hanging from a hook above a rough workbench whose surface was littered with various tools.

Whatever this place was, its thick stone walls made it dank and heavy with the odor of mold. There was no sign of Molly Janek or Sara anywhere in the gloomy cavern, but she noticed another closed door on the far side.

He misunderstood her probing. "Wondering what chance you've got of someone rescuing you? None," he taunted her. "No one knows about this place but me. In the early days, the ice that was cut out of the lake in winter was stored here underground for summer use. Then when the hotel got refrigeration, this place was abandoned and forgotten."

He approached her, chuckling cruelly. "Smart, huh? Makes the perfect hideaway. Because even if someone did wander this way, they wouldn't know we were down here. Wouldn't even hear you if you screamed your head off."

Dim though the flickering light was, he stood so close that Lauren had her first clear sight of Anthony Johnson. She didn't like what she saw.

Though he resembled Ethan, his features were sharp and cold, his mouth twisted in a mocking smile. The blue-green eyes that stared down at her were intense, smoldering with what must be the bitterness of the legacy that had been denied him. He hadn't shared in the Brand wealth, and now he never would.

Lauren thought he was despicable, but she refused to let him see her fear. "Where's my daughter?" she demanded. "What have you done with her?"

Before he could answer her, the door on the far side

opened, and Molly Janek appeared. She was startled by the sight of Lauren, her guileless blue eyes in her thin face nervously looking from Lauren to Anthony. He rounded on her angrily.

"Didn't I tell you to stay here with the kid?"

"She was all right. I left her sleeping like the little doll she is. I had to go out, hon. The formula was all used up, and I knew she'd be ready for another feeding when she woke up."

"First it was diapers, and now it's formula. Didn't that stupid little brain of yours stop long enough to think about the risk you were taking? She followed you here, and if I hadn't sneaked up behind her from the other path after snitching the boat and setting it adrift, she'd have blown it for us."

"I'm sorry, hon. I was only trying to take good care of—"

"Shut up, and let me think." He eyed Lauren, and then cast his gaze in the direction of the workbench. "Okay, maybe this isn't so bad. Maybe we can use her as our ticket out of here after the kid is delivered."

"How so, hon?"

"Never mind. Right now, we need to make sure she doesn't get away before we're ready for her. Get me those handcuffs I took from the security supplies at the hotel last winter. Looks like I finally got a use for them."

Molly obediently went to the workbench and poked through all the clutter he must have accumulated in this secret workshop over a period of time. While she was searching for the cuffs, Anthony confiscated Lauren's shoulder bag. She regretted having it taken away from her. If the opportunity presented itself, she'd hoped to use her cell phone. It was something she should have done long before now, had she been thinking clearly.

She ought to have known Anthony was too cunning to overlook the possibility of a phone. He found it immediately, looked through the other contents in her purse, pocketed the phone and tossed the bag on the floor. Molly returned and gave him the handcuffs.

"Hold out your wrist, the right one," he ordered Lauren. When she hesitated, he growled a menacing, "You won't feel good if I have to persuade you."

She extended her wrist. He clamped one of the bracelets over it and snapped it shut.

"I want both of you in the other room. And this time stay there," he instructed Molly. "I've got work to do at the bench in here, and I don't want any distractions."

Lauren had the uneasy conviction his work was connected with her and how he intended to use her to get himself and his girlfriend safely away from Windrush. Whatever that twisted brain of his was in the process of devising, she knew it couldn't be pleasant.

Useless to ask him. He wouldn't tell her. In any case, her major concern was for her daughter's welfare. She longed for some assurance that Sara was all right, which was why she permitted Anthony to lead her across the room and into the other chamber from which Molly had emerged.

Oil lamps burned here, as well. There was a large basket sitting on a crude table against one wall. Sara had to be lying inside that basket, although Lauren was allowed no glimpse of her.

Anthony dragged her in the opposite direction. They stopped at a metal rack holding rusted saws and tongs that must have been used long ago to remove ice from the lake. The rack was tightly bolted to the wall. He locked the other bracelet over one of the bars that formed the rack. Lauren was helpless now, chained like a felon to the wall.

Without another word, her captor retreated from the chamber, closing the door behind him. She and Molly were alone, buried underground in what felt like a prison cell.

Ignoring Lauren, the blonde busied herself at a camp stove. *She's preparing the formula for Sara's feeding,* Lauren realized, watching her anxiously. When the bottle had been warmed to Molly's satisfaction, she went to the table and leaned over the basket, making cooing noises to its occupant.

Then she carefully lifted the baby out of the basket, settled herself on a stool, and just as carefully began to feed Sara with the bottle. There was a tender smile on Molly's face, a little girl playing mother as she looked down at her charge cradled in her lap.

Lauren gazed at the scene in frustration, unable to satisfy herself with even an adequate view of her daughter's face.

That should be me. I should be holding her, feeding her, not some woman who has no right to cuddle her.

As if suddenly aware of Lauren and sensing her need, Molly looked up from her task.

"I'd let you hold her," she said, her tone both sympathetic and friendly, "but if Anthony came in and caught us, he'd be awfully mad about it. But, hey, don't worry. I've been taking real good care of her. Anthony didn't want to, but I made him take me to get those extra diapers back in Elkton. She sure goes through them, doesn't she?"

Lauren stared at her. That's when she realized two things about Molly Janek. She was either mentally challenged or incredibly naive. Like a simple child, she seemed unable to understand how seriously wrong all of this was.

She was also completely under Anthony Johnson's control. Although Molly was at ease now, even cheerful, Lauren remembered how nervous she had been in Anthony's presence, how anxious to please him. That being true, it wasn't likely that Lauren could convince the young woman to help her. But Molly did seem to possess both an innocence and a basic decency, so maybe…

"Listen to me, Molly," she pleaded earnestly. "I want you to get that handcuff key away from Anthony. You can manage it somehow."

The young woman looked at her, not understanding. "Why would I do that?"

"So you can unlock me. Then I'll stand a chance of helping not just myself and Sara but you, too. It will be in your favor when they catch you. Because both of you *will* be caught. But if you free me, I promise I'll do everything to see to it that they go easy on you."

"No," Molly said solemnly, shaking her head, "I could never do anything like that."

"Are you so frightened of him?"

"Anthony can be sweet, you know. He can be awfully sweet."

"But sometimes he's mean, isn't he? Mean enough to kill."

"It was his grandfather's fault. He wouldn't listen to Anthony and wanted to throw him out of the house."

"And what about his aunt? She was trying to help him, and yet he killed her, too, didn't he?"

"No, that wasn't very nice," Molly admitted. "But waiting in that farmhouse until everything could be settled about the baby broker got on his nerves real bad."

"Was that a reason to kill his aunt?"

"Well, Hilary *was* being difficult. She wanted to go straight back to her house in town so she wouldn't be suspected. But Anthony said no, that she had to stay because she was in on it with him. Then she got scared and wanted him to forget the whole thing and give Sara back."

"And he wouldn't."

"He said it was too late for that."

"So he killed her."

"Only after Hilary sneaked his gun away from him and hid it. I guess she was afraid he might use it. She wouldn't tell him where it was. They had a terrible fight about that, and he knocked her down. She had only herself to blame, because he never meant to kill her."

"Molly, you have to get away from him before he ends up hurting you."

"Anthony would never do that. He loves me."

"You can't trust him. He's sick."

But Molly had stopped listening to her. There was a dreamy look now on her pale, pinched features as she bent her head with its wispy blond hair over Sara again.

The young woman was immune to all reason. There was nothing more that Lauren could do. Her thoughts turned to Ethan and how desperately she missed him. What if it all ended here and she never saw him again? That very strong possibility, along with forever losing her precious daughter, gripped her with pangs of anger and despair.

No! Either she or Ethan, or perhaps both of them together, had to find a way to defeat Anthony Johnson. But how, when Ethan didn't know where she was? Or even that she was gone?

IT WAS ONLY AFTER a long search on the lake that Ethan and his partner, Fred Griggs, found the missing boat tucked behind a tiny island not far from shore.

They approached the craft with caution, but it was apparent before they reached it that it was empty and adrift. Boarding it, they inspected it and learned there was still plenty of gas in its tank and that nothing was wrong with its engine.

"He must have waded to the beach after leaving it," the security man surmised. "It's shallow enough here to wade all the way back to shore. But what was the point of taking it out and then just abandoning it?"

Ethan had a fearful certainty of exactly why the boat had been stolen and then hidden behind the island. A decoy. And it had to have been Anthony Johnson who was responsible for it. Something to keep them busy, to lure them away from the true rendezvous with the broker. But if that meeting wasn't to occur somewhere out here on the lake, then where—

Fred Griggs had a call on his two-way. Ethan waited impatiently, knowing from the security man's responses and the expression on his round face that something was wrong.

"What is it?" he demanded when Griggs ended the call.

"It was Dick Frazier. He said Ms. McCrea is missing. Seems she left her partner and went up to the village to look around. There was some kind of mixup, so they didn't learn until a long time later that she hadn't turned up back at the hotel."

Ethan tried to suppress his alarm and failed. "And they waited until now to tell us about it?"

"Well, they've been up there looking for her, but they couldn't find her or anyone who knew where she could be."

Ethan grabbed his cell phone clipped to his belt, extended its antenna, and punched in the digits for the number to Lauren's cell phone. He waited anxiously, hoping she would pick up, but she never answered.

His heart had been in his throat from the second Griggs informed him that Lauren had been reported missing. Now it dropped like a stone down to his stomach. "Let's get back to the hotel."

"What about the abandoned boat?"

"Leave it. It can be picked up later."

With the throttle wide open, their small craft roared across the lake in the direction of Windrush.

Standing rigidly in the bow with legs apart to brace himself, Ethan expressed his growing fear by swearing under his breath. He was angry with himself for permitting her to go off with another partner. And he was angry with Lauren for leaving that partner to search on her own.

Whatever his mood when they'd parted in the lounge and he'd gone off to pore over a map of the hotel, whatever his disappointment in her after that emotional scene in front of the television set, he should have kept her with him. Because if anything happened to her, if Anthony Johnson had somehow gotten hold of her—

And that was when it struck him with the force of a blow. He was in love with Lauren! He couldn't lose her! How could he live without her, or his daughter, either? They were both of them as vital to him as the blood that coursed through his veins.

As swiftly as the boat traveled over the blue waters, it wasn't fast enough to suit Ethan. He was frantic by the time they reached the landing. Leaving Fred Griggs to moor the craft, he swarmed up the ladder onto the dock.

How could he find them? Where could he possibly search that hadn't already been covered by the teams? And how much time was left to him?

Looking up, he checked the position of the sun. It was already in the west, the shadows of the mountains beginning to spread across the lake. Late afternoon was approaching, and if they didn't soon locate and prevent that rendezvous…

Sick at the thought of what the outcome might be, he started to lower his gaze. That's when he saw them high on a wooded ridge over to the left of the hotel.

He had only a brief glimpse through a gap in the evergreens before the trees swallowed them again. But it was enough for him to know there had been three figures. A man and two women. At this distance he'd been able to distinguish little else. Except one of the women had auburn hair and the other was a blonde. A blonde bearing something in her arms that could be a baby.

His daughter! Ethan was convinced of it.

"That ridge," he called down to Fred Griggs, who was still busy fastening the lines. "What's up there?"

The security man gazed in the direction he indicated. "There's a trail along there."

"Where does it go to?"

"The station for the cable car that runs up to the scenic overlooks on Mt. Evans. But there's no one there. It's been shut down for the season and the trail closed. Too cold on the mountain this late in the year."

"How do I reach that trail?"

"Over to the left on the far edge of the lawns. Path is marked, but what—"

"I don't have time to explain. Contact Dick Frazier for me and tell him where I've gone and to get up there with help as fast as he can, because I think Johnson is headed for that cable car."

Not waiting for a response to his request, Ethan raced up the length of the dock and across the lawns. He found the marked path and tore along it at top speed, his brain burning with his fear for the safety of both the woman he loved and his daughter.

Anthony had managed somehow to capture Lauren, and if he hurt either her or Sara—

Don't think about that. Just concentrate on reaching them.

It seemed clear to him now what Anthony intended. The cable car was going to carry him and his captives to the rendezvous with the broker at the top of the mountain.

They had all overlooked this possibility. Learning that the broker was to fly in, they had assumed he would arrive by floatplane. None of them had considered a helicopter. And what better place for an illicit exchange than a remote mountaintop, which meant there had to be some safe, level spot up there for the chopper to land.

Never mind that the cable car was shut down. As mechanical as he was, Anthony would know how to activate and operate it.

Ethan was sure this had to be the scenario, but could he get there in time to stop it? His long legs and the rigorous, special forces training that had conditioned his body were in his favor. The path, when it turned and began to climb steeply toward the ridge, was not.

Ethan met the challenge by exerting his energies to their full force. He was winded when the path joined the main trail on the crown of the ridge. But he didn't let that slow him. Pausing only long enough to catch a quick breath, he pounded along the trail, his heart pumping a litany.

Hang on, Lauren. I'm coming…coming…

The route was level now and that made the going easier. But it seemed to take forever before he trotted around a bend and saw a clearing ahead of him. Using the trees as a cover, he approached the opening with caution.

There it was, the small cable-car station. But there was no sign of the three adults, one of them carrying a baby, who must have reached the place some minutes before him. Risking exposure, Ethan moved out into the clearing.

It wasn't until he neared the building that he heard the throb of an engine inside. There was only one door, a heavy one. When he carefully, silently tried it, he found it locked from the inside.

They were in there, he knew, but there was no way to reach them. No windows to break through, only the open end at the back from which the cable car had yet to emerge. When he crept around to the side, he could see that the structure was perched on the sharp edge of an abyss. Its back end hung precariously over the chasm. It would be impossible for him to reach that opening.

Frustrated, Ethan eyed the stout pine tree that grew against the side of the building. Its branches were as good as the rungs of a ladder. All right, if not the walls, then maybe the roof.

Without hesitation, he scaled the pine, not knowing yet what he was going to do, only that he was determined not to let that car inside get away from him.

It was a shed roof, its higher end above the opening. The roof's relative flatness made it easier to navigate once he was on it. He had no idea whether they realized he was up here. Maybe not. He'd been as quiet as possible, and the hum of the machinery down there should muffle any sounds on the outside.

He'd reached the upper edge of the roof, and was wondering as he crouched there whether he could swing himself down and through the opening, when he heard below him the sound of what must have been the drivewheel turning. It was followed by the rumble of the rolling cable drum, then the clang of a bell announcing the imminent departure of the car.

They had to be inside the gondola. In another second, the brake would be released. They would be on their way if he didn't act. Forget Dick Frazier. He and whatever help the Mountie might be bringing with him were obviously delayed.

Ethan didn't think when the car suddenly swung out from the opening. It was instinct born of need that enabled him to launch himself under the cable lines and down onto the roof of the gondola as it passed beneath him. Whatever generated his action, the special ops officer who had trained him would be proud of his feat.

Maybe less proud, Ethan realized, if he failed to survive his situation. It was a perilous one, with the rapidly moving gondola suspended over a chasm whose depth he didn't want to think about. All he could do until they reached the upper station was to flatten himself and hug the roof with spread arms and legs. Any other effort would be suicidal.

The ascent was marked by a series of cable towers located at intervals along the tops of ridges. Every time the car bumped through one of these towers, it threatened to spill Ethan into space. The wind that tore at him out here in the open didn't help, either.

Clinging to the roof, he came to the conclusion that his ordeal atop the train long hours ago had been a stroll in a meadow compared to this.

Ethan was able to measure the halfway point when the empty gondola from the upper station, that counterbalanced the whole operation on parallel cables, passed them on its descent. Hopefully, Dick Frazier would be waiting at the lower station to board it and follow them. But Ethan couldn't count on that.

The next few minutes tested not just his strength but his

endurance against blasts of air that grew more frigid as they climbed above the treeline. His entire body was numb with the cold by the time they arrived on the summit.

The car, slowing on its last steep ascent, crawled into the station and came to a rocking halt inside its stall. Ethan eased himself up from the roof into a crouching position on its edge. With the blood already circulating again through his limbs, he was ready to spring on Johnson the instant he emerged from the car.

Would surprise be in his favor? It was still his hope, but it proved to be a wasted one. The occupants of the car were aware of his presence on the roof. That was evident when the gondola door slid open just wide enough for a harsh voice to call out to him. "Whoever's up there, and I'm thinking it's probably you, *Cousin* Ethan, then you'd better stay just where you are. Because if you don't, then your girlfriend and what she's carrying are gonna end up being on your conscience the rest of your days. Do we understand each other?"

Ethan had no choice. "We understand each other."

"Keep your distance, then. We're coming out."

The car's side door rolled back all the way. Anthony appeared first, followed closely by Lauren. He was leading her like a dog on a leash. One of the bracelets on a pair of handcuffs encircled her wrist. The other bracelet was in Johnson's fist. Lauren's free arm bore Sara wrapped snugly in a blanket. The blonde, Molly Janek, who at some point must have transferred the baby to Lauren, emerged last. She was trembling like a frightened child.

Lauren, too, was frightened. She looked up, her gaze seeking Ethan's. "Please," she appealed to him, "do what he says. If you don't, Sara will die."

Johnson laughed. "I've got insurance here, Cousin. Show him," he ordered Lauren. When she hesitated, he growled an insistent, "Turn around and *show him.*"

Her captor swung her around by the handcuffs, exposing

her back to Ethan's view. She had some kind of pack harnessed to her. What in—

"Wanna know what's in the pack?" Anthony chortled. "Plastic explosives with a magnesium charge. And this—" he held up a small, black remote clenched in his free hand "—this is the little baby that signals the charge. All I have to do is back away out of harm's way and press this button here, and *boom*. Cool, huh?"

The sick bastard had rigged up a bomb and strapped it to Lauren's back!

Ethan felt himself shaking with both rage and his inability to make use of his hands, rolled into fists down at his sides. But he could, and did, deliver a savage warning to the man smirking up at him.

"If you hurt either her or my kid, then I promise whatever it takes I'll find you. And when I do, I'm going to send you to hell."

"She won't suffer, or the baby, as long as you both do what I tell you." He rapidly issued his instructions. "This is how it's going to work. You're going to stay right here inside the station, Cousin. You and Molly together, while your girlfriend and I go out to meet that chopper."

"You're not going to leave me, hon!" Molly wailed.

"You can't come. The chopper was told to expect one man and one woman with the baby. If they spot a third adult, or anything suspicious, they won't land."

"I don't want to be left with him!"

"He's not going to hurt you, because he knows what will happen to his girlfriend if he touches you. He's going to be a good boy while I hand over the baby and get the money. Aren't you, Cousin?"

"But it's all gone bad, hon. How can we get away now?"

"The same way we got up here. You and I, Mol, are going back in the cable car. Brand and his woman stay here. As long as I keep this remote, they won't try to stop us. And once we're down the mountain—" He shrugged. "Well, the re-mote won't work at any distance, so everybody ends up safe."

The cunning Anthony had anticipated all obstacles. Sup-ported by the explosives, a weapon as vicious as the mind that that had crafted it, his ultimatum left Ethan without a choice. He had Sara's life to preserve, as well as Lauren's.

"You'd better not come back here alone, Johnson."

"That's up to you, Cousin." He turned to Lauren, tugging at the handcuffs with a sharp "Come on, it's time to go."

Helpless and hating it, Ethan watched him lead Lauren out of the building. At the doorway, she looked back at Ethan over her shoulder. The expression on her face was pure torment for him. He knew what she was feeling, that in order to make sure her daughter survived, she had to go out there and without a struggle hand her over to a stranger. It was killing him, too.

They weren't gone more than a few seconds when he was seized by a wrenching regret. *What have you done?* But he knew what he had done. He had let them go. He had trusted Anthony Johnson to keep his promise, a man without con-science who had already murdered two people. And if he didn't try to stop him before it was too late—

Without hesitation, Ethan clambered down from the roof of the car. Molly backed away from him.

"What are you doing?" she cried.

"I'm going after them."

"You can't! You heard what he said. He means it!"

"I know what he wants us to believe, but I think it was a lie. He's not coming back for you, Molly. He realizes if he goes down that mountain the law will be waiting there to grab him, if they're not already on their way up here. He's leaving you and going out on that helicopter."

Unless the occupants of the helicopter agreed to remove Anthony from the scene, and this already could have been ar-ranged, it was not a certainty. It was, however, a strong pos-sibility. And if Johnson didn't take Lauren along as a hostage, then he would leave her dead. Either way, now or afterwards, her life was bound to be sacrificed. It would be his last, perfect act of vengeance against the grandson of the man who had rejected him.

Ethan intended to make sure that didn't happen.

The helpless, timid Molly made no effort to stop him when he charged out of the building. There was no sign of Lauren and Johnson, but there was only one way they could have gone.

The terrain both straight ahead and to the right was far too rugged to manage on foot bearing a baby. That left only the other direction where a trail winding around the side of the mountain had been hacked out of the rock. Since the drop in most places was deep and precipitous, a strong guard rail had been erected all along the trail's outer edge to prevent any mishaps. At intervals, there were overlooks that commanded spectacular views.

But Ethan wasn't interested in the scenery, only in overtaking Lauren and Johnson. Sprinting along the trail, immune now to the biting cold, he was careful to check around each bend before proceeding. He didn't want to suddenly run into them, not when Johnson had his finger ready to depress the button on that remote.

He must have traveled a quarter of a mile when, peering around a shoulder of rock, he sighted them. They had stopped where the trail ended. This had to be the site of the rendezvous. Beyond the barrier, where it turned back from the drop and joined the mountain, there was a natural flat area. Large enough, Ethan thought, for a helicopter to set down, though he could see stretches where ice had formed on the ground.

There was no sign yet of the chopper Johnson was waiting for. Unless Ethan acted before it arrived…

Pulling back out of sight, he searched his mind for some means of rescuing both Lauren and his daughter. Anything he tried would put them at serious risk, but he was determined to save them. How?

Maybe if he got above them, waited for his chance…was that possible? Turning his head, he could see enough clefts and knobs of rock to provide him with a means of scaling the wall to a ledge that ran parallel with the trail.

As silently and as swiftly as possible, Ethan climbed the wall until he was standing on the wide ledge. Hunched over and dodging from boulder to boulder to conceal his presence, he worked his way around the shoulder until he was looking directly down on his objective.

He could hear an impatient Johnson, as he searched the sky out over the barrier, complaining about the delay. Then Ethan, who had already assumed his familiar position of a fighter waiting to attack, with crouched body and coiled hands, got his break.

"I'm gonna be busy when that chopper gets here," Anthony said to Lauren. "Think maybe we'd better see to it you stay put, just in case you get any cute ideas about trying something. This ought to hold you."

Head lowered, he busied himself clasping the dangling bracelet of the handcuffs around the pole that formed the horizontal bar of the guard rail. Ethan didn't know whether Lauren sensed his presence or whether, hating the sight of herself being locked to the barrier, she looked away and up.

There was a startled expression on her face when she glimpsed Ethan looming above them. Then, quickly composing herself, she used the moment to both distract Anthony and to provide Ethan with his opportunity.

"Please," she implored, "take Sara and put her down somewhere safe away from me and the bomb. You don't want to risk her now that you're so close to getting what you want."

Good girl, Ethan told her silently, admiring her courage.

Anthony considered her request. Then, apparently deciding there was nothing suspicious about it, he slipped the remote into a pocket of his jacket in order to free his hands.

Praying Johnson wouldn't look up and discover him on the

ledge, Ethan watched him remove the baby from Lauren's arm that had held her against her breasts. Johnson took Sara several yards away from the railing, found a sheltered spot in a mossy hollow behind a boulder, and placed her there.

Satisfied, Anthony started back toward his captive. Ethan waited until he was passing underneath him. Then he leaped from the overhanging ledge, smashing into his target and knocking him flat. The impact of his attack stunned Anthony, but only briefly.

In the next second, clawing at Ethan in a ferocious rage, he fought to get one of his hands inside his pocket. Ethan had him pinned down with his weight and had succeeded in seizing both of his arms. He longed to render Anthony unconscious with a blow to his jaw but knew he couldn't release either hand long enough to deliver it. He had to keep Johnson from getting one of his fingers on that button.

Anthony twisted and heaved. In his struggle to throw Ethan off, the remote slid out of his pocket with such force that it went spinning across the flat surface of the trail in Lauren's direction. Ethan dived after it, missed it and watched in horror as the remote skidded over the sharp edge and went sailing into space. He waited in helpless terror for the explosion that would destroy the woman he loved, but to his vast relief nothing happened. Wherever it had landed below failed to trigger its signal or was too distant for the signal to be effective.

Whatever the explanation, Ethan knew he had to get that pack off of Lauren's back. He sprang to his feet, prepared to deal first with Anthony. But Anthony's fury had been diverted by the roar of an approaching engine.

The three of them looked up as the helicopter came swinging into view from around the back side of the mountain. When it reached them, it hovered low over the scene for a moment.

Its occupants, looking down, must have realized immediately that something wasn't right. Two men and a woman when there should have been *one* man. Not trusting the situation, the chopper started to retreat.

"Nooo!" Anthony howled.

Ducking under the barrier that divided the trail from the open area where the craft had been meant to land, Anthony ran after it. In his fury and frustration, he was oblivious to everything but the helicopter that was deserting him.

When, in his headlong charge along the brink of the precipice, he struck a patch of ice, he was unable to save himself. One second, he was there; the next, he went tumbling with a scream of terror into the void.

"Dear God!" Lauren cried.

"Forget him," Ethan commanded. "It's too late for him."

It was too late for Anthony Johnson's soul long ago, he thought, reaching Lauren's side. By now, the helicopter had sped away and was no longer in sight.

"Sara," she said.

"She'll be all right for a few minutes. The three of us are going to be just fine. Let me get at that pack."

She obliged him by turning sideways. The thing was a bitch, Ethan thought. Harnessed on her so that the straps passed across her chest and both over her shoulders and under her arms. In the back, they were tied in a series of tight knots intended to defeat any easy removal.

He was angrily starting on those knots when Lauren halted him, a quaver in her voice. "Ethan, wait! Look down!"

He followed the direction of her lowered gaze, his heart stopping when he saw it. The remote hadn't landed somewhere far down the mountain. It was only a few feet below them, caught on the lip of a tiny shelf of rock.

Poised as it was, it looked ready at any second to lose its balance and go bouncing off the shelves below it. Ethan knew he had to get that remote before it detonated the explosives.

Flattening himself on the ground, he stretched his arm toward the shelf, straining to reach the remote. No good. There were too many inches between his fingers and the device. Nor could he try to climb down there. The face of the cliff was too sheer, the shelf too small to accommodate him without disturbing the remote.

His only choice was to get rid of the bomb pack, because the railing was so strong that he could never break through it in time to remove Lauren a sufficient distance from the signal. Surging to his feet, he fiercely attacked the knots. His fingers by now were numb with the cold, hindering his frantic effort.

It was coming, though, the straps beginning to loosen. He hurried. "Hang on, I think—there!"

The straps slid away, allowing him to lift the pack out of its harness. Handling it carefully, bearing its weight in the palm of his right hand, he drew his arm back and hurled it with all the strength he could command over the side of the mountain. At that instant, the remote must have slipped off the shelf. He could hear it crack against the rocks below.

There were a few seconds of silence, long enough for Ethan to wrap his body protectively around Lauren. His ears rang with the blast that followed. He could feel pebbles raining down on his hunched shoulders. But nothing else. The explosion had occurred too far below them to do more than kick up dust and bits of rock that were already settling.

"You okay?" he asked Lauren.

"Yes," she said, releasing her breath on a long, shaky sigh. "Or I would be if I weren't handcuffed to this rail."

Turning her around so that she faced him, he grinned down at her. "That's all right. This way, you can't get away from me."

He proceeded to take advantage of her captive state by framing her face with his hands and covering her mouth with his in a long, molten kiss.

He would have gone on kissing her if their daughter hadn't

reminded them of her presence with a loud wail that said she had been ignored long enough and didn't like it. Releasing Lauren, Ethan went behind the boulder, picked up Sara, made sure the blanket was still tucked around her warmly and carried her back to the railing so that her mother could see she was unharmed.

He could hear shouts back along the trail in the direction of the cable car station. "Sounds like the cavalry has finally arrived," he said to Lauren. "Let's hope they know where to lay their hands on some tools to get you unlocked, because now that I know how much I love you, I'd sure hate having to leave you up here on this mountain."

Chapter Fifteen

"They'll be sending up the first rockets in just a bit," Donna Cardoni said to her. "Are you sure you wouldn't like to go out and watch?"

Lauren turned her head in the direction of the French doors. All of them had been left open to ease the flow of the guests onto the terrace. People had been streaming through the lobby for the past twenty minutes. Both the terrace outside and the lawns below it were packed now with spectators waiting to be dazzled by the display over the lake.

"It's quite a show," the hotel manager encouraged her. "Windrush's traditional way of ending each season."

Donna was a kind woman. Lauren knew she was concerned about her. But mingling with the crowd on the terrace to watch the fireworks, no matter how spectacular, was not going to relieve her anxiety. Only Ethan could do that.

"Thanks, but I think I'll just wait here."

She had no longer been able to endure the awful vigil up in their room and had come down to the lobby. Besides, the easy chair she occupied offered her a view of the front entrance. She wanted to be right here to meet Ethan when he walked through that door. And if he didn't—well, she didn't want to think about that.

Lauren leaned toward Donna seated in the chair next to hers. "I don't suppose you've heard anything?"

The manager, looking sympathetic, shook her head. "No, but try not to worry. These things drag on, and they did have a lot to cover."

It was taking all day, Lauren thought. And she couldn't help being worried. She had been apprehensive about the outcome ever since they had taken him away long hours ago.

Two RCMP officers had arrived from Kingstown early that morning. After questioning Lauren and taking her statement, and because Ethan had insisted on it, they had permitted her to remain here at Windrush with Sara.

But the Mounties weren't that easily satisfied where Ethan was concerned. There was the matter, not just of Anthony's death, but of Ethan's involvement with Buddy Foley's death. He had been forced to accompany the suspicious officers back to Kingstown for an intensive, in-depth interrogation.

Dick Frazier had turned Charlie Heath over to his superiors. The lawyer, together with Molly Janek, had also been transported to Kingstown.

They'll hold Molly and Heath. But Ethan…what if they don't release Ethan? What if they drag up all the business about his grandfather's murder? Don't believe what he tells them because of his connection with that, even though he was acquitted? What if they arrest and charge him?

Lauren couldn't stand it!

"I tried phoning Kingstown," she said to Donna, "but they wouldn't tell me anything or let me talk to Ethan. They said I'd just have to be patient. But all this time, and being so late now…"

"It's a long way back from Kingstown. Give him time to get here. He'll come. He won't want to spend a night away from you and Sara." Donna gazed at the sleeping baby in Lauren's arms. "You must be tired holding her. Wouldn't you like me to take her for a bit?"

Tired? No, Lauren wasn't tired holding her. Now that she had Sara back in her arms, thankfully unharmed and healthy after yesterday's horrendous events on the mountain, she couldn't bear to be separated from her.

"I'm fine," Lauren assured the manager. "And I appreciate you for sitting with me like this, but you must have a million things to do. Wouldn't you—"

"Look!"

Lauren's head swiveled in the direction Donna indicated. There, coming at last through the front entrance, was the tall figure of Ethan. She was so weak with sweet relief that she staggered when she pushed to her feet.

Donna had also risen from her chair. "Here," she said, "you'd better let me take Sara. I think you're going to want both of your arms free."

Donna was right. Lauren surrendered her daughter to the manager without an objection this time. Then, steadying herself, she flew across the lobby and into Ethan's waiting arms.

She no longer had to live off the memory of the love he had declared for her yesterday on the mountain, which was exactly what she had been doing throughout this eternal day. He was here in reality, and she couldn't get enough of that love as she wound her arms around him. Pressed herself against his solid length. Lifted her head to welcome his hungry kiss.

She was reluctant to end that kiss, but she needed to know if he was all right. Leaning away from him just far enough to look up at him, she searched his strong face. He looked tired, but he was smiling.

"Was it very bad?" she asked him.

"It took forever," he explained, "because they had to check out everything I told them, first with the police back in Seattle, then the sheriff and Agent Landry in Elkton, and after that the crew on the train. But in the end, they put it all together and believed me."

"Thank God. And Charlie Heath and Molly?"

"The lawyer will certainly stand trial, maybe both here in

Canada and in the States. As for Molly Janek, I don't know. She's in a state of shock over the loss of Anthony. Could be she'll end up in some psychiatric facility."

Poor Molly, Lauren thought. Even though the young woman had played a major role in Sara's abduction, Lauren couldn't bring herself to feel anything but sorrow for her.

"What about the baby broker?" she wondered.

"They'll try to find and prosecute him, but that won't be easy when they have so little to go on. As for you and me…" Ethan took a quick breath, then released it slowly. "Well, we're going to be all right, Lauren. We're going to be just fine."

"Yes," she said.

Ethan looked around. "Sara?"

Lauren linked her arm with his and led him across the lobby to where Donna was waiting with their daughter. The manager, with a grin on her face, transferred the baby to her mother.

"I think this reunion needs to be a private one," she said, accepting their thanks with a little wave as she walked away.

There was a moment of silence when they were alone, and then Ethan turned to Lauren with an abrupt "Family."

"What are you saying?"

"I want us to be a family."

"What does that mean?"

"Marriage," he said decisively.

"You're asking me to marry you?"

"Yes. That is, if you wouldn't mind living in Seattle where my work is, because you can take your own work just about anywhere, can't you? We'd keep the log cabin in Montana for vacations and things. And since we'd have my income, this could be your chance to write that novel."

"You've been thinking about this, haven't you?"

"Yeah, all the way back from Kingstown over that miserable road." He gazed down at her, those wonderful blue-green eyes registering both his eagerness and his suspense. "What do *you* think?"

"That I love you very much, and—" Sara was awake now and stirring in her arms. Lauren looked down at their baby, realizing that Ethan's anxious proposal needed to be acknowledged with action, not words.

"Here," she said softly, "this is long overdue."

Her answer, when she gently placed Sara in her father's arms, couldn't have been more clear or definite. She was telling him not only that the time had come for them to share their daughter equally and together, but of her trust and deep love of him.

Lauren knew by the joy in his eyes as they met her gaze that he understood she'd accepted his proposal. That she wanted them to be husband and wife as much as he wanted it.

She watched Ethan as he looked down at Sara, a tender, paternal pride on his face. Her heart swelled at the touching sight of father and daughter together.

The perfect moment was augmented by the boom of the first rocket outside. Lauren and Ethan turned to watch the rocket soar into the night sky, where it burst high over the lake in a shower of brilliant stars.

Ethan was as excited as a boy. "Let's go out there on the terrace and introduce Sara to her first fireworks."

"That sounds like a plan."

"I have another one."

"What?"

"I was thinking," he said, a gleam in his eyes and a promise in his voice, "that afterward we'd go upstairs where you and I will make our own fireworks."

She smiled at him. "I like that one, too."

"Yeah? Good." One arm cradling Sara and his other arm sliding around Lauren's waist, Ethan led his family toward the French doors.

"Donna told me that the fireworks mark the end of the season here," she said.

"That might be true for Windrush, but for us…"

Yes, she thought, *for us they mean a beginning.*

Her mind and heart embraced that precious thought as they walked through the open doors into their future.

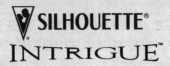

❖ SILHOUETTE®
INTRIGUE™

SECRET CINDERELLA by Dani Sinclair

Millionaire Roderick Laughlin wasn't prepared for the
woman who begged for his help only to escape a crowded
ballroom, leaving him with the memory of the sweetest lips
he'd ever tasted. But with a killer on her heels, Melanie
Andrews had no one to turn to except the man she'd
deceived…

COWBOY ACCOMPLICE by BJ Daniels

McCalls' Montana

Regina Holland desperately needed a cowboy to star in her
commercial…and JT McCall was just the man for the job.
But when she finagled a position on his cattle drive in order
to convince him, she hadn't counted on becoming a killer's
target – or falling hard for the rugged rancher.

UNAUTHORISED PASSION by Amanda Stevens

Matchmakers Underground

She was just a job…thought former lawman Jack Fury, and
if he had any sense, he'd keep his chance encounter with
Celeste Fortune a purely professional affair. He'd been hired
to shield her from a dangerous predator, but Jack wasn't sure
he could resist Celeste's tantalising beauty.

THE SUBSTITUTE SISTER by Lisa Childs

Eclipse

When her estranged twin disappeared, Sasha Michaelson
had gone to her sister's lakeside estate to care for her child.
Haunted by her dead sister's cries, Sasha was losing control
– until she met Sheriff Reed Blakeslee. But could she trust
this man…or was he keeping something from her?

On sale from 18th November 2005

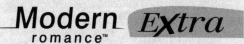

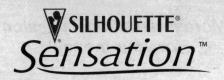

EVERYBODY'S HERO
by Karen Templeton

The Men of Mayes County
It was an all-out war between the sexes – and Jo was losing the battle. Would his need to be with Taylor withstand the secret he carried?

MIDNIGHT HERO by Diana Duncan

Forever in a Day
As time ticked down to an explosive detonation, agent Conall O'Rourke and bookstore manager Bailey Chambers worked to save innocent hostages – and themselves.

ALONE IN THE DARK
by Marie Ferrarella

Cavanaugh Justice
Patience Cavanaugh had vowed never to date a cop, but detective Brady Coltrane was the type of man to make her break her own rules…

Don't miss out!
On sale from 18th November 2005

FREE

2 BOOKS AND A SURPRISE GIFT!

We would like to take this opportunity to thank you for reading this Silhouette® book by offering you the chance to take TWO more specially selected titles from the Intrigue™ series absolutely FREE! We're also making this offer to introduce you to the benefits of the Reader Service™—

★ **FREE home delivery**
★ **FREE gifts and competitions**
★ **FREE monthly Newsletter**
★ **Books available before they're in the shops**
★ **Exclusive Reader Service offers**

Accepting these FREE books and gift places you under no obligation to buy; you may cancel at any time, even after receiving your free shipment. Simply complete your details below and return the entire page to the address below. You don't even need a stamp!

YES! Please send me 2 free Intrigue books and a surprise gift. I understand that unless you hear from me, I will receive 4 superb new titles every month for just £3.05 each, postage and packing free. I am under no obligation to purchase any books and may cancel my subscription at any time. The free books and gift will be mine to keep in any case.

I5ZEE

Ms/Mrs/Miss/Mr...Initials ....
BLOCK CAPITALS PLEASE

Surname ....

Address ....

....

....Postcode ....

Send this whole page to:
The Reader Service, FREEPOST CN81, Croydon, CR9 3WZ